SHELTER ME

When friendship is all that remains

Judy Shine Logan

SHELTER ME
Judy Shine Logan
Copyright © Oct 2013
All rights reserved

This book Book is a work of fiction and any resemblance to any person, living or deat, is strictly coincidental. This book is protected under the copyright laws of the United States of America. No part of this publication may be reproduced or transmitted in any form or by any means, electronic or mechanical, including photocopying, recording, or by an information storage or retrieval system, without written permission from the author/publisher.

Line/Content Editor: Denice Whitmore
Cover: Maxwell Alexander Drake
Interior Design: Audrey Balzart

ISBN: 978-1-936525-96-6
Second Edition - Released 10/2014

www.iqpublishers.com

Published and Printed in the United States of America

Forward

Judy Shine Logan's Shelter Me details the harrowing life of a woman neglected by her alcoholic mother and abused by her sadistic husband who transcends her personal suffering in a struggle to be a loving mother, an effective office manager, and a compassionate friend. Ms. Logan provides a riveting account of the shame, guilt, fear, and anger experienced by abused women and the secrets they keep, the lies they tell, and the painful decisions they make in order to survive. Through a relationship with a recently widowed, childless woman who is forced by circumstance to return to the workplace, the central character develops the strength to escape from abuse and begin a new life. At the same time, she helps the widow to overcome grief and develop enough independence to start a new life. This powerfully written novel about two women who help each other is a testament to the power that caring relationships give to people who struggle with overwhelming grief or paralyzing fear, anger and despair. It should be required reading for all professionals who work with victims of domestic violence and their families. It will serve as an inspiration to those who suffer from such violence as well.

Ethan S. Rofman, M.D.
Associate Professor of Psychiatry
Boston University School of Medicine

Acknowledgement & Thanks

No book is created in isolation. Shelter Me belongs to all those, whose generosity of love, patience, encouragement, and faith kept its embryo nourished until birth.

First and foremost, I want to thank my parents, William (Bill) and Pauline (Brooks) Shine for their genes and genius in creating siblings and me. There has never been a better brood than us!

Each of my siblings contributed her/his support and gifts over the course of the book's gestation and labor. Janice, a retired Deputy Sheriff, whose stories about responding to Domestic Violence calls, prompted my heart to explore this horror; my sister Kristeen (called Ainee), who encouraged me non-stop, read the novel, and cooked copious amounts of food to sustain me both following my cancer surgery and the death of my husband; my brothers Bill and Ed, who were the male role models after our father's death, and Terri, the baby sib, who has been a great cheerleader throughout the twenty plus years it took for this novel to see the light of day.

To my older sister, Joan (Brackley) Dixon, a scholar, who enticed me with the idea of college way back in the early '60s, and whose intelligence I always admired.

To my nieces and nephews, Heather, Jason, Aiden, Felicia (rest in peace with Uncle Buckle), Little Eddie, Laura and Kyle, Christopher, Lisa, Alyssa and Avery Jade and my sister-in-law, Susan Shine, and brother-in-law, Richie Bopp.

Frank, my husband of 38 years, who believed in me so much that he made me go out in the rain to carve my initials in the wet cement when he was putting in the kids' swing set in the early 70s. I know he's watching from heaven, and is very proud right now!

For my children, children-in-law, and grandchildren: Frank III, my oldest son — strong of mind and body, his beautiful wife Kristen, and his children, Katherine Alexandria and Frank IV; my gorgeous and accomplished daughter Kristeen and her awesome husband Matt; and, my youngest son Michael — great friend and confidant — all of them are God's gift to me; never have children loved and supported their mother more than mine! I love you all!

For my wonderful Aunt Catherine, and cousins, Priscilla Sammet and Jim Shine, and many others, too numerous to name—many thanks for sharing the journey and for the encouragement.

What would life be like without friends who rally and rouse you to better and bigger goals and accomplishments? So many of you were at Boston Regional Medical Center (BRMC) with me, and must be recognized: my former boss, and forever friend, Ethan S. (Sam) Rofman, MD, a psychiatrist of great compassion and wisdom (and his wife Elaine), who gave me the first dot-matrix printer as a department gift when I left the Medical Center.

BRMC CEOs extraordinaire, Wolfgang von Marck, and Frank Perez, two wonderful Christian men who supported me in my employment and my education, especially during family crises.

And, of course, to the "women" of the psychiatry department who were its backbone; the receptionists, secretaries, billing specialists and transcriptionists, we undergirded the whole shebang.

To my very special friends, Rachelle and Steve Doherty, and Yvonne Staffier (rest in peace). To my three spiritual mothers: Priscilla Barnard (rest in peace), Bette

Weiscopf and Charlotte Luscombe; to my Otis Street Church friends, most of whom have now passed, and to my Hillside United Methodist Church friends, Teresa Buckley, my "bud," Imogene Williams, Sandy Bancroft, Rosemary Couture and Betsy Dixon. To Paul Cakanic and Kim Pannerton (for wonderful friendship and great gourmet meals!)

To Judy DiFranco-MacDonald, Jean Bertrand, Eileen Calnan-Haynes, Amy Rossi, Victoria Blight, Deb Kenez (rest in peace), Donna Arnold, Tess Marts, Ray Dumais, Gary Ruppert (AMEX financial planner extraordinaire), Jami Carpenter, my first professional editor, Jo Driscoll, Myfanwy & Peter Morgan, Nicole Oneail, Patti Falbo-Toupin, Ofe Polack, Paul Lantieri, and my friends in the QHS class of 1966 - all exceptional wonders.

And to my new (and special) Las Vegas friends, Daryl Haynes, Annette Morris, Kate & Larry Christiansen, Pat Martinez, Pat Paulin, and Angel Valesky.

To my writing companions and peers at the Henderson Writers' Group, the Las Vegas Writers' Group, and the Las Vegas Creative Writers Critique group – I've never been surrounded by more creative, generous people all with an eye to improving each other's writing. Many thanks!

Of course, my heartfelt thanks go to Jo Wilkins (who championed this book) and Maxwell Alexander Drake, Ink and Quill publishers, and Denice Whitmore, editor extraordinaire, for their work and faith on behalf of my book, and to Steve Gibson, Attorney at Law for his advice on my book contract.

And most importantly, I want to thank GOD for the talent he gave me, the friends, family and associates He put in my path to encourage and support me, and for Psalm 139 from the Hebrew bible in which He tells me, 'When you were being formed in secret in your mother's womb, I knew you (and loved you).' All praise, honor, and glory are Yours. Amen.

Judy Shine Logan

SHELTER ME

Chapter 1

Anne couldn't remember who called, only that he said Joe was dead. She didn't remember how she got to the hospital after that, either.

"Has your husband been sick, Mrs. Craig? Who was his regular doctor? Has he been in this hospital before? Did he have a history of heart disease?"

Their rapid-fire questions were like blows to her head, disorienting her. Anne couldn't understand what they were asking. "I want to see my husband."

"I'm sorry, Mrs. Craig, your husband is gone."

"What do you mean gone?" Anne raised her voice. "I want to see him!"

"That's not a good idea, right now, he's…"

"You let me see him now—," Anne's voice rose with her hysteria, eyes blazing. "—or there'll be more trouble for you and this hospital than neither of you can handle. Do you understand me?"

The doctor sighed. "I do, Mrs. Craig. Come with me, please."

He led Anne down the hall to an elevator marked STAFF ONLY, motioning her inside. He pressed the LL button and they rode in silence. Anne's heart pounded, her hands shaking.

Maybe they made a mistake. The emergency room was full of people on gurneys, maybe they thought it was Joe who died, but it might be someone else. Mistakes have been made before.

When the elevator opened, the doctor gestured for Anne to follow him through a long, poorly-lit corridor, until stopping in front of two huge steel doors. Anne felt a rush of cold air and shivered.

When the doctor opened the door, the young attendant looked up from his desk fronting the morgue suite. "What can I do for you, doctor?" he asked, rising from his seat.

"This is Mrs. Craig. She'd like to see her husband, if you can arrange it, please." The two men exchanged a look, silence falling between them.

The attendant nodded and pursed his lips before he spoke. "Certainly, doctor. This way, please, Mrs. Craig."

He led Anne to a small room off the suite's corridor. A steel sink took up most of the wall opposite a bank of cabinets from which the doctor took two hospital gowns, two elasticized bonnets, and four-foot coverings. "Please put these on, Mrs. Craig," he said, handing her half the materials.

"Why?" Anne asked.

"Hospital rules."

Anne focused on his quiet voice. She struggled with the gown, head bonnet and booties. "All right. Now, may I see my husband, please?" Anne's voice wavered.

"Of course." he said, turning away from her.

Gesturing toward the hallway, he led her to another door that opened onto a cavernous chamber lined with steel drawers on three walls, and a bank of sinks with surrounding countertops on the fourth wall. Scales and other devices were laid carefully along the countertops. Six metal tables were lined up side by side in the center of the room. An enormous clock hung over the equipment on the wall.

Anne realized she'd stopped breathing and gulped in a painful breath that stuck in her windpipe. The ticking of the enormous clock, reverberating through the place like a mechanical heartbeat, broke the shroud of silence, counting down the last seconds of her former life.

"This will be difficult, Mrs. Craig. Are you sure you want to see him now, before the funeral director can prepare him for viewing?"

"Yes," Anne whispered, her voice so small that the doctor hesitated a second before motioning Anne to the bank of steel drawers on one side of the room.

The attendant reached up, grasped one of the steel handles, and pulled on it, withdrawing the interior tray from the wall. He backed away to let Anne stand beside her dead husband.

Even covered by the sheet, she recognized Joe instantly... his contours in Basque-relief. The shape of his head, his nose, his torso, his hammer-toes that pained him throughout his life...his misshapen knees injured in football, his sturdy legs...every part of him memorized during their twenty-five years of marriage.

The doctor stepped up again, looked at Anne and drew back the sheet.

Anne gasped. She had never seen a dead body before... the cardboard eyes, the slack face, the open mouth with its surrounding ring of white, the mottled blood collected in grotesque, dark patches beneath his skin. Joe looked like an eggplant gone bad.

Anne fainted.

Gone—two months had passed already. Every moment a lifetime. Every day an eternity.

Anne felt like she had grief-walked through those days, remembering little, and handling the trauma like a hospital—giving energy and attention without feeling. Only the busyness of her husband's death drove her: probate, insurance, bills, deed, car, and finally, financial priorities now that she lived alone.

She was luckier than some new widows, the lawyer said, "At least you know how to balance a checkbook."

Now there was nothing left to do. The busyness was done…death's dues paid, time empty. She sat in her kitchen waiting…waiting for something to need her attention, but there was nothing.

Anne walked to the wall phone. With trembling hand, she picked up the receiver, and dialed the familiar number. She hadn't seen or spoken with her best friend since the funeral. It was time to reach back into life.

"Hello," the well-known voice answered.

"Bette?" Anne's throat tightened.

"Anne, I don't believe it," Bette stammered. "How are you? I mean now that…um…you know…things are…um?"

"Okay, I guess. Everything's done," Anne's voice trailed off. She rubbed her forehead with her free hand. The sun reflected off her diamond ring, sending a laser light across the room.

"Good. No. I don't mean good that he's, you know, I mean…"

Anne nodded. "I understand."

"I can't imagine how you're, ah." Bette hesitated. "Coping, but I—"

"It's awful, Bette." Anne sobbed, pulling a tissue from her pocket to wipe at the tears spilling down her face.

Bette rushed to fill the air. "But you're doing okay now, right?"

"No. The house is so empty I hear my heart beating. I don't know what to do with myself." Anne paced back and forth as far as the phone cord permitted.

"I understand. I'm sorry I haven't called. I just figured you were…you know," Bette said defending herself.

"I'm a mess. I need to see you. Can you please come for lunch today?" Anne stretched the phone cord taut walking across the room to take hamburger from the freezer. She laid the cold package on the counter, and walked back to the wall that held the phone.

Anne knew her life had to begin again. Where better than with her first friend? Long before school started, or husbands found, they were friends, sharing everything from toys to teens to matrimonial triumphs. It was only natural for them to reconnect now.

"Bette? Did you hear me?"

"Sorry, dear I got distracted. What were you saying?"

"Lunch, today. Can you please come?"

"You know, it's funny you mention lunch, dear. Just yesterday Bill and I agreed that we should invite you to dinner, though…I hadn't heard from you in two months, so I…"

"I'm sorry I haven't called sooner, Bette," Anne wiped her face again. "It's been so…awful."

"I'm sure. Now, listen, why don't you come for dinner real soon, then? It'll be fun, won't it?"

"I was hoping we could just get together, just to talk," Anne said pleading.

"I'm sorry, dear. I just can't today."

"How about tomorrow, then? Please, Bette." Anne's voice cracked.

"I know dear, I'm so sorry, I have to…um, oh, look at the time. I have to run, Anne. My daughter's waiting for me. Please set a date for dinner with us when you're free, then, all right? Bye-bye, dear."

Click.

Anne pulled the receiver from her ear, her mouth open. She stared at the phone. "I am free!" she yelled at the taunting silence, her throat tightening again. Her eyes shot angry tears. "I am free, damn it!" She slammed the phone into its cradle on the wall.

What was that? You acted like I was some stranger. Like I didn't matter. I don't get it. We've been friends for years. Anne walked to a chair and dropped into it. For a long while, she cried until anger left while sorrow returned. *See, what's happened, Joe? You left me, now my friends don't want me either! I can do anything I want, but there's nobody to do it with!*

Eyeing the bundle of meat on the counter across the room, she leapt from the chair, sprinted toward it, then struck out with a powerful sweep of her arm, sending the package flying across the room where it hit the opposite wall with a thud, sliding to the floor.

"Who cares if I eat, either?" Anne dropped down onto the floor, sobbing. She realized that even now she wasn't really talking to anyone.

I hate you, Bette. You aren't my friend — Joe is my only real friend. He gave me everything: his name, his love, his life, his strength, his fidelity. Everything except his future.

Unlike Bette, Anne realized that Joe shared more than the surface of her life. He shared her secrets, her heart. *He used to say he'd chosen to ride the river with me, but our boat hit a rock called death and he was swept overboard.*

Anne sobbed until, like a river in summer, the heat sucked up the water, leaving only small pools between the rocks.

For a long time she sat on the floor, not hungry — though she hadn't eaten — nor tired, though she hadn't slept in days, nor angry, nor sorrowful, for the tears had washed everything away.

She sat there feeling nothing. She felt no pulse, no breath, no aches, no pains...nothing physical, or emotional. She had no urgency, motives, or directives. There were no duties urging her on or demanding her attention, her time, or talents.

Life with Joe was always urgent. Do this, do that, see this, buy that, arrange this, discard that, hurry, start, stop, do, think, go, worry, hurry, hurry, hurry.

Maybe she was dead. Dead to the world and its musical chairs of start, stop, shove, sit, smile, win, lose. She saw it now, life was a game of musical chairs--everyone eager and healthy in the beginning, the snappy music new — people racing round and round vying for the chairs they'll grab when the music stops.

Everyone happy, thinking the game will go on forever, and since only one person gets bumped off at a time, nobody notices. As the game goes on and on, though, the players get older, less agile, while the music becomes like a metal spoon scraping the bottom of a pan, the last few notes scratched out in painful strains, as everyone drags himself round and round until there is only one player left to win.

Anne wondered if winning that final chair was really winning at all. Joe was lucky; he left the game early, his running was done. *What about me? I don't want to keep running. I want to be with him. I want to be dead, too!*

Thinking of the knives across the room, Anne tried to pull herself up from the floor. Her legs gave way beneath her. She fell down and sobbed.

I can't even kill myself, Joe. How am I going to do this death march alone? Isn't that what life really is? A death march in four-four time? Distracted victims marching to their death?

She spied the soggy meat lying in a pool of bloody water beside her and shuddered. *Oh, my God. I could have laid here rotting. Who would have found me? Who would have buried me?*

She pushed into a sitting posture, and then picked up the dripping mess.

"I'm not dead yet!" she yelled to the empty room, angry activity dragging her back into the game, "and until there's somebody to lay me down beside you, I'm not going to die, either! I have to be without you in life, but I sure as hell am going to be with you in death."

Using her free hand for balance, she rolled onto her knees and stood. Spying the trash bin, she walked over and dropped the squishy meat into it.

Turning back, she saw the red river that trailed behind her. *I'll clean that up tomorrow.*

Chapter 2

Her legs aching, Terry carried the basket of clean laundry up from the cellar, placing it on the kitchen table.

She had been running around working all day. First going to church with the kids and then coming home, doing the wash, straightening up the house and finally fixing dinner.

Despite her best efforts, though, the dinner was lousy, her husband was in a bad mood, the kids were cranky, and the house was a mess again. It felt like trying to harness Jell-O, and she was exhausted.

Now, the kids were in bed, her husband sat in front of his electronic babysitter, and Terry had a few minutes to herself. She looked around before retrieving a journal and pen from under the clothes in the laundry basket and sat at the kitchen table.

Dear Diary,

Another Sunday in hell. We fought again today because he wouldn't go to church with us. How am I supposed to make this a religious family if he won't go? He's the one who wanted the kids to be Protestant in the first place, just because his father used to say, "We sure as hell aren't Catholics." That's right. They weren't Catholic, they weren't anything, but he says, "If the kids are Catholic I'm not going with you." That's all he said, so I found a nice Protestant church and converted, and what good did it do me? Now I take the kids to church every week, and he still won't come with us!

No offense, God, but religion sucks. It's just man's way of controlling the masses and my man's way of controlling me by keeping me from Mass.

"Hey, that's pretty good," Terry said aloud, pleased with her pun.

"What's good?"

Terry jumped. "What?" She turned to see her husband standing behind her.

"Now what're you writing?" he said, looking at the open notebook.

"Nothing," she shut the book, covering it with her arm.

"You were having a pretty good time in here laughing and writing nothing, weren't you? Let me see it." He lunged toward her, grabbing at the book.

"What?" Terry pulled it behind her back. "It's nothing, I was just writing." She twisted first left, then right to avoid his grasping hands. "Please, Mack, it's mine!"

"Nothing is yours," he wrapped his big hand around her throat. "Anything you got is mine. Give it to me."

"Please, let me go. I have a lot to do before work tomorrow."

"Screw work and your book," he said. He tried to lift her from the chair. When she resisted, he squeezed harder. "I said, let's go."

"Mack, please."

Terry saw his neck veins bulge beneath his face, pushing the blood to his forehead. He lifted his free hand in front of her face in a fist.

"You okay, Mom?" Cara asked from the doorway, dressed in her Wonder Woman pajamas.

Mack dropped his hands and pulled them behind his back.

"I'm okay, sweetie." Terry jumped up. She pushed past Mack to join their young daughter in the hall. "What do you need?"

Mack charged through the door, knocking Terry against the wall. "You'll pay for this one, bitch," he mumbled. "Just wait."

Cara glared at her father as he retreated down the hall. "What's the matter with him?"

"I wouldn't let him see my book," Terry held it up.

Cara shook her head. "Why didn't you just give it to him, Mom? You know he can't read."

"Out of the mouth of babes." Terry started to cry.

"I'm not a baby, Mom. I'm twelve."

"I know that, honey. You're a lot smarter than your mother!" Terry wiped away her tears and forced a smile. "Why do I always fight with him, Cara?"

"It's not you, Mom."

"When I fight back, I make it hell because you kids have to listen to it, too."

I can take care of myself, but when I fight with him it upsets the kids — that was my fault. He would never hurt them. It's my resistance that makes him crazy, sometimes making his anger spill over onto the little ones because of me. Now Cara's upset, he's upset, and I'll have to fix it all somehow. Thank you, God, that I can get out of here for work tomorrow. Maybe let things cool down a little.

"I'm sorry, sweetie," Terry said, still weeping. "Let's get you back to bed. All right?"

Cara shrugged.

"Is Tommy still asleep?" Terry asked.

"I'll go check." Cara started down the hall.

"No, no, no," Terry caught the girl by the arm. She pulled Cara into a hug. "That's my job. Your job is to be my pretty girl, now get to bed, okay?"

"I love you, Mom." Cara's voice trailed off, though she didn't move.

"I know, sweetie. Now go to bed, please."

Cara shuffled off to her room, turning back twice to look at her mother. Terry moved toward Tommy's bedroom.

When she peeked in his room, she thought Tommy was asleep in his Spiderman bed. She pulled the door closed, but stopped when Tommy called out.

"Mommy?"

She walked into his room and sat on the edge of the bed, the light from the hall barely illuminating the six-year-old's face.

"What, honey?" Terry wiped her eyes.

"Did Daddy hurt you?"

"No, baby, Daddy just got mad for a minute, that's all. It's okay, now." She tucked the blankets around his little form.

"Cara, okay?"

"Cara's fine, too." Terry bent down and nuzzled his face with hers.

"When I'm a big boy no one's going to get mad at you because I'll beat them up."

Terry smiled at her little man.

"I know, you're my big, strong boy. Now, go back to sleep, honey, okay?" Terry kissed his cheek, adjusted the blankets again, and stood to leave.

"Mommy," he said, grabbing at her retreating form, "I love you!"

"I love you too, big boy. Nighty-night." Terry sighed, pulling the door shut.

Why can't I just get along? Why do I have to be so stubborn? What was the big deal about letting him see the book anyway? Now everyone in the house is upset. It's all my fault. I'll never fight with Mack again. From now on I'll be a good wife and get along with him, if only for the kids' sake.

She went into the den, but Mack wasn't there. She turned off the TV. She felt her shoulders drop. He must have gone to bed. *Thank you, God.*

Terry slumped onto the sofa to wait a while before going upstairs. *Maybe he'll be asleep by then. I can start fresh tomorrow after work. I'll make a nice dinner, not like the mess today, and I'll be extra nice to him. Then things should smooth out. If I play my cards right, the family can get back to normal. I'll just have to do more to make this home a happy one.*

She picked up a book to read. Soon, she drifted far away to an enchanted land where a feisty heroine remained undaunted — no matter what terrible things happened to her.

If only I could be like that. Why am I so moody? No matter how hard I try, I can never stay upbeat for very long.

Pep talks, women's magazines and church hadn't helped her maintain a good mood. Sometimes things felt out of control, and when things felt out of control, she got scared — like she should be doing something more, though she didn't know what, or what trouble it would bring for not doing it. Always, some unfinished business hung over her, the weight of which made her tense and gave her headaches.

When she was too tired, or the kids too needy, or Mack too demanding, or work too busy, it made her sick with headaches. She wanted to scream, *Stop, please. Let me get my bearings. Let me catch up. Please, one thing at a time…wait, wait, wait!*

She felt herself being swept away as though she stood at the top of a blender being sucked down into the blades, her vision getting more and more unfocused, until she saw only a dizzy blur, and buckled, the weight of the world crushing in on her from all sides, pulverizing her.

She imagined herself gone, except for little pieces of fleshy bone that spun away from the blades in a frenetic whirl, whipping at the edges of her consciousness. Peace settled upon her because she felt nothing as opposed to feeling everything.

Suspended in this bliss of nothingness, she continued to float until someone screamed from the shore bringing her back together again. Lately, only her kids could call her back.

Terry got sleepy. She closed the book, turned off the light, then trudged up the stairs to her bedroom. She entered, afraid of waking him. She didn't turn on the lamp, instead using the tiny glow of the night-light in the hall to get her bearings.

Squinting, she saw his eyes were closed, but she couldn't see how his chest moved. If it rose and fell in quiet rhythms, it was safe, he was sleeping, though too much noise would wake him and he'd get angry. If his chest moved in high, rasping sighs like a bellows, he lay awake waiting for her. Sometimes she couldn't tell. The tension made her heart palpitate, not knowing what to expect. Tonight she couldn't tell.

She undressed, dropping her clothes on the floor instead of in the hamper, in case the lid slipped and crashed down, waking him. She held her breath and slipped gingerly into the bed. She didn't try to get comfortable, either. She just stopped moving as soon as her body touched the mattress.

She lay there letting the minutes pass, listening to the sounds of his breathing. If his breath flapped gently, like a curtain in the breeze, he was about fifteen minutes into sleep. If his breath sounded like wind bouncing off of rocks, he was well underway.

The quiet stage before sleep carted him off made her most tense, because if she made too much noise, he'd wake and blame her for thrashing around. If he awoke and she didn't speak to him, he'd accuse her of ignoring him.

She liked to be in bed asleep before him, which was impossible since he didn't help get the kids ready for bed, for school, for church, or anything else that might have lightened her load. Sometimes, his lack of support made her angry though she couldn't say anything about it.

Mack took in a huge gulp of air that bounced off the walls of the room. She almost jumped off the bed, catching herself in time, managing to keep still. She couldn't stop her heart from ricocheting off her ribcage, though, prayed he didn't hear it.

Finally, he snored.

Thank you, God.

Terry drifted off to sleep, her headache coming again. The pulse of the blender in the background accentuated the spinning of the room.

Chapter 3

Terry punched in at exactly 8:00 a.m. and walked past the empty receptionist desk on the way to her office.

We've got to get that job filled. Already things are backed up without having to cover that job, too. I'll have to talk to Mr. Clark again today. He's got to hire someone soon.

"Morning, Terry." A young, perky girl flew past her moving toward the secretarial area.

"Morning, Beth." Terry said. "Listen, when you get settled, would you please take the reception desk this morning?"

"Sure thing, Terry."

"Thanks a lot."

A cluster of women walked past Terry, each greeting her. "Morning...Hello...Hi there."

Terry smiled, returning their greetings, pleased with her staff. They were all good girls...intelligent, hardworking, a pleasure to supervise.

Mr. Clark, on the other hand, is a bit challenging. It's taken a while, though he trusts me now. So, who cares if he takes credit for all my ideas? It is the cause, not the credit that counts. Getting the problem fixed is what's important.

Once settled in her office, Terry buzzed Beth, asking to be told when Mr. Clark came in.

At 9:00, Terry's intercom buzzed. Mr. Clark had arrived.

Terry gave him a few minutes to get settled before going to the break room to fix him a cup of coffee just the way he liked it.

"Morning, Mr. Clark." She handed the cup over to him, smiling.

"Ah, my coffee," he smiled at her, reaching for it. "If only my wife were as good to me as you are."

Every morning, the same old joke, though it still made her blush. Compliments unnerved her.

"Mr. Clark, have you given any thought to hiring someone for the receptionist position?" Terry asked.

"There's someone out there, now," he blew on the streaming brew, taking a sip.

"Yes, though she's needed in the secretarial pool. Sales leads are piling up, the reports need to be typed so the expeditors can place the orders, and—"

"Well, have her do it half-time, then put someone else in there the other half," Clark rubbed his balding head.

"Yes sir, that might work, but just imagine how much more we could get done if Beth went back to the typing pool. Especially if we had someone just for the receptionist position."

"Who's Beth?"

"The girl at the reception desk, sir."

"Why, she doesn't want the job?"

"It's an entry level position, sir. Beth's been here five years. She's one of my best typists."

Mr. Clark sighed, shaking his head. She knew he hated details.

She saw his shoulders slumping and gathered her determination. "I could handle everything. I'll put a sign out front and an ad in the paper. I can do the interviewing, so you only have to pick from the finalists, all right?" She nodded her head in encouragement, eyes open wide.

"I don't have time to worry about this right now. Where are the reports I need for my meeting?"

"On the credenza, sir," Terry said, pointing.

"Then leave me be so I can study them."

"Yes, sir. What if I just start interviewing people, then when you're ready, you pick the one you like? Would that work?"

"For heaven's sake, Terry, please." He dismissed her with a wave.

"Consider it done, sir. I'll handle everything." She smiled at him, and backed out of the office.

Mr. Clark sighed, picking up the meeting materials. "Fine, now, please…"

"Excellent, thank you!" She closed the door, brainstorming on what she'd put into the advertisement.

Chapter 4

For weeks after calling Bette, Anne stayed in the house, walking aimlessly from room to room picking up objects, each resurrecting a memory. The porcelain ballerina Joe bought, calling it the Billerica girl, the crystal clock engraved with Timeless Love that he gave her for their anniversary, pictures of them laughing and cavorting in their world within the world.

She cradled each treasure in her hands, kissing each one before returning it to its place of honor, only to pick it up again the next day and the day after that. Endlessly, every object, every memory, gave her something to hold onto--something that kept Joe present.

She moved into the living room, picking up a photo of them together in Maine — bright smiles, beautiful scenery. The ache in her heart was so bad she could hardly breathe. *Where are you, Joe? Why did you leave me? Why did you die? God, if you really exist, please tell me where Joe is!*

The river filled and spilled again, the force wrenching rocks from their bed, bouncing them off the banks of her gut. She felt sick and had to sit in Joe's chair. She filled her lungs with his lingering scent. Even with her eyes closed, the tears leaked out.

Anne must have dozed because night had darkened the outside world by the time she finally opened her eyes. She turned on the lamp beside the chair, and a haggard old woman, her cheeks hollow and eyes empty, stared at Anne through the adjacent window.

Screaming, Anne jumped up and ran to the kitchen. She had heard stories about crooks that targeted homes of the recently deceased and her heart pounded.

She rummaged through the utensil drawer in the dark, looking for a knife when her fingers ran over a sharp blade that sliced through her skin. She didn't cry out for fear of being discovered, but instead moved her hand further down to the knife's handle.

Anne crept into the living room, hugging the walls. She moved toward the window, the knife in her shaking hand. Once there, she stopped to catch her breath, then peeked around the trim. She saw no one.

Carefully, she crouched down, duck-walking to the lamp beside the chair to turn it off. She waited a few seconds, then moved back beside the window and peeked out again, relieved to see an empty porch. She exhaled, and dropped down onto the floor, still shaking and clutching the knife. Her heart pounded. *Thank you, God.*

For a long time, she waited in silence, not moving, barely breathing. When she thought it was safe, she rolled onto her knees, peeked out the window again and sat back. The porch was empty.

She pulled herself up using the window frame and crept off to her bedroom, where she tucked the knife between the mattress and box spring. Putting her full weight onto the mattress, she sat on the bed directly above the knife to pull it out. It slipped out easily.

Satisfied, Anne went to clean the blood from her hand and saw the old woman looking back at her in the hall mirror—gaunt and hollow-eyed, she stared back at herself.

By the third month, Anne was getting cabin fever, and the food in the house was almost gone, the perishables long ago discarded.

Instinct, more than hunger, forced her to eat small amounts of food every few days. Mostly pasta—pasta with butter, or canned tomatoes, or occasionally a bowl of oatmeal without milk because there wasn't any. The food didn't matter anyway, because she couldn't taste it, but her body demanded something.

She washed up, dressed, and put a kerchief on her head in case she met someone she knew, because she hadn't curled her hair in months. She didn't want to look disheveled—that would reflect badly on Joe.

She walked out of the house to the garage, which smelled musty, not having been opened in two months. She climbed into the car and turned the ignition. It started right up, but the gas gauge needle sat very close to empty.

Damn it. Now I have to feed the car, too. She drove around for quite a while looking for a service station that still provided full service, having no idea where one was. Joe had handled all the car's needs.

Come to think of it, I've never changed a tire, or filled a gas tank, or registered a car, or had one repaired. You did everything, Joe. Anne began to sob. *I was the lady of our home, my happy domain by day, your happy castle by night. Why did it have to stop?*

She pulled over to the side of the road. She didn't notice that the sun was shining or the flowers were blooming because her eyes sat behind the torrential downpour that ran over her nose and down her chin.

Blindly, she searched her purse for a tissue and finding one, swiped it across her face to clear her vision. The tissue disintegrated in her hand, leaving snotty strips of shredded material. She threw the remnants onto the passenger-side floor and, pulling off her kerchief, used that instead.

The tears finally abated and she pulled the car onto the road again. She drove the streets, obeying the traffic lights, keeping the right distance between her and the car ahead of her, still looking for a gas station. If asked how she got from point A to point B, however, she couldn't recall--she couldn't seem to remember things anymore.

Just ahead, a service station sign read 'Full Service'. Relieved, Anne pulled into the lot and alongside the pumps. A tall, skinny boy with acne and filthy overalls came out of the garage bay.

He walked up to her car window. "What'll it be, ma'am?"

Anne cranked down the window. "Gas, please."

"You wanna filler up?"

"I guess...all right, fill it up, please." Anne nodded.

"You got it." He smiled at her.

Anne turned in her seat and watched the young man fill the car with gas. She heard the car sucking up gas like a dog lapping water. When the boy came around to the front of the car with a squeegee in his hand, she felt self-conscious, but she couldn't help watching him clean the windshield. He didn't seem to notice her, the windshield acting like a one-way mirror.

When the gasoline pump clicked off, Anne jumped. The boy dropped the squeegee into a pail and walked around to the back of the car. He pulled the spigot out and replaced it on the pump, tightened the gas cap and then walked around to the driver's side, again.

"That'll be twenty-five dollars, ma'am."

"Twenty-five dollars? That's highway robbery!"

"Yes, ma'am." He nodded.

Anne reached into her purse. She saw from the corner of her eye that the boy looked down into the car. She turned her body slightly before opening her wallet, took out the correct amount of cash and turned to face him again. She handed him the money. "Thank you," she said.

"Yes, ma'am," he took the money. "Thank you for coming by." He turned back toward the office.

"Just a minute, young man," Anne called after him. She reached back into her wallet, pulling out a dollar bill. "This is for you."

"No, ma'am…you don't have to do that. This here's my job," he said, his face turning red.

"Please, take it." Anne offered the dollar again, "I hate pumping gas, so I'm very happy that you're here doing it."

"Okay, ma'am, thank you," he said, avoiding her eyes.

Anne stopped at the market, bought a few groceries and the daily paper, and headed for home.

She parked the car in the garage, but instead of going into the house through its adjoining door, she went around to the front of the house, which hadn't been opened since the funeral.

She recalled the dozens of people who followed her into the house like one long, black snake winding its way up the driveway — distant relatives, Joe's co-workers, the church ladies who set up the buffet, and of course, the pastor who performed the service.

They had all milled about, eating and whispering to each other, yet when they spoke directly to Anne, they yelled as though she were deaf. She couldn't remember what they said exactly, though mostly the same thing over and over in slight variations; "I'm so sorry…He was a good man…We'll miss him…Sorry…I'm here for you, if you need me…It must be awful…I'm so sorry…Please call if you need me."

Only the minister's departing remark rent Anne's heart. "We can never understand these things, my dear," he said, nodding. "But we do know that it's God's will."

Anne wanted to slap his face, hard. What a stupid, awful thing to say! Why would God take her husband when she needed him! Was she supposed to feel bad for feeling bad… like how dare she compare her grief with God's need? Or worse, compete with God for what was His to begin with… What was wrong with people? God wasn't a monster. People were the monsters.

Anne glared at the man in black through slit eyes, her lips pulled in a hard line. She agitated a tiny piece of tissue between her fingers to control her anger. She wanted to hit him so hard that his head would spin for days. But she'd been raised right, so she kept her rage to herself.

By the time the church ladies cleaned up, the man in black left to spread more good news, and everyone else had departed, Anne was spent. She went to her room and collapsed onto the bed.

She thought back to that awful day when Joe died, remembering only snatches of conversation, much of it now shrouded in fog.

Anne tried to open the front door, but it stuck. She pushed harder, felt it give a little. She peeked through the mail slot, seeing mounds of mail scattered all over the floor, pushed through, one day at a time, now blocking the narrow passage. She had forgotten to retrieve it daily, now it looked like hundreds of pieces barricaded the passage.

She went back to the garage and entered the house through the adjoining door, shaking her head. God only knows what was in there, probably bills that needed to be paid. It made her angry. She never liked handling the bills and now it was one more thing thrust on her like the aftershocks of a quake. Where did she begin? How?

She felt weak, and knew that her body needed food. She shuffled to the stove and turned on the burner to make a cup of tea, though she couldn't face making a meal. Instead, she put a piece of bread in the toaster and dropped a glob of peanut butter on its center after it popped up. It reminded Anne of dog droppings on a dry lawn, but she managed to get it, and the tea, down. She headed for bed. The mail could wait until tomorrow. Within the hour, she fell asleep for the first time in weeks.

Chapter 5

Terry was in a panic. *I've got to make up for yesterday's fiasco. I'll stop at the market, get a nice steak for him, feed the kids early, and put them to bed. Then I'll shower to get pretty before waking him for work. That should put us on good footing again. With any luck, the evening will help put things to rights. Be with me tonight, please, God.*

Terry rushed through the market grabbing too much food. She knew better than to shop when she was hungry, and even worse she bought twice as much food as they needed when she tried to appease Mack, like if the first thing didn't work, the next thing might.

She chose a huge piece of steak, some Portobello mushrooms, frozen squash, and for dessert, both chocolate and vanilla ice cream. Terry bought a pack of cigarettes for him, too.

Just before six o' clock, she pulled into the driveway. The children ran out the door to greet her. Mack had picked them up from their grandmother's house, for once, saving Terry a trip and a headache.

"Hi, Mom," the kids said, hugging her.

"We missed you today," Cara said.

"I missed you, too!" She kissed each child.

She regretted every moment she was away from them, but she had no choice. If she didn't work to help Mack pay the bills, they would live in poverty. Still...she would give anything to stay home with them.

The kids took the groceries from Terry, brought them to the kitchen, and put them on the countertop. "Mom, I started supper." Cara announced, pointing to a pan of near boiling water. "Can we have spaghetti with butter tonight, please?"

"That's not much of a meal, honey,"

"That's what we want!" Tommy said, pleading.

"I bought steak for all of us tonight," She picked up the meat to show them.

"Please, Mom, we want spaghetti." Their little faces hopeful — they held their folded hands to their chest, making Terry laugh.

"All right, you two monkeys!" Terry put the steak along with her good meal plans aside for the moment.

The kids giggled, jumping up. "Thanks, Mom." Tommy hugged Terry around the waist.

"Okay, now you two go watch TV until I get this done." Instantly they obeyed.

Terry reached up into the cabinet above the stove and pulled down the spaghetti box and olive oil. She poured the oil into the boiling water, took a small handful of brittle pasta sticks from the box, broke them in half, and dropped them in too. She stirred the spaghetti so it wouldn't stick together. Taking out plates, she set them on the table with big slices of Italian bread. The butter dish went on the table, too.

Okay, I'll get the kids' dinner finished first, then I'll start Mack's. No big deal. The kids can bathe themselves for one night. I'll be able to spend some time with Mack before he goes to work to make up for yesterday's blunders.

Terry felt happy while she strained the spaghetti then dumped it into a bowl. She called the kids to the table, piling the spaghetti onto each plate. The kids scooped up blobs of butter to drop onto their pasta.

They laughed and pointed at the steaming piles.

"Look, Mommy, my butter looks like me when I slide down the hill on the snow!" Tommy giggled.

"Hey, my butter is going down a slide…weeeeeeeeeeeee…" Cara laughed.

They slurped the spaghetti, spraying butter all over their faces, thrilled at the chance to be messy.

Cara grabbed up a huge forkful of pasta, shoved it into her mouth and let the rest hang down her face. "Look at me, Mom. I'm a walrus."

They laughed at Cara's antics, Tommy following his sister's lead. Seizing a handful of spaghetti, Tommy put it onto his head, saying, "Look Mommy, I'm a mop!"

They were giggling and guffawing, nearly choking on their pasta and their delight.

"What the hell is this?" Mack shouted, standing in the doorway. He moved into the kitchen, breathing hard and stood next to Terry. "Can't you make them anything better than freaking spaghetti?"

"That's what they wanted, Mack!" Terry whispered.

"When did they become the goddamned parents in this house? Who said that they should tell you what they're going eat? Who's the freaking mother here?" He lunged toward her. "I suppose you were going to give me that crap, too, huh?"

"No, I bought steak for you, Mack," Terry backed away from him. "I was going to cook it when the kids were done."

"Well, isn't that nice! I get steak while my kids get spaghetti. Real nice, lady, but this isn't your goddamn mother's house!" He moved to the table and swept Cara's plate to the floor. "What I get, we all get…do you understand me?"

Terry cried.

"Why can't I have meat, too, Mama?" ten-year-old Terry said, whimpering. "Why do we get cereal and he always gets the meat?" Terry pushed the corn flakes back at her mother. "I want meat, too."

Instead of a steak, her mother slapped Terry across the face.

"You're a goddamned, spoiled child, Terry," mother said.

"You know goddamn right well that your father has to work. He needs the meat, but no, you're never satisfied, are you? You always want what someone else has? God's going to punish a selfish little girl like you. You just wait, and see if he doesn't." Her mother staggered from the room.

Terry knew she was wrong, but she couldn't help it. She loved the taste of meat. She waited until her father finished his meal and left the table. Looking around, she listened intently, then snuck back into the kitchen, grabbed up the delicious rim of fat left on her father's plate, then ran to the bathroom, locking the door.

She sucked out all the juice, first, savoring each delicious swallow. Then, she chewed on the glob of fat for as long as it lasted. It left a greasy film on her tongue and the roof of her mouth. Nothing ever tasted so good, or made her feel so bad.

"Hey! Did you hear me?" Mack slapped Terry across the face, bringing her back to her own kitchen. "I'm talking to you!"

"Ow! Yes, I hear you...I'm sorry — you're right. I should have given the kids steak. I'm sorry...I'm really sorry..." Terry bent over to pick up the smashed plate and scattered spaghetti. "I've spoiled everything, again." She sobbed.

The kids stared at the floor.

"All right...stop crying," Mack's voice softened. "Just cook the meat. We can all have some with the spaghetti. Okay?" he said, putting his arm around her.

"Okay," she said, still crying. "That's a good idea, honey.

I'm really sorry." She felt like a stupid woman and a lousy wife and mother, but sometimes he helped her see her mistakes. "Thank you, Mack."

He left the room and the kids stared at Terry. No one spoke.

Hours later, lying beside her husband in their double bed, Terry was happy that the evening and the dinner had finally turned out well. The steak was delicious, complimented by the spaghetti, while everyone loved making their own ice-cream sundae.

The kids gave Terry no trouble about taking their baths or going to bed either, and Mack surprised Terry by calling in sick for the night—something he rarely did. It was nearly midnight, now. The house was quiet and peaceful.

"Well, what about it?" he said in the dark.

"What?" Terry asked, her mind on Morpheus, the god of sleep, not Mack.

"You know what," he said, his voice clipped. "Get over here." He grabbed her nightgown to pull her on top of him. "Get them off!" he said, yanking on her panties.

Terry wiggled out of the barrier, squirming left, then right so she could stay on top of him without falling off the bed.

"Oh, that's it...move like that again."

Terry gyrated, moving to a silent rhythm. He settled into her, matching his thrusting with her pushing, his retreat with her withdrawal, until finally he climaxed and told her to stop moving.

"You really got into that, didn't you?" He laughed.

"Yeah." She smiled in case he could see her in the dark. She rolled off him to sit on the edge of the bed. From the floor, she picked up his dirty tee shirt and tucked it between her legs.

"Night, honey," He rolled over, his breath rising and falling in quiet rhythm.

"Night," she whispered, pulling her bathrobe on and hobbling to the bathroom, the tee shirt still tucked between her legs.

She hated the sticky feeling of sex and couldn't wait to wash away the last of the day's work. Sticky or not, it was better to milk him and get it over with than to remain clean and have to listen to him bellowing like a cow. Peace had its price, and it was cheaper than war.

Terry felt woozy. *Please, God, give me strength.* She limped down the hallway. *See how easy it is to make a happy family? My mother was right. I am a selfish little girl who always wants what everyone else has; a sneak-thief who steals fat from her father's plate, but denies her own kids meat; an ingrate and a troublemaker who even resents her husband's needs.*

Terry's world spun. She barely made it to the toilet, where she plopped down to put her head between her knees to stop from fainting, the smell of him there making her gag.

She blacked out.

Terry awoke before the alarm. Mack still slept beside her. She snuck out of bed, going downstairs to make breakfast. She would surprise everyone by making pancakes this morning since she had a little extra time today before getting ready for work.

She loved the smell of cinnamon floating in warmed maple syrup. It filled the kitchen with delicious aromas.

"Hey, good-looking," Mack said, taking his place at the head of the table.

"Hi, honey," Terry answered.

"Hi Mom..." Two voices chimed in together.

"Morning, kids. Go wash your hands."

Terry placed a huge stack of pancakes in front of Mack, who dug right into them. "Damn, these are good! Where's the bacon and juice?"

"What?" Terry's mouth dropped open. She stood rooted beside the table, her eyes wide open.

"Just kidding," he laughed. "I don't need bacon, when I got my little piggy right here…ha ha ha." He pinched her rear end.

Terry felt her face turn red. She wanted him to stop in case the kids heard him, but she didn't want to start any trouble, either. She kept her mouth shut. Too late.

"Who's a piggy, Mommy?" Tommy asked.

"No one, honey. Daddy was just teasing, that's all." Terry smiled first at Mack, then at Tommy.

Cara returned to the table and Terry saw her shoot her father a dirty look. Terry winced at Cara, who brought her face under control before Mack could see it.

The meal was pleasant, albeit a little tense, and ended with enough time for Terry to send the kids off to dress for school, and for her to grab a shower, too. She was pleased as she bent down to kiss Mack.

He grabbed a breast and squeezed hard.

"Ow…what are you doing?"

"What? I can't show my wife a little affection? The hell with you, then," he said, pushing off his chair, shoving her away. "I'm going back to bed."

"I was hoping you could walk the kids to the bus stop so I can get to work a little early today."

"What do I look like, the goddamned babysitter? That's your job." He shrugged, walking out of the kitchen.

Terry's shoulders slumped. She hadn't realized how tense they were until they released. Now they hurt. She stretched her neck first to the left, then to the right and back again, but it didn't help with the pain. She headed for the shower to get ready for work.

Terry didn't arrive at work any earlier than usual, though her days held more work lately.

The ads she placed for the receptionist position during the past month hadn't brought anyone suitable. They were either too giddy, too dull, or too chatty. Terry wasn't comfortable bringing any of them to Mr. Clark's attention. She knew she had one-shot and couldn't waste it.

At 9:00 am, Terry glanced up at the clock, rubbing her temples to ease her pounding head, *Please, God, send someone good! I can't do this much longer.*

Chapter 6

By the time Anne hefted all the mail out to the kitchen, and dumped each load onto the kitchen table, she was out of breath and overwhelmed. Huge piles of mail overflowed the table, falling to the floor.

How can I do this? Where do I start? Damn it! Anne felt the anger rising from her stomach to her throat, bitter and burning. Why did she have to do this anyway? She couldn't think straight, never mind do the mail or pay the bills. *Damn it!*

She sat staring at the task for a long time. She went to the laundry room for two laundry baskets. Into one she threw all the junk mail, circulars and newspapers, cutting the mountain by two-thirds. Retrieving a trash bag from under the sink, she dumped the junk mail into it, knotted the end, and pushed it across the room.

She returned to the remaining mountain. Some of it looked like sympathy cards and correspondence. She dropped those into an empty basket. What looked like advertising hidden in more sophisticated envelopes went into a second trash bag to join its sibling across the room. It felt good to toss the bag away from her.

What looked like real correspondence remained, though Anne was too exhausted to deal with it. She scanned return addresses, thinking she would start on them tomorrow, but a letter from their accountant caught her eye. She tore it open.

"*Dear Mrs. Craig. Please call me at your earliest convenience. I've been trying to reach you for weeks, and it's imperative that we talk about your late husband's investments and your current financial situation. I look forward to hearing from you soon. Sincerely, Bill Dixon, CPA, MBA.*"

The letter was dated a month ago. Anne's stomach started roiling, again. What could be imperative? *We talked right after Joe's death. Maybe Bill just wanted to change our investment strategies or something. Don't get tense. I'll just call him, that's all.*

"It's your Black Tuesday," Bill said, once Anne was put through to him. "I'm afraid your husband's accounts were nearly depleted. You should take out what little is left to preserve the capital, but that means you won't have any dividends or other returns to live on right now. I'm so sorry, Anne."

"What am I supposed to do now?" Anne said in a small voice.

"Unfortunately, you're twelve years away from collecting Joe's Social Security, which means you have to go to work."

Anne felt like she'd been punched in the stomach; she couldn't breathe and she wretched.

"Anne, did you hear me?"

Anne couldn't answer him for a moment. When her voice returned, she said goodbye and hung up the phone. She walked to the liquor cabinet. Taking down good-old Johnnie Walker from the shelf, she opened the bottle and poured a full tumbler of the amber liquor. Joe would not have approved, but what difference did that make now? This pain could be no worse than all the rest of them. At least this one would eventually take away the tension.

Anne couldn't sleep. She was too nervous and her mind kept racing. *What should I wear? My blue suit? Is it too formal? Is it too feminine? Is it feminine enough? What kind of questions will they ask me? What if I can't answer them? What if they hire me and I can't do the work? What if they don't hire me?*

This was only her first interview after weeks of filling out applications.

"We're sorry, but you have no work experience," they kept telling her, and without experience no one was willing to let her work to gain it. When she mentioned that she had been a homemaker for twenty years and did a lot of volunteer work, they just smiled and said, "Homemaking and volunteering aren't considered real work."

One man had gone so far as to say, "Look, little lady, the difference between working and volunteering is like the difference between performing under pressure and visiting one's friends. The first is an entrapment and the second is an engagement."

If Anne hadn't been so worried about getting that job, she would have given way to the anger welling inside her and told him off, good. What did he think being a homemaker meant? Sitting home eating chocolates all day or lying around watching soap operas, or lunching with one's friends while your husband is breaking his hump to pay for them?

Were houses cleaned by magic, or groceries obtained by telepathy? Were people cared for by intentions or activities? Joe always said that a job had no reciprocal regard for its disciples, but a family had the power to raise the dead and rear the living to achievements far beyond any job. Yet, these people upon whom Anne must now depend said that in being a homemaker, she'd backed the wrong race. The only good race was the fast track and she'd been left behind cleaning out the stables.

Anne was furious, but what could she do? She needed to find a job. She had no choice but to swallow her anger and keep her mouth shut. She remembered reading Henry David Thoreau back in college — his observation written centuries ago that now made sense. "Most men live lives of quiet desperation." Anne was desperate and had to remain silent, but anger could remain so long as she hid it.

It was too early to get out of bed, but Anne decided there was no point in remaining there, wide awake and worrying. She pulled on her robe, gathered clean underclothes, and headed for the shower, hoping the lack of sleep wouldn't show on her face.

Nature had been good to her, though, and her fifty-five years looked like forty. Staring into the mirror, she couldn't see the effects of sleep deprivation. Thank God. Anne noticed the small window behind her and to the left. She turned from the sink, remembering the day she and Joe bought it. They agreed on frosted glass, both for privacy and for light, but Joe wanted pink glass, Anne beige. She teased him, saying maybe he should get rose-colored glasses, too, so his world would always be pink.

He laughed and hugged her. As long as they were together, he said, his world would always be rosy. In the end he bought the beige glass to please her. Now he was dead and her whole world was beige. He had taken the rosy hue with him.

Tears filled Anne's eyes and she wished she'd let him have the pink window, and everything else he ever wanted, because nothing — no choice or argument or possession was worth winning if he weren't there to share it. She would give up everything for just one more day with him. What good was anything without him?

What did she have now…only their history and their house, but the history couldn't help her because it had no arms to embrace her, and the house was empty, devoid of his presence. Her life was a shell now, like a book whose pages have been read and the book put away on a shelf. She had nothing real to hold onto.

It was so unfair. How could history reduce Joe's life to a set of facts and figures instead of the reasons and resolutions of his heart and mind? How could it reduce their love and their dreams to little more than an accumulation of pictures in an album, or dishes and a dining set? She wept as she took off her nightclothes and stepped into the shower.

Anne stood under the hot water for a long time, hoping to ease the tension in her body and her head, though the steam did not reduce her depression. *Where are you? How can you really be gone? Where did you go? Why haven't you let me know you're alright?* Had his soul risen from his body like this steam rising from this water, as the minister said? Were the rains from heaven washing his flesh into the ground, just as this water washed away the sweat from her body?

"Joe," she screamed aloud. "Why did you leave me? Why do I have to go out among strangers and work in their world, instead of yours? I loved taking care of you and your home. Why did it end? Why can't I die, too? Why should I have to live without you?"

She took in a mouthful of water, gagging and choking, her tears forcing their way up through the rubble inside her, meeting what she had just swallowed, creating a painful bubble in her chest. She tried to belch to release the blockage, hoping it was a heart attack. The bubble burst and left only more pain in her outstretched windpipe, though not enough to kill her.

She stayed in the shower until her tears were spent and her fingers wrinkled. When she finally shut off the water and stepped out, she shivered in the colder air, goose bumps rising all over her skin.

Anne dressed, her former obsession with style now unimportant. She put on her bra, panties, and a bathrobe, and applied make-up, following the rituals she practiced her whole life. *Funny how a simple habit doesn't change no matter what else happens.* She watched her hands choose and apply the materials.

"You're getting to be quite a philosopher in your old age." She snickered, picturing a long-haired philosopher interviewing for today's receptionist position.

"We're sorry, you lack the work experience needed to greet people. No, it doesn't matter that you've studied four thousand cultures and met millions of people in your work as an anthropologist; you have no experience in office reception." Anne laughed out loud, picturing herself in her suspect blue suit, arriving at some newly-discovered island to interview the lost tribes of a stone-age people and then trying to justify it as relevant work experience in receiving people.

Before she knew it, she stood before the mirror, her make-up done, dressed and feeling lighter. The mechanics of everyday living provided her a respite from the mind games that provided a ride from depression to laughter, at least for the time being. Now she was ready for coffee.

Maybe this wouldn't be too hard to take. She sat watching the news and sipping coffee. She still had twenty minutes before she had to leave. *If I do get this job, I could be up early each morning. It might even be fun to get dressed and out each day. The house is clean and there's no one to mess it up, so what's so hard about working and keeping a house clean at the same time? If it weren't for Joe's absence, this might not be too much to manage after all.*

With a new sense of control, she finished her coffee and headed for the door.

The tension didn't overtake Anne again until she entered the parking lot, choosing a space close to the wall. Her stomach did somersaults and her heart pounded, making her regret the coffee. Why couldn't she just turn around and drive back home? Before the thought was an action someone stood outside her car speaking to her.

Anne nearly jumped out of her seat. "What?"

"Sorry I startled you." The young woman laughed. "Are you here to interview with Mr. Clark?"

"Who?" Anne was still off guard.

"Mr. Clark," the woman repeated, smiling.

"Oh, yes, yes, I'm sorry," Anne tried to regain her composure and her manners. She rolled down the car window. "I'm sorry...my mind was somewhere else."

"That's okay." The younger woman smiled again. "I'm Terry, Mr. Clark's office manager. I knew there'd be a new face here today. No one comes here unless they have to." Terry laughed. "C'mon inside."

Anne's tension shrank. "Thank you." She climbed out of the car. "I'm Mrs. Craig, or Anne, if you prefer."

"Anne it is, then. Let's get a cup of coffee before Mr. Clark arrives. We've got plenty of time. He's not usually here until nine."

"I was told to be here at eight."

"I know." Terry smiled. "C'mon, I'll show you around."

Anne followed Terry inside to a spacious foyer decorated with greenery overflowing in huge pots at both ends of a massive oak reception station. The modern furniture looked fresh while the floor and the windows shone in the early morning sunlight.

"Obviously this is where the receptionist...you'll sit...if you accept the job." Terry winked. "Over here is the—"

Anne's nervous laugh stopped the lecture.

"What's so funny?" Terry asked.

"You said 'if I accept the job.' I'm not so sure they'll accept me! I've never worked outside my home before. I don't have any experience working, so..."

"I know, but there's a first time for everything, right? Being the receptionist is the best place for you to start because you'll get to know everyone — everything — who gets what calls, how often, for what reason. This job is the pivotal point for information about the company, its people, and besides, it's the best place for you to get a foothold," Terry said matter-of-factly.

Anne's eyes grew wide as she listened to the responsibilities of the job. Maybe she couldn't do it without experience.

Terry laughed. "Don't worry. You'll get the job if you want it."

"How can you be so sure?"

" I'll tell Mr. Clark to hire you," Terry said.

"Why would you do that?"

"I don't know." Terry shrugged. "I guess because everyone deserves a break at least once. Now, how about that coffee?"

"All right," Anne said stepping back to look at Terry. *I may not have worked outside my home, but thanks to Joe, I've seen enough people working their trades to know a game when I see one, and to know that not all business is done on the job. I'll have to watch this one very closely.*

"Anne, we have a business dinner on Friday night. Can you do it?" Joe asked.

"I guess...but what do you want me to wear?" Anne said, picking up her cue.

"I'd like it if you were naked," he laughed, "but you better wear something or the boss will like you better than he likes me."

"He already does."

"Hmmm...that's okay, as long as you're willing to bring home the bacon."

"That's your job," Anne teased. "Mine is to take care of whatever you give me. What would you like to give me...hmmm?"

"Come over here...you'll find out." Joe reached for her, catching her in his arms. They giggled and kissed.

Business dinners were no big deal for Anne, having hosted lots of them. She loved playing party and was at her best when entertaining. She devised a cataloging system so that no theme was ever repeated or a dress worn twice for the same guests.

When Joe teased her about the system, she explained it. "When someone wears the same old things all the time, people think he's poor. Being poor is equated with being stupid. So the sin isn't in being poor, only in looking poor. Everyone knows that opportunities and money are not given to the poor, because they only consume the resources rather than compound them like business people must. So if we want our share of opportunities, we have to look like we don't need them."

Joe laughed at Anne's logic, though agreed that she was probably right. Being a talented seamstress as well as a careful manager, Anne created many of her own dresses and Joe's ties and shirts, making them look well-dressed on very little money. Since most people assumed that their clothes were very expensive, the couple was given their share of opportunities and had done well financially.

"You know what? I like you better without clothes," Joe teased, bringing Anne back to their conversation and leading her up to their bedroom.

"Mrs. Craig? Mrs. Craig, are you ready to see Mr. Clark?" Terry said, snapping Anne back from her former world.

"Sorry." Anne jumped to her feet, her face hot. She followed Terry into a large office where a middle-aged man sat behind a huge desk, mounds of papers littered over the surface.

"Mr. Clark, this is Mrs. Craig," Terry said.

"Mrs. Craig, this is Mr. Clark." Terry finished the formalities and left the room.

"Have a seat," he said, without rising. "Terry tells me you've had quite a background. Is that true?" He leaned forward, scrutinizing her.

"I'm, not sure...ah...what background she meant?"

"Well...ah," Clark searched frantically for Terry's notes. "Ah, wait a minute...oh, here we are. Terry said you've maintained a home for twenty years and that you volunteered a lot. Is that right?"

"Well, yes, I have but..."

"Tell me about it."

"Yes, I, um..." Anne wanted to run away. Her face was hot, her mouth dry.

What did I tell her? Had I slipped — mentioned something personal when we were having coffee? Lately, at the store or the gas station, I've had no control over my mouth. Things just spilled out —

personal things...private things. Things about me, Joe, our dreams, plans. It's as if I say things aloud to keep him alive. I can't help myself. Everything reminds me of him – the blue sky – summers at the beach. The cruises we took. The places we visited or planned to visit. Even how Joe had used the daily newspaper to wrap up potato peelings before throwing them away.

Nothing happened in her life that he was not a part of – he was her constant support – her partner. Like at parties, when someone asked Anne personal questions, Joe's wink gave her permission to play with the inquisitor.

Anne recalled the time that a rival colleague of Joe's asked whether Anne was planning on having children and if so, where they would raise them. Anne answered innocently, "Well, if we're doing things right we could have a child someday. Of course, I'd want to raise the child wherever Joe and I were."

Everyone laughed except for the embarrassed interrogator.

Now Joe was gone and this stranger was asking her probing questions again, this time without Joe standing across from her, winking and encouraging her to speak or supporting her playful answers.

"Where did you do volunteer work? For your...ah...your husband's company?" She sensed the phony sensitivity that civility without caring creates.

"Yes," Anne answered. "I mean, I worked with several groups, including my husband's charities. I've listed names of the organizations on the application if you'd like to check with them." She wanted to run away.

"I'm sure, but we need to make it perfectly clear that whoever gets this position will commit to a one-year assignment and promise not to run off and get married or pregnant."

Anne couldn't believe her ears. It was like Clark's brain had flipped a switch and he went into automatic stupidity. *Run off – get married? What was he saying? What had Joe been – A first installment – A one-night stand? There were thousands of nights — millions of days of investment, a lifetime of joy with Joe. Run off — get married? To whom? There would never be anyone as good as Joe or as sexy, or loving, or gentle, or as singularly hers in the entire world. Run off and get married?*

Already she hated Clark, though she couldn't answer him or tell him to go to hell, or to keep his lousy job. Joe didn't stand on the other side of the room making it all right. He was no longer there to defend her or help her to defend herself. She knew that this was only the beginning of her vulnerability. Without Joe, she stood on her own. This moron was only the first assault on her fragile future.

Clark leaned back into his chair. "Do you want the position or not?"

"I...ah...I mean, I...ah...yes, of course; I need this job." Anne couldn't believe it. If Clark was offering her the job, why did she feel like she'd been beaten up? Was she being too sensitive? Had she imagined it? She was uncomfortable with Clark and this place, but she needed the job. *Beggars can't be choosers* she remembered her old grandmother's saying. Anne had no choice, but at least, now, she had a job.

"Yes, I'll take it, thank you," she exhaled, realizing she'd been holding her breath. It wasn't a big job or even a well-paying one, but she had nothing, and sometimes victory was relief rather than riches.

"Fine, fine," he said, dismissing her. "See Terry on your way out. She'll tell you what to do." Clark waved her out of his office, lowered his head and picked up his newspaper again.

Anne stood up and showed herself out. She found Terry waiting within earshot and Terry threw an arm around her shoulder.

"Well, how did it go?" Terry asked, not waiting for an answer. "When can you start? Is tomorrow too soon? Oh, I knew he'd like you." She stopped to catch her breath.

"I'm not sure he likes me. He did offer me the job." Anne squirmed out from under Terry's arm.

Terry smiled. "Great! I knew he would. Is tomorrow too soon for you to start?"

"No, that's fine. What time?" She enlarged the space between them.

"We usually start at 8:00 am, but why don't you come in around 8:30 am. I'll have your paperwork ready by then, okay?"

"Yes, thank you, ah…" Anne hesitated, trying to pull the woman's name from memory.

"Terry. My name is Terry," she smiled again. "I'm sure we'll be great friends." Terry's head bobbed up and down. "See you tomorrow."

Terry guided Anne to the door, then turned and went back into her office.

"Yes, thank you," Anne said, not sure how much thanks this woman deserved or expected.

I have to start somewhere on the firing line, remembering the metal ducks that she and Joe shot at when the carnival came every spring. *But this doesn't feel like fun, and I'm getting scared, Joe. Why aren't you here to protect me and to make things right? Why did you have to die and leave me?*

Anne hurried to her car before she began to cry. *Maybe that man was right, work is an entrapment and now the fun is over. Joe, I'm afraid.* She cried as she drove home, alone.

Between coordinating the switchboard coverage, maintaining her own assignments, interviewing for the receptionist position, and then taking care of Mr. Clark's secretarial work, Terry was working faster than ever. Her shoulders cramped with pain. It was only 9:30 am.

Thank God, Clark hired Anne. The search had gone on for weeks. I was getting frantic. Soon things will settle down and I can return to my usual pace.

"Terry, come in here," Mr. Clark called from his office.

"Certainly," Terry said without hesitation, slipping her pen over her ear, and grabbing a notebook.

"Terry, why do you want to hire that dingbat?" Mr. Clark demanded as soon as Terry walked into the office. "She doesn't have any office experience at all, for crissakes!"

Terry closed the office door. "Mr. Clark, I think she'll work out fine if you give her a chance. She's very bright, she dresses beautifully and you know those are definitely good qualities for a receptionist."

"Every time I asked her a question, she stuttered," he yelled. "She's stupid, I tell you!"

"She'll be fine, Mr. Clark. I promise. She was just nervous — she'll be fine before you know it. I promise!"

"It'll be your mistake, if she isn't," Mr. Clark said, rising from his desk and walking toward her. He stood directly in front of her now, his breath hitting her face. "You know I've always trusted you, Terry, because I think you're so... capable," he drew out the last word. He cocked his head, putting a hand on her shoulder.

"Yes, sir," Terry answered, retreating a few steps, letting his hand fall back to his side. "She'll be fine, I promise. I take full responsibility for her. Don't you worry, sir. I'll make sure she learns quickly. You can bank on that, sir. Thank you, so much, Mr. Clark." Terry turned to run from the room, nearly colliding with a dark-haired stranger standing just inside the door.

"Oops, sorry." Terry felt her face flush.

"Hi, there." The stranger grinned down at her.

"Terry, wait!" Mr. Clark ordered.

Terry turned to see Mr. Clark beckoning her. A sudden rush of fear engulfed her. She was trapped between the two men, and her heart pounded. She looked first left, then right searching for an escape, but the stranger blocked her way.

"Come back in here for a minute," Mr. Clark said. "and bring Gary with you."

Terry didn't move. Her hands were sweating, her stomach pitching. For a moment she stood transfixed staring at the stranger, her mouth dry, and her body frozen.

Terry's heart ricocheted off her ribcage and her breath came in little gasps. Her shoulders pulled up tight around her neck, making her head push forward like a cowering child.

"Terry, this is Gary Shine," Mr. Clark said. "He's training here before he takes over the Bangor Division."

Terry turned to face Clark and realized the stranger stood right behind her. She couldn't speak.

"What's the matter with you?" Mr. Clark snapped his fingers. "Don't tell me that stupid woman is already rubbing off!"

"No, no. Sorry, sir. My mind was somewhere else for a second. Sorry," She pulled herself erect, turned around and took a step backward to make more room between her and the stranger.

"Hi, my name's Terry. Terry Woods," she said in her professional voice. "Welcome to Boston." She extended her hand.

"Hello, again." Gary grinned.

"Nice to meet you." She pulled her hand back.

"Terry's my…ah…assistant—right, Terry?" Mr. Clark smirked at her.

"That's what the job description says, sir." She felt her face get hotter.

"That makes you chief cook and bottle washer, right?" Gary laughed.

Terry laughed, too. "Yes, I coordinate everything around here, so if you need any help, just yell."

"I will." Gary winked at her.

Terry stood transfixed. Something internal, something unexpected responded to this man.

"As a matter of fact, Terry, I'm making you responsible for Gary," Mr. Clark said, resuming command. "I expect you to coordinate both his time and his training here. Do you understand?"

Turning back to Clark, Terry pleaded, "But Mr. Clark, I have to train Anne first because we've been without a—"

"If that dingbat can't learn quick enough, then we'll get someone else. I want you to help Gary, not some broad who's never worked before! Goddamn it, Terry, you're not a social worker."

"I know, but just in the beginning, she'll need a chance to learn, and—"

"Chances are for the ponies, Terry, not for dingbats. One week. That's it. One week, you understand me? You get that broad trained in one week or get rid of her."

"Yes, sir; she'll be fine. I promise." Terry nodded repeatedly.

"Alright, now Gary and I need to talk, so get started on his schedule," Mr. Clark waved a hand, dismissing her.

Terry turned back toward the door, but as she passed Gary, that internal thing clicked on again. She felt a rush of heat go through her. Her face tingled. He smiled at her and she averted her eyes.

Oh, God, please. If I can just keep Mr. Clark at bay until Anne gets good, and help Gary get good while keeping him at bay, I'll have it made.

Terry knew that life was difficult, and that the measure of one's worth was the number of things you could juggle at one time and the number of concessions you could make to the wills of other people. Some days were just more difficult than others, but if you stayed focused you'd always be okay.

The day flew by after her meeting with Clark, and Terry was so pleased they had hired Anne. Despite her initial nervousness, Terry felt Anne would learn the routine quickly, and besides, Terry looked forward to teaching her. It's good to start over in life, and every new person you meet is a chance to become someone new yourself.

Terry looked forward to the challenge. She had some serious work to do here. But first, there was home.

Chapter 7

Since Joe died, Anne barely slept. When she did, she awoke by 5:30 am, too early to get out of bed, too wide-awake to go back to sleep.

Instead, she lay there looking out at the winter sky still dark with night. She wondered why she continued to live. There would be more dark nights and even darker days ahead, so what was the point? What was the attraction in continuing to breathe, or sleep, or eat, or work? Who cared if your house was clean, or your yard was groomed, or your lights went on or not? Who cared if you wore the same old clothes every day or whether you had enough money to buy perfume, or dusting powder or soap.

What difference did it make if you bathed, or smelled bad, or brushed your teeth? Who cared if you'd shrunk from lack of food, or wasted away with disease, or rotted away from lack of hygiene? Nothing mattered when you didn't want to live.

Why didn't she give in and give up? Why was she still trying to live when she only wanted to die? Why was she still going through the motions of life, putting in her time here when all she wanted was to be there with her dead husband? How can it be over? It can't be over. It just can't.

The sky lightened outside her window and, as if a lever were thrown, daylight brought activity. *I don't know why I'm doing this.* Angrily, she threw off the covers and put her feet on the floor. *I have to get ready for my new job, before my new friend gets concerned.*

Already Anne disliked the young woman who had sewn up this employment. What was Terry's angle anyway? What did she want?

Whatever it is, I don't feel like playing. I feel like chucking this whole stinking mess and leaving this life. But no, I have to show up for work because Miss Goody-two-shoes went to bat for me. I never asked her to do it, and God knows I don't want to work with that idiot Clark, either. He hasn't got the brains he was born with, so why should I be a birdie between those two players?

Anne pulled her robe off the chair. She stomped over to her bureau, grabbed clean underwear, and headed for the shower.

Already she resented work, though she hadn't worked a single day yet. Though her resentment came from a desire to die rather than a desire to live, she now realized that work prevented her from doing what she wanted to do in life. It was a game in which everyone was forced to participate. Despite putting herself into the game, she hated Terry and Clark for calling her onto the field.

∞∞∞∞∞∞∞∞∞∞∞∞∞∞∞∞∞∞

It was a good morning when Terry got the kids and herself ready to leave, and the house picked up before Mack got home from work, or in this case, woke up. Today looked like a good day. She'd been up since five, but with everything done, it was only 7:30 am. Mack still slept, having stayed home from work the night before.

The kids were anxious to get going, so Terry bundled them up in their winter clothes, and walked them across the street to the bus stop. Other young mothers were already there chatting among themselves, youngsters in tow.

"Good morning," Terry said.

"Morning," they chorused back.

"Going to work today?" one of the mothers asked.

Terry laughed. "Oh sure, work as usual."

"I have so much to do at home that I can't image how you work and get your housework done, too."

"Oh, my house is a mess!" Terry said lying.

"Really?" the woman sniffed. "My husband works and I take care of our house."

"I'd love to stay home, but…"

"Where's there's a will, there's a way."

"My husband provides everything we need," a short blond smirked.

Terry felt her face burning. "Mine does, too, but I don't think it's fair for him to have to do it alone."

"You're not one of those women-libbers, are you?"

"What's a libber?"

"She-males." The other mothers laughed.

"I work because I have to," Terry said, but the gaggle had turned their backs to her already and resumed talking among themselves.

Tommy and Cara drew in closer to Terry, waiting in silence for the bus. When it arrived, Terry watched her children board, and then walked across the street alone.

Great! Now, I have to go to work to teach Anne and Gary the ropes. I wonder how badly I'll screw that up, too.

She got to work at five minutes to eight and rushed to get ready before Anne arrived. Luckily, Gary wouldn't be in until ten.

Terry still felt terrible about this morning's failure with the mothers. She was determined to do better at work. She pulled out the forms Anne needed to sign and rushed to collect the answering machine messages and distribute them before Anne arrived. By 8:30 am, Terry was ready.

Terry saw Anne at the front door and hustled to open it "Good morning, Anne."

Terry extended her hand and grasped Anne's sweaty palm.

Anne entered the foyer. "Good morning, Terry."

"Okay, I've got all your paperwork ready so when you're done with that I'll show you how to get the messages, work the switchboard, where to find names, how to read the room schedules..." Terry stopped to gulp air.

"Then, I'll explain sick time, vacation, and —"

Anne put up her hands in front of her. "Whoa, Terry. I can only absorb so much at a time."

"Sorry," Terry's face flushed. "Of course, it will take time. I was just rattling on. Okay, how about a nice cup of coffee before we start the day? Then we can begin, all right?"

"That sounds good. Do you need help making it?"

"No, there's always a pot brewing in the lounge, or at least there should be. Come on, I'll show you where that is."

Terry led the way through the foyer past the offices and through the main secretarial area where women looked up from their typewriters. Some smiled, some stared, and some snuck peeks at Anne.

"Those are the girls in the secretarial pool," Terry whispered. "You'll meet them at 10:30 am when we all stop for coffee. They're a good bunch. I'm sure you'll get along fine with them."

The bottom half of the walls in the break room were painted a pale pumpkin color, while the top half was papered with huge orange and white flowers. Anne shuddered. Comfortable-looking couches sat against two of the walls with some folding chairs spread around the room. The fourth wall had a door to the lavatory.

Anne saw a large table set up with a toaster oven, a coffee pot, and a small refrigerator off to the left side. The table held stacks of cups, plates and condiments.

"How many girls work here?" Anne said.

"Fifteen."

After fixing their coffee, the women returned to the reception desk. Terry handed Anne the employment paperwork. "Look these over, fill them out while I work the console, and if you have any questions, I'll be right here to help you."

After a few minutes, Anne complained. "I don't understand this part."

"What?" Terry looked over at the form. "Oh, deductions? That's asking if you have any kids at home"

"Why do you need to know that?"

"It's the law."

"No, we don't...I...don't have any children." Anne looked away, her eyes clouding up.

"Okay, then just put a zero in there."

Anne turned back to the task, continuing to question every entry. When she finished the forms, she passed them back to Terry.

"Ok, great." Terry smiled. She handed a blank notebook to Anne. "Maybe you can take notes as I work the console."

Anne sat back, pen in hand, ready to learn the job. But, despite taking five pages of notes, nothing made sense. She sat there confused and frustrated watching Terry's fingers fly over the keys—all those buttons blinking at once. She gave up trying to learn and decided to observe her new supervisor instead.

Anne guessed Terry's height at about 5'3". *Much shorter than me*, she mused, considering her own height at 5'7". Joe said that her slender body, and the fact that she carried herself stiffly, added to the impression of being tall.

She smiled at the memory of her mother's impatience with slouching, and her insistence on making Anne walk around with a book on her head. Obviously, the book-walk was successful because Anne never slouched, wiggled her posterior, or swung her arms. She even overheard someone say that she looked like a British sentry on guard duty. *Hmmph...what did they know?*

Anne noticed that Terry did slouch a bit, and her body was more solid than stately. It was earthy, slightly Rubinesque and maternal-looking. Her work clothes were neat, though not fashionable, and in beige tones.

Terry wore her dark brown hair, short but functional and she wore minimal make-up. Her hands looked strong, with clean, unpolished nails, complimented only by a thin gold wedding band. An inexpensive watch sat on her left wrist.

Despite this plainness, though, Anne saw a certain charisma that easily drew people to Terry.

"Take messages for me this morning 'till I get back from Springfield, will you, hon?" a handsome young man asked, winking at Terry. He zipped by the desk.

"No package from Houston, yet, Terry. Check on it for me, will you?" a heavy-set man shouted from an adjacent doorway.

"Where's the cleaning lady, Terry? My office is a mess!" Another man, shaking his head, held up a dusty hand as proof before heading to the washroom.

Amazed, Anne watched how Terry took care of everyone and everything with speed and diplomacy.

"Alright, Anne, let's have you try it." Terry motioned to the console, jolting Anne back to the task. "I'll be right here so don't worry."

Anne and Terry swapped chairs, but before she could pick up a call, a bustling redhead stood in front of the desk, hands on her hips, eyes zeroing in on Terry.

"Yo…any calls from Angel?"

"Not yet." Terry smiled, shaking her head.

When the woman left, Anne whispered. "Angel?"

"Hardly," Terry shook her head. "That's Flora. Angel is the man she lives with, who by the way, never calls. Don't let her intimidate you, Anne. She's just a big mouth."

"It wouldn't take much to intimidate me right now," Anne said. "I'll never learn this job, or all these faces, or be able to answers all these questions."

"Sure you will. Just give yourself time. It'll all fall into place. It's like my macaroni analogy." Terry nodded.

"Your what?"

"It's like this…water boils at 220°, right? So when you drop in the macaroni it takes eight to ten minutes for it to cook. No matter how high you turn up the gas, you can't make the water boil more or make the macaroni cook any faster. It is what it is."

"Where'd you hear that?" Anne was stunned.

"I made it up...do you like it?"

"Very graphic, but I don't want to think of myself as macaroni."

"Okay, then, think of this...show confidence until you have competence — then you'll really have confidence." Terry sat up straighter.

"What?"

"Show confidence until you have competence — then you'll really have confidence."

"I heard you the first time, but I don't understand it. How can I show confidence if I don't feel it?"

"Easy, once you realize that confidence is only denial of the negative possibility, then you just remain positive until your skills catch up with your belief."

"I'll have to think about that one." Anne frowned. "But right now I have enough to learn without adding in philosophy, too."

"Don't worry. Really, you'll do it." Terry coached Anne until a shadow fell across the desk.

Looking up, Anne saw Mr. Clark's scowling face hovering over the console, his mouth pulled down and his eyes homing in on her.

"How's she doing?" he asked Terry without taking his eyes off Anne.

"Very well, Mr. Clark. She's picking it up very fast!" Terry said, lying. "She'll be fine in a week or so."

"We don't have a week or so to waste on a simple switchboard." He pulled his eyes from Anne to Terry, "Especially if you have to train her. I need you working with Gary." He shot another look at Anne. "She'll have to be ready by the end of the week. Do you understand?"

"That's not much time, sir, but...we'll do it." Terry said.

Anne felt like a surgery patient being discussed by the doctors before the anesthesia took effect.

When Clark stomped off, Terry turned to Anne.

"Do you think you'll be ready to work alone by Monday?"

Anne couldn't help but see the hope on Terry's face. "I'll try, but what happens if I can't?"

"Don't worry about that right now. Just remember — show confidence until you have competence — confidence is just the denial of the negative possibility...denial is a cure. It'll be alright, Anne, trust me. Let's start again."

When Anne looked up at the clock again, it read 10:30. Break time.

"I really don't need another cup of coffee, Terry," Anne shook her head. "I'll stay here — try to learn this material."

"No, everyone has to take a coffee break. Besides, I want to introduce you to the other women." She showed Anne how to put the phones on voicemail, and guided her back to the lounge.

What if I don't want to meet them? Anne's chest constricted and her jaw tightened. Still, she let Terry guide her along. When they entered the lounge all eyes turned toward her. She felt her face flush.

"Ladies, this is Anne Craig, our new receptionist," Terry put her arm around Anne's shoulders. "I hope you'll make her feel welcome."

Terry walked to the coffee pot, leaving Anne in the middle of the room where a group of women crowded around her, all speaking at once.

A perky redhead extended her hand. "I'm Jane. I work in sales."

"My name's Beth. I work in sales, too," another redhead piped in.

Anne wondered if the entire sales force were redheaded.

"Bobbie's my name," another woman grabbed Anne's hand, pumping it. "I work in shipping."

From the strength in your hand, it's good career choice. Anne smiled.

"Hi, I'm Angela," a tiny, sweet-voiced woman said, "I'm in OS&D."

"Pardon?" Anne frowned.

"Overages, shortages, damages...like claims, you know?" Angela giggled.

Not a bad choice, either. Anne felt certain that few customers, no matter how angry they were, would hassle this little doll.

"I'm Flora," Angel's girlfriend announced, pushing another woman aside. "I'm in the training department." Flora's bulging eyes and thick lips reminded Anne of a puffer fish, though she suspected Flora was actually a piranha in disguise.

"Don't let her intimidate you, Anne," a pleasant-faced young woman said, stepping in front of Flora. "She's all mouth. Believe me, you'll hear her before you see her, so you can run if you want to."

The women laughed while Flora shot a hateful look at the general assembly before storming over to a couch and plopping onto it.

"Hi. My name's Beth Anne. I'm in finance," the young woman continued, extending her hand.

"She probably takes home more money than she makes, too," Flora snapped from across the room.

Beth Anne spun around to face Flora. "Want to say that to my face, bitch?"

"Okay, that's enough," Terry intervened, rescuing Anne from the center of attention. "Let's forget the sibling stuff for one day, huh? Let's just enjoy our coffee break."

Within minutes the customary chatter began and small pockets of women collected to exchange their daily bread, forgetting all about Anne.

Curiosity finally won out. "Anne, where did you work before coming here?" All conversation stopped and ears opened.

"I...um, haven't...um...." Anne cleared her throat. "I haven't worked before," Anne's face tingled. "I was a homemaker, and—"

"Isn't that nice?" Flora mocked, tilting her head coyly, adopting a plastic smile. "Did you like being home?" she asked in honeyed tones.

"As a matter of fact, I did." Anne said, her lips and eyes compressing.

"Don't worry...it won't be much different here!" said a young woman, sitting alone in the corner. "At home you just clean the toilet, here you work in it!"

Flora moaned. "Oh, jeez; there she goes again!"

"Shut up, bitch," the young woman shot back. "Listen, lady," the girl spun in Anne's direction so fast that she jumped, "this place is a crap-house and we work at the bottom of the toilet bowl. If you make bubbles, they flush, so maybe you should have stayed home where you controlled the handle!"

"For heaven's sake, Cindy, shut up," said a large-boned woman with graying hair.

"Screw you!" Cindy turned her face away from them, crossing her arms over her chest.

"Why did you decide to come to work, now?" the large woman asked.

"I just...um...I just became a widow." Anne's voice cracked despite her intention.

The women's shocked and saddened faces displayed the emotions that Anne would not. In unison, they expressed their condolences.

"I'm sorry...You're so brave...God, I couldn't take that... You must be scared...How are you doing"

The women chimed into the collective potpourri. One woman jumped up to embrace Anne, who pushed her away, though not before the scab that held Anne's emotions in check was dislodged.

Anne's pain erupted, sending hot tears running from her

eyes in ugly black waves of lava down her face. She ran into the lavatory. *Why didn't I keep my mouth shut? Now they all know my business.*

Anne felt exposed and vulnerable. She hated that feeling. She hated the women, too for knowing her business. Worse, she hated them to see her emotions.

No one tried to retrieve her from the lavatory and eventually Anne walked out to the reception desk long after the break ended.

Terry looked up, smiled and motioned for Anne to take the receptionist chair, again.

Anne couldn't smile back. She was ashamed of her behavior during the coffee break, and only having to answer the phone brought words to her mouth for the rest of the morning.

"Anne, use this key, not that one." Terry pointed to the transfer key.

"Alright, alright!" Anne banged the key with a rigid index finger. "Is that correct, now?"

"That's fine," Terry said just above a whisper. "I'm sorry if I was sharp with you."

"You weren't sharp with me!" Anne said, regretting her tone. "I'm the one who was cross. I'm sorry."

"No, no, no. I'm pushing you too hard. It's my fault."

"I know when I've been cross, and I said it was my fault. Now, please, stop taking the blame for something I did!" It was one thing to be wrong, but quite another to be excused without apology. Anne felt guilty.

Terry's eyebrows pulled in, making her forehead wrinkle as she stared at Anne.

"I said it was my fault. Now, can we please continue?" Anne said.

Terry stared, not really at Anne but through her.

Anne's heart stopped. *Is she mad at me now. Oh God, I can't afford to lose this job.*

Terry continued to stare.

"What's the matter?" Anne said, afraid to hear the answer.

"Nobody ever took the blame before..." Terry whispered, "or said they were sorry."

Anne pulled her head back, her brow furrowed. *What? What an odd thing to say.* Anne watched the young woman from the corner of her eye with renewed curiosity.

The switchboard buzzed back to life. Anne took the call. "Hollicorp," Anne announced, "Yes, sir, I can help you; I'm the new receptionist."

By lunchtime, Terry had snapped out of her silence, impressed and pleased to see Anne buzzing along taking calls and doing well.

There was a break in the calls. "What are you doing for lunch, Anne?"

"I hadn't thought about it, really. What does one do for lunch here?"

"Well, you can always bring a lunch if you're short of cash," Terry said then worried that she'd insulted Anne. She knew that widows were always poor. "Of course, if you want to go out, there are several nice restaurants locally. I'll be glad to take you to one of them."

"I didn't bring a lunch, so I guess I'll have to go out. Would you mind taking me to one of those restaurants?"

"Heavens no, not at all. And, since it's your first day here, why don't I treat you?"

"That's not necessary. You've done enough already."

"No, really, I want to. Actually, I insist. After all, I am your supervisor." Terry laughed.

"If you insist. I'll buy some other time, alright?"

"Sure." Terry nodded. "I don't go out every day, just once in a while when I can afford to, or, when I can't afford not to." Terry snickered.

"Pardon?"

"There are just some days, broke or not, when you can't

stay in. So, even if you drive around the parking lot for an hour, you have to get out of here."

"I think I feel that way today."

"You've only been here one day!"

"It's been a long day already." Anne shook her head.

"It doesn't take much to become a working woman, I'm afraid. Welcome to the world of work." Terry stood and gave Anne a ceremonious bow. "Now, let's get out of here and have lunch."

"Sounds like a plan." Anne switched on the auto pickup and Terry gathered their coats. Once the machine blinked green, they left the building.

Terry settled for a small restaurant less than a mile away. Once seated, she and Anne made small talk while they waited for their server.

Finally, a waitress appeared with a pad, pencil and a scowl, "What'll you have?"

"Can you wipe down the table, please?" Anne sneered at the lumpy surface beneath her menu.

"Sure." The waitress shoved the pad and pencil into a pocket of her soiled orange uniform. She pulled the ragged remains of a dishtowel from the other. She reached in front of the women, and swept the lumps toward the edge of the table, letting them fall to the floor. She tucked the cloth back into her pocket, retrieved the pad and pencil, sighing. "Okay, now what'll you have?"

Anne's nostrils flared.

"Cobb Salad, please." Anne sniffed. "Terry, you?"

"The same, please. Oh, and can I get some water with lemon?" Terry smiled at the server.

"Whatever." She rushed away through the crowded, noisy room.

"Is it always this busy?" Anne asked.

"Yes. Sorry, it's close by, and the food's not too bad."

Anne dismissed the apology with a wave of her hand. "I hope the food is better than the waitress."

Throughout the room, loud conversation was punctuated with slurps of drink and the clanking of silverware. Someone blew his nose, and Terry noticed Anne cringe. *Oh God, this wasn't a good choice.* Terry slumped in her seat.

The server brought the food and drinks to the table, some of the water sloshing over the glasses onto the surface.

Anne gave her a look.

"I know. Will I wipe the table, please?" The waitress retrieved the cloth from her pocket again and slapped it around the plates.

Anne shuddered when the server turned away.

"Anne, how long did you look for work before applying to us?"

"Weeks," Anne said groaning. "Nobody wanted to hire me because I hadn't worked before."

"I can imagine," Terry said, although she couldn't. She'd been working since her pre-teen years. Actually, she couldn't remember when she hadn't worked at least part-time. Even in grammar school, the neighbors sent her to the store for them and gave her a few coins for her help. Always, Terry gave the money to her mother.

"How long have you worked at Hollicorp, Terry?" Anne asked.

"Um…about three years, now, I think. Let's see…Tommy was four when I started, so…" Terry's eyes looked upward, as she calculated. "Yes, three years last November. I had just put Tommy in nursery school and decided to work days while my husband worked nights."

"How many children do you have?"

"Two. A daughter named Cara who's twelve and my son, Tommy. They're great kids," Terry said.

"That's got to be rough, though. How do you manage that?"

"What?"

"Two kids, a full-time job, and a husband!" Anne said.

"Oh, it's nothing."

"Yes, but if you work full time, then you go home and your husband goes to work, when do you see each other? Who helps you with the children?"

"We almost never see each other for long during the week, and nobody helps me with the kids. That's my job. When I get home, I fix them dinner, get them ready for bed, get my husband up and fix his dinner. When he leaves I get our clothes and lunches ready for the next day. I have it down to a science by now, so it's not bad"

"Science or not, that's a lot of work!" Anne said, shaking her head.

"I manage okay. Sometimes my husband gets angry because I take on too much, but I've cut back this year."

"Cut back? What did you do before?"

"Well, I was trying to go to college at night."

"Why?"

"I've always wanted a college degree because my father had one and I admired him so much."

"Is he gone?"

Terry chuckled without mirth. "Well, he's gone but not dead."

"Oh, I see. But, why didn't you go to college right after high school, then?"

"Well, Mack — that's my husband — wanted to get married right away, so we did. I was trying to go to school at night like I said, but I had to stop."

"It was too much work, hmmm?"

"Not for me—for Mack. He had to take care of the kids at night before he went to work. It made him too tired and cranky."

"Even without going to school, that's still a lot of work, Terry."

Terry laughed. "Do you have kids, Anne?"

"No, I think I already mentioned that I don't have children," Anne said.

"I'm sorry, Anne; I forgot." Terry worried about her short-term memory. She couldn't seem to retain information for very long lately.

"It was just Joe and me," Anne answered. "Now there's… just me."

Terry wanted to cry. She couldn't imagine having no one in the whole world that needed you. No husband, no kids, no one. Sure, it was tough to do all that she had to do, but at least she had people who needed and loved her. What good was life if no one was there for you? What would be the point in living?

"I'm glad you came to work with us, Anne," Terry said. "I really needed someone good on the switchboard. I know you'll do well."

"Hell will freeze over eventually, too!" Anne snickered.

"But not at Hollicorp," Terry said, breaking the tension, choking back a laugh. "That place will always be hell!"

"Well then, here's to hell!" Anne raised her water glass.

"Amen," Terry answered, raising her cup. "To hell with hell. Uh oh, look at the time! We'd better get back there or there'll be hell to pay!"

"Yes, let's go to hell, Terry." Anne laughed "Imagine, I've only been working there one day, and already I've told my supervisor to go to hell."

The two women still laughed as they drove back to Hollicorp.

Terry caught Gary watching her. It made her nervous. Twice, she left the switchboard to work with Gary, but it was getting more difficult to run between the two of them. Terry hated doing things halfway.

"Hey, slow down there, Terry. You're trying to do too much."

"I've heard that before," Terry sighed, thinking about her conversation with Anne about Mack's constant complaint.

"That's my job, though." Terry gave him a weak smile.

She picked up the statements and reviewed Gary's work. "These look good. What else shall I give you to work on?"

"Everything." He smiled.

Terry looked away. "Okay, it's getting late today, anyway. So, tomorrow…" she said, "I'll put you in some of the formal classes. You won't have to wait for me to give you a moment or two."

"I'm perfectly willing to wait for you." His eyes twinkled.

"Yes…well, um…okay. Take home the brochures I gave you earlier and call it a day. I'll be more organized tomorrow."

Terry left the office chuckling to herself once she walked out of earshot. *The best way to handle things now is to send one of the kids outside to play, then help the other one.* With Gary gone for the day, things felt more manageable.

"I don't mind just hanging around today," he said, behind her.

Terry cringed. "I didn't know you were behind me, sorry."

Gary frowned. "Sorry for what?"

"Nothing, nothing. Ok, then, I'll see you tomorrow." She turned around and headed toward her own office.

"Okay…see you tomorrow then." He shrugged.

Terry felt Gary's eyes on her back, and she shivered. *Why does he unsettle me, so? It doesn't matter. I have too much work to worry about that right now. Anne needs training, and I need a schedule for him for tomorrow or I'll have the same problem I had today.*

Terry picked up the phone and dialed Flora's extension. When Flora answered, she said, "What do you have set up tomorrow for Gary Shine?"

"I haven't been able to work it all out yet. I've got him in the P&L class at 9:00 am, the Claims class at 11:00 am, and then of course he'll break for lunch at 12:00 noon, but I don't have anything for him after that, yet."

"That's it?"

"I could put him in some other classes in the afternoon if you want."

"I need his entire day scheduled with classes, tomorrow." Terry tried not to sound as testy as she felt. "Can you please get that set up and put a schedule on my desk before you leave today?"

Flora responded in kind. "Whatever."

"Thanks," Terry said, her voice clipped.

"Remind me never to get on your bad side," Gary laughed, again, standing at her door.

Terry groaned. "I thought you left."

"I forgot to say goodnight…and thank you," Gary said, placing a candy bar on her desk.

"What's that for?"

"Defending Anne yesterday, and for being so sweet in training us both today. Goodnight, Terry." He winked.

"That's my job," she said to the empty doorway, her heart fluttering. She was afraid to leave her office until she brought her pulse under control. Finally she left and headed back to Anne's desk, hoping her face wasn't red, though a smile kept creeping across it.

Anne noticed the smile. "What's so funny?"

"Nothing!" Terry said, a little too quickly.

Anne turned back to the console, but not before Terry saw her smirk.

◇◇◇◇◇◇◇◇◇◇◇◇◇◇◇◇◇◇◇◇◇◇

My first full day of work under my belt, Anne thought, driving home. *With a headache to boot!* She opened the car window and the chilly night air rushed in. It felt good, and it helped her to air out her thoughts. Her mind found it difficult to remember everything that she'd seen and heard all day. Her concentration distracted, she wove in and out of two lanes.

A man in a monster truck behind her beeped and cursed. "Hey, you stupid broad, get the hell out of the way." He cut out from behind her and sped on ahead.

Must be in quite a hurry, Anne sniffed, suddenly aware that she was not. *Of course he's in a hurry. Probably rushing home to a ready dinner. Maybe his wife will give him what-for if he's late. But what do I have to hurry home to? There's no one waiting for me – not to cook for or to expect me there.* She began crying, and once started, couldn't stop. She pulled over to the side of the road, dropping her head on the steering wheel, she felt sorrow revisit.

Chapter 8

The overhead light still shined when Gary pulled into the space marked 48. He realized he had left the light on since last night. He had really tied one on at the local pub, stumbling back to his room in the wee hours. He wasn't much of a drinker, but he'd been lonely and the pub was the first open, inviting place he found. Going there hadn't helped. The more he drank the more lonely he became talking with people he barely knew. People with whom he had nothing in common except the loneliness of an evening and the emptiness of a life without events. Now he could remember neither their faces, nor their words — only their invitation to 'come back if you're in the neighborhood.' *The neighborhood? A neighborhood without neighbors, and an invitation without interest — just a momentary meeting — not of minds but of empty schedules and lonely hearts.* He came back to the room feeling more alone than ever wondering why he agreed to relocate in the first place.

It was the money. It was always the money. Despite being a manager at the old place and quite successful by all accounts, the headhunter called, offered him more money, and he left.

It wasn't too hard to pull away, either. He had done all there was to do on that job, and had gone about as far as he could with the people. Some of the women had let him go all the way, then clung and cried for commitment. That was their problem, not his. He'd never made any promises and actually prided himself on keeping his options open. After all, he never knew what stood around the corner, so why foreclose a better prospect by fencing himself in prematurely.

Still, he had always been lonely, because open options meant never having any real friends, only acquaintances — peripheral people — people perfectly outside himself who never got close. Peripheral people were playmates, not soul mates. They might be great in bed but not in the bulrushes. Peripheral people only took, and Gary was tired of taking on others' needs while his own went unnoticed, unfulfilled.

Isolating himself from real commitment and keeping his options open worked for him. It was better to be lonely than always on loan.

He opened the door to the room, dropped his briefcase onto the bed, like a coin into a fountain, and headed for the pub, again.

No matter what Terry did, it wasn't enough. She tried suppers, sex, gentleness, generosity, patience and praise, but nothing ever pleased him. The suppers were lousy, the sex never good, the gentleness an invitation for abuse, and the praise always suspect.

She could never placate him or pacify him. It made her crazy, because she didn't know what else to try. Now, he was starting again.

"Do you have to make that freaking noise out there?" he screamed from the living room.

Terry and the kids were making cookies in the kitchen. "I'm sorry, honey," she said, shrugging her shoulders, giving the kids a quizzical look. "We'll keep it down," she yelled back.

Cara shook her head. Tommy's eyes grew big and fearful.

"Don't worry kids, it'll be alright," she whispered to them. "We'll just be quieter."

"We weren't doing anything wrong!" Cara said rolling her eyes.

"Shhh. I know, honey, but there's no sense in upsetting him."

"He's always upset anyway!"

"I know, but let's not make him more upset, please? We'll just have to be a little quieter, okay?"

"Sure." Cara picked up a glob of cookie dough, squeezing it through her fingers until it oozed out in long, sticky ribbons from between milk-white knuckles. "I'll be good and quiet."

"Good is not always the same as quiet, Cara, but right now I think it's best, okay?"

"Yeah." Cara pouted.

"Hey! What are you doing out here anyway?" he said from the doorway, making them all jump.

"Ha ha ha...that's pretty funny," he cackled. "You people all jumping like that. Ha ha ha. I must of scared you, huh? Ha, ha, ha," he continued laughing as he drew closer to them.

Terry noticed her son quiver. "We're making cookies for you, honey." She stepped between her husband and son.

"Well, what's taking so long, then?" he bellowed.

"We just started."

"Well, hurry it up, for crissakes. I'm starving and I don't have all goddamn night. I have to go to work soon. That's all I have to do....be late to work! Then none of you will be eating cookies." He scowled.

"We're trying to have some fun at the same time, Mack." Terry shrugged her shoulders.

"Fun?" He leered at her. "You want fun? How much fun will it be cleaning this up?" he grabbed the bowl of cookie dough and tilted it above the floor.

"No!" Terry grabbed it from his hands, yanking it back. "You get out of here now and let us do this."

Mack stood there for a second with his mouth open before

realizing what had happened. He turned around and stormed out of the room.

"Get it done quick," he hurled back at the threesome.

"Okay... let's make those cookies!" Terry said.

Cara smiled, licking her sticky fingers, while Tommy moved beside Terry and wrapped his arms around her hips.

Within an hour the cookies were piping hot, their fragrance drawing Mack back to the kitchen doorway. "Well, am I going to get any?"

"Sure, honey, just a minute." She raced to get a clean plate, her anger forgotten.

"Well, hurry up, will you? I told you I have to get to work to feed this goddamn family."

"Okay, okay, I'm hurrying." Terry handed him a plateful of fragrant cookies.

He snatched the plate from her, scrutinizing the food. "You call this shit cookies?" he said, popping one into his mouth. "They taste like shit, too. I've seen better cookies in the road after a horse has had a dump," he said, throwing more into his mouth, turning back toward the living room.

Terry's heart sank. "Okay, kids, let's have some cookies."

The kids dug into the gooey pile of goodness, but Terry didn't take any. She'd lost her appetite.

Hours later, the kids were asleep, Mack had gone to work and Terry went to her room. She looked over her shoulder before she slipped her hand beneath the mattress and pulled out her journal. She brought it into bed with her, picking up a pen from the nightstand.

Dear Diary:

Today was the worst day I can remember in a long time. Everyone in work was demanding my attention at once, and poor Anne was trying to learn the switchboard with Mr. Clark breathing down our necks. Mr. Clark also gave me responsibility for Gary Shine's training, too. God, it felt like I needed to be triplets to take care of everybody. I probably let them all down anyway because Anne had a million questions and was so nervous I thought she'd faint. Then Gary kept watching me all day, waiting for more work because he's so smart he finished whatever I gave him quickly, and then waited for more. Cara and Tommy both needed me so we tried to make cookies, but Mack came bombing into the picture demanding my attention. I just can't seem to be everywhere or do everything by myself anymore. God, please help me.

She stopped writing when an acute loneliness stole over her. She began to cry. Everyone's problems rested on her, and she had no one to help her sort them out. She was alone, fighting a million battles and wishing to God that she had a comrade, or a friend to help her out or even to talk to. But neither ever came.

She ached for physical solace too. Like her life, she lay alone in her bed, and she wished Mack were there to hug her. Still, she knew that wouldn't help because he wouldn't understand. He would think she was horny and he would expect to get milked in exchange for a hug. Her heart ached thinking that no one in the whole world could uphold her without a price. Why did everyone need to be relieved before offering relief?

She wasn't horny and she didn't need to get laid, she needed to get loved. Though, after his tantrum tonight, Terry didn't want Mack, either. She was only having fun with the kids when he got angry and she didn't know why. If she asked him, he wouldn't tell her, so how could she stop making him angry? She couldn't win. With each new battle she lost ground and energy. She laid there and cried until she had no tears left.

Then she remembered Gary's gift. 'Thank you for

defending Anne yesterday, and for being so sweet in trying to train us both today,' he had said. More tears came from deep inside her. She wondered what it'd be like if Gary hugged her.

Chapter 9

Oh, no! The alarm hadn't gone off. Anne was late. She jumped from the bed and ran to the bureau, tearing through her underwear drawer. Nothing. Damn! She'd done the wash the night before but forgot to bring it upstairs. Now she'd have to run down to the cellar. She didn't know what time it was, though from the sunlight flooding her room she knew it wasn't 6:30. If it wasn't 6:30, she'd be late no matter what time it was right now.

Why is it taking longer and longer each day to get ready for work? Maybe because at night I have no energy left to get clothes ready for the next day. Maybe it's just the change of pace. Once I get used to it, it'll be fine. This week she was so tired she could barely make dinner before flopping into bed. Her habit of reading before falling off to sleep was gone. Bedtime now was more like falling off a cliff in a high wind. The moment she hit the bed, she para-sailed away. Now she had overslept.

Barely closing her robe, she raced from the room, and down two flights of stairs to the cellar. She grabbed the laundry from the dryer, but it was still damp. *Damn it. I can't wait to dry them. They'll just have to do.* Dumping the clothes onto the table beside the dryer, she pulled out panties and a bra, and raced back upstairs.

No time for a shower, either. In the bathroom, she tore off

her robe and nightgown, turned on the faucet and swished a face cloth under the hot water, scalding her hand. "I don't believe this," she yelled.

She picked up the soap and rubbed it onto the cloth and gave each armpit a once-over, then swished the cloth again, re-applied soap and ran the cloth between her legs. The friction made her pee and she realized she hadn't yet emptied her bladder.

Anne dropped onto the toilet seat and relieved herself while trying to wash the pee off her inner thighs. *If only I could reach the sink from here*, she stretched out her arm, but her reach was a little short. She threw the cloth toward the sink but it fell to the floor, instead.

I'm batting a thousand today. Hopping off the toilet, Anne grabbed toilet tissue with her other hand to dry her thighs. She stepped onto the washcloth, kicked it aside, and pulled the plug from the sink. Squeezing out a quick ribbon of toothpaste onto the toothbrush, she pushed it across her teeth, striking her gums. *Oh, God that hurt.* Anne looked up at her face in the mirror. Ten hours of work wouldn't help this mess. She spit the toothpaste into the sink and didn't take time to gargle.

By 8:15, she sat in the car heading to work.

⊸∞∞∞∞∞∞∞∞∞∞∞∞∞⊸

Terry distributed the messages, waiting for Anne. *I hope she hasn't quit. Mr. Clark can be callous, but I figured Anne was smart enough to know his bark was worse than his bite. Maybe I should call her house.*

Terry searched the staff roster. She couldn't find a listing, and then realized that Anne hadn't been there long enough to be included. When Gary came in, Terry was deep in thought.

"Hi there!" he said.

"Oh, hi," Terry felt her face warm. She hadn't heard him come in and his entry had surprised her. "You're early today," she said, feeling self-conscious. He was acting funny and his face turned red. Maybe he knew she'd been thinking about him last night. *Anne, please get here so I can go to my office.*

"How's it going today?"

"Fine." She smiled at him, noticing that he looked peaked.

"Good." He smiled back at her. "I need coffee, though. How about you?"

"I'd get it for you, but Anne isn't in yet," she said, rising to her feet.

"You don't have to get it."

Terry felt his hand on her shoulder, pushing her back down onto the chair. A tingle went through her.

"Just tell me again where the coffee is," he said, pulling back his hand and turning away from her, "I'll get it myself."

"It's outside Mr. Clark's office." She pointed to the left though he didn't turn around to see the gesture. "Help yourself."

"Fine," he said walking toward Clark's office.

Now he thinks I'm a jerk. He just started here and already I've messed things up. Terry wanted to cry as some internal critic kicked into high gear. *I came on to him like a slut, for heaven's sake. Now he's disgusted with me and I'm to blame.* Hot tears rose to her eyes and a throbbing ache seized her throat. Terry wanted to hide in her office, but Anne wasn't there to relieve her at the desk. Already, this day was bad!

Arriving five minutes later, Anne bustled through the door.

"I'm sorry I'm so late!" she said before reaching the desk. "My alarm didn't go off. Oh my God, what time is it? Quarter to nine...I'm sorry, the traffic was terrible." Out of breath, she pushed her things beneath the desk and pulled off her coat. "Here, let me get that." She dropped her coat on the second chair to grab the buzzing phone.

"Don't worry about it, I've got it," Terry said. "I'm just so happy to see you."

"Terry, please let me do that," Anne said, punching in the key first. "I can do it, really."

Poor thing. She sounds just like Cara after she's done something wrong. Anne must feel guilty for being late.

Anne handled the call well.

"Do you want to try it alone for a while, then?" Terry asked, knowing that the phones never got busy before 10:00. Maybe that would help Anne feel better, and allow Terry to hide out for a while, too. Her jaws ached from forcing a smile. Her head swam with pain.

"Yes, I can do it, really. Thank you." Anne said. "I'll be fine."

"Good, I need some coffee, anyway." Exhausted, Terry turned from the switchboard and headed for the lounge, but Gary intercepted her first.

"I found the coffee."

"Good." Terry continued toward the lounge.

"Where are you going?"

"I need coffee."

"It's right over there, remember?" Gary laughed, pointing toward Clark's office, his composure reinstated.

"The women have some in their lounge, too." She hurried away.

"I know, but get some from Clark's pot and come join me." He stepped in front of her to block her path.

"Well..."

"I insist. I was a little brusque with you earlier," he said, taking her arm. "Certainly you can spend five minutes with your other errant charge, can't you?"

"Alright." She submitted, but shook free of his grasp. Again his physical presence unnerved her, and her face felt prickly. She hoped it wasn't turning red, too.

In silence they walked to Clark's office.

When they both reached for the same coffee cup their hands touched, Terry jerked hers back, and looked away.

"I have to get to work," she said, grabbing another cup and filling it, sloshing some onto the table. "I'll have your schedule ready in twenty minutes. You can pick it up then, alright?" she said, walking away.

Anne smelled the coffee and needed some badly, but seeing Terry walk back from Clark's office, she knew better than to ask. Something was wrong. Terry's face was red and she walked fast. Gary trailed behind Terry with a look of confusion.

He glanced over at Anne, and when he saw her watching him, he walked toward her instead.

"Good morning," he said, extending his hand. "My name is Gary Shine. I don't think we were introduced yesterday."

"Hi, I'm Anne." She returned his smile.

"How's the new job going?"

"Very well, thank you. This is my first day all alone."

"Good."

"Terry trained me, so I think I can do it now."

"Terry's a good teacher. I'm sure you'll be fine. See you later." He turned back toward Clark's office.

"Thanks," she said to his back.

What a handsome young man, but what's going on with him and Terry? Anne laughed. She'd been there less than a week and already she saw plenty. Terry had been right. It was like a soap opera and Anne was enjoying the panorama. She'd just have to keep her eyes and ears open, and, as always, her mouth shut.

The redhead was back. "Hey! Did I get any calls, yet?" she yelled, jolting Anne back to the job.

"I'm sorry?"

"Why, did you do something wrong?" Red laughed.

"What was your question?" Anne forced her face to remain calm.

The woman stopped laughing and snapped each word out. "Did I get any messages today?"

"No."

"Are you sure?" The Flame burned.

"Positively," Anne said with maximum politeness.

"Well, maybe I'd better check with Terry then, just in case," the woman said crossing her arms.

"Be my guest." Anne smiled. The Flame leapt toward Terry's office, leaving Anne furious.

Several minutes later, Anne saw the redhead fly from Terry's office and hurl a dirty look in her direction before continuing toward the secretarial area. *I hope you get pregnant and he leaves you!* Anne still needed that coffee. Ten-thirty couldn't come fast enough.

Gary didn't get a break again until after the first two classes. His mind was muddled. *So much to learn, so many details to remember.* His head, not in the best shape today, made it hard to focus on the classes. His thoughts lingered on Terry. *Why did she act so strangely this morning? Why does she jump every time I touch her? I couldn't have hurt her. Yet when our hands brushed against each other, she jumped a mile. Christ, most women can't wait to be touched. Maybe it's because she's married, though that hasn't stopped others in the past. Not that I want to get involved with a married woman, again, but…*It was too much for him to figure out this morning. He needed some food to get straightened out.

Gary left the office and headed for a restaurant, stopping at the first one he saw. Once inside, the food smells made him nauseous. He ordered the chicken soup to go.

Outside in his car, with the steaming foam container balanced on his lap, he nursed the hot soup, trying to make his stomach stay still. It was January, the temperature only in the thirties, so he had to keep the car running.

After a while, the exhaust fumes bothered him. He closed the foam container, thinking that might help. He pulled out his work notes, trying to study them, but every noise and movement distracted him. He couldn't concentrate. Putting the papers away, he headed back to work.

At noon, Anne asked Terry if she would like to call in her rain check for lunch, but Terry declined.

"I brought in my lunch, but thanks." Terry smiled. Today she looked forward to sitting in her office alone, with the door closed and the radio turned up loud.

After Anne left, Terry closed her office door, discarded her shoes and raised her legs onto a stool. She sat sprawled out relaxing, skirt slightly raised, her mind adrift with the music when someone knocked at the door.

"Just a minute." She adjusted her skirt, dropped her legs down from the stool and put her shoes back on. Crossing to the door, she opened it a crack and timidly peeked through. "Yes?"

"Are you at lunch?" Gary asked.

"Yes, but that's alright. I was almost done anyway." She opened the door.

He started to walk away. "Go ahead, finish your lunch. I'll catch you later."

"No, wait. It's okay. Come in. I'm done, really." She beckoned him into the room.

"You're sure?"

"Yes, please, come in." She reached out for his arm, but stopped and made a sweeping motion with her hand toward the other chair in her office. "Have a seat." She left the door wide open, returning to her chair. She wanted to act nonchalant after their earlier encounter.

"Thanks. What were you doing with those?" he asked, seeing the ledgers open on her desk.

"Oh...I was working on the accounting books before lunch."

"Um... I thought I should talk to you about my schedule this afternoon."

"Sure, what is it?"

"This class on overages, shortages, and damages."

"Yes, OS&D," she corrected him.

"Right. There seems to be a lot of law involved here. How can I get much knowledge from a single class?"

"Actually, the class will give you a foundation in the concepts, Gary, but you'll learn most of it as you go along. Mostly, when the customer yells." She chuckled. "Then you'll learn quickly. Don't worry about that right now. It'll be enough if you learn the lingo, so to speak." She smiled at him.

He smiled back. "You know a lot about this industry, don't you?"

"I guess," she said, looking away from him.

"Is your degree in this field?"

"I don't have a degree." She cringed.

"You don't? How do you know so much about this business, then?"

"I just love to learn. And I'd love to get a degree, but right now I have all I can do to keep up with work and my family."

"Even without a degree, I think you could be a terminal manager."

"Oh, no, I couldn't. Besides, I have a family to take care of, too. My husband has the career. I have a job — just to help out."

"Yes, but if you have to work, why not work for the most money you can get?"

"I'm paid pretty well. Besides my husband works too, you know."

"Oh, yes, he has the career. What does he do?"

"He's a factory worker. Been there ten years, now." Terry nodded.

Gary frowned. "Wouldn't he be glad if you made more money?"

Terry was shocked. *If I make more than him, Mack would go crazy.* "I don't know. I haven't asked him."

"It seems a shame for you to know so much and not reap the rewards for it." Gary sighed. "I didn't mean to be blasphemous." He made a cross with his index fingers.

Terry giggled. "You weren't blasphemous, and thanks

for your compliment. It's nice to hear once in a while." She looked away.

"Christ, more often than once in a while, I hope," Gary chuckled, "Otherwise, why would any of us go on, eh?" He winked at her and rose to leave. "Okay, I have class in ten minutes. Thanks for your encouragement. See you later."

Terry couldn't believe what she'd just heard. *He said I'm capable of doing more and better instead of telling me that I don't do anything well. He doesn't think I'm a jerk, after all.* She felt her mouth and cheeks rise into a smile.

Anne was getting the hang of it. Call forwarding, voice mail, direct inward dialing, conference calls, camp-ons... all of it mysterious and marvelous — at first beyond her comprehension, now her expertise.

Terry was right about getting information on people here, too. Anne was now privy to many of the shenanigans and secrets among the workers, as well as the wheeling and dealing of the brass.

Good old Clark. Cheating on his wife while trying to put the make on Terry, burning the candle at both ends and walking on the top of it to survey the field. Then how about Billy in shipping? Meeting the guy from accounting for lunch every Tuesday after receiving a special package from the Route 1 truck driver. And loud-mouthed Flora. Telling everyone about living with her boyfriend for years and begging him to marry her because she was old-fashioned and wanted to have a baby. What a tramp.

"Hey, you haven't been passing on messages from Angel! What's up with that?" Flora wagged her finger in Anne's face.

Anne lost her patience. "I can't forward what hasn't come in. Maybe you should stop making excuses for your boyfriend and get one who's more available and conscientious."

"You shut your mouth, old woman," Flora yelled.

Terry ran from her office and guided Flora to the lounge to calm down.

Nothing more was said, and although many of the women whispered their condolences to Anne, none chose to put herself in Flora's direct line of fire.

That was fine with Anne. She knew one didn't have to openly challenge an enemy to consider her one. Silence was often misconstrued as agreement, anyway. Better to say nothing, than let your enemies know how you felt. Then, you had less trouble getting by, or getting even later, when the time was right.

Despite all that Anne had learned about the others at Hollicorp, Terry remained an enigma. She never received or made personal phone calls or shared anecdotes from her personal life. Still, she was always solicitous and anxious to please. Surely she had an angle, too, but what was it?

Anne recalled a time, long ago, when someone thought she also had an angle. At one of Joe's company functions, a handsome, young man had approached her, his hands tucked behind his back. He bent his short, stocky frame slightly forward.

"Hello, Mrs. Craig. My name is Frederick Henley." Anne stepped back to survey his entire frame since she towered over him.

"Oh," he said, *"I didn't mean to startle you."*

"You didn't." Anne smiled.

"Yes, well, as I was saying, my name's Doctor Henley. I'm the new company psychologist. How do you do?" he said without extending a hand.

"I do very well, thank you," Anne answered, pleased with her twist of phrase.

"Yes, yes," he nodded. *"Are you enjoying the company function tonight?"*

"Very much, thank you." She decided to have some fun.

"Actually, my father was an executive for a similar company years ago, just as my mother did what I am doing now. I fell into this role quite naturally." She baited him.

"Ah, yes," he said nodding on cue. "So this is familiar to you, then?" She nodded back, still smiling.

"Tell me, would it have been your choice if your mother hadn't modeled this lifestyle for you?" He leaned his head in closer to Anne.

"I'm not sure." Anne tried to look contemplative.

"I see." He raised his eyebrows and opened his eyes wider. "Why is that?"

"Because I actually wanted to be something more than a work-driven WASP," Anne said, enjoying her game.

"I see." He nodded, knitting his eyebrows together. "And is your husband a work-driven WASP like your parents?"

"Oh, yes, he's work-driven alright. But he's not a WASP."

"Ah, so there's a difference in your religions as well?" The doctor was getting excited. The company wanted its executives and their wives to have solidarity. That's why he'd been hired, to find those little chinks of dissent and report them.

"Not exactly a difference," Anne leaned in and whispered. "Let's just say there is a difference of opinion."

"Do you want to talk about it?"

"No." Anne shook her head, wrinkling her nose.

"Well, what about the difference in your work habits, then. Let's talk about that, shall we? How are they different? You said you wanted to be more than a work-driven WASP. Have you done more?" he asked in rapid succession.

"I've done much more than I ever planned to do with my life by being Joe's wife."

The doctor wouldn't let go. "So you've given up a WASP role for yourself and chosen to be the wife of a work-driven man then, yes?"

"I haven't given up anything, Dr. Henley." Anne smiled. "I enjoy being a wife, and I adore my husband. There are no differences or problems between us," she said, ending the game by walking away.

The little bulldog followed her. "Yes, but you did say that you wanted to do something different, isn't that right? More than just copy your parents' lifestyles. Do you feel you've done enough differently?" He was hot on the trail now.

Anne was getting annoyed. "Well, to tell you the truth, Doctor, I really wanted to be the president of the Soviet Union when I was young, but..." she let the bait hang to see how high he'd jump.

"Were your parents communists?" he said, his goatee quivering.

Anne burst out laughing. "No, Doctor Henley, they were not communists, nor was I ever interested in politics. Nor am I unhappy doing what my mother and father did before me. I love my husband, his work, my place in the scheme of that and, my own life. I was only teasing." Anne said, walking away from him, shaking her head and laughing.

"But, Mrs. Craig, humor is often used to..." he followed her across the room, his frame still bent forward and his hands still tucked behind him, "...suppress anxiety or pain."

"We've had a lovely chat, Doctor, thank you." She continued walking away from him, but like a hound on a fox's scent, he continued to dog her.

"Mrs. Craig, did I upset you? Let's just chat a bit."

Anne stopped and turned around. She stooped so she could be nose to nose with him.

"No, we will not talk." She smiled at him. "I was only teasing with you – not everyone has an angle that needs to be unbent." She spun away from the flabbergasted man. Later Joe told her that the good doctor diagnosed Anne as a very passive-aggressive woman.

Anne laughed at the memory. The poor psychologist. Of course, she'd been wrong teasing him, but it was his conviction that she was sick that caused him to over-analyze everything she said until he found what he was looking for. Ultimately, his value depended on her infirmity.

Perhaps I'm playing psychologist with Terry now. Maybe she doesn't have an angle either, but nobody's that private or that positive. Something's missing and I just don't know what.

The phone rang and Anne put away thoughts of Terry.

Terry had been working on the budget projections all day and was exhausted. Mistake after mistake took their toll on her nerves and her production. She threw her pen across the desk and cursed.

"Boy, that must be some problem," Gary said, poking his head into her office.

"What?" She nearly jumped out of her seat.

"I said that must be some problem you're working on." He laughed.

"Yeah." She laughed, shaking her head. "It's a beauty."

He picked up the pen and brought it to her. "Have you ever tried using a pencil, instead, when you're doing figures?" He laughed, looking over her shoulder, and pointing to the rows of messy inkblots.

"No, I never thought of it. But I'll try that. Thanks!"

"Great. Now, have you ever tried that little place down the street for lunch?" he asked, raising his eyebrows, and twisting his face ever so slightly, giving him an elfin look.

"No, is it good?"

"The best. How 'bout if I buy you lunch there tomorrow?" he asked.

"Oh, no, I don't think so, Gary…thanks," she said, dismissing the idea entirely.

"Why not? You've been working on these budgets for my division and you've seen to my training. I owe you that much."

"I get paid for doing that, but thanks anyway." She shook her head.

Seeing her distress, Gary said, "I'm sorry, Terry. I didn't mean to embarrass you. I just wanted to thank you for all your hard work, that's all." He turned and left her office.

Now, she knew her face was red. She felt foolish for handling that so poorly. After all, he was a nice guy. He hadn't meant anything by the invitation. He was just trying to be friendly. *So why is my stomach turning and a wave of heat moving up my body?* She had never felt like this before. *That's all I need to start flirting with Gary. Mack would kill the both of us.* She shuddered. *I'd better start behaving myself.*

She reached for a pencil to work on the ledger again. She made another a mistake. *Damn.* She reached for the white-out, and realized that she was using a pencil. The error could simply be rubbed away.

Five o'clock came and all the employees were heading for the door with their paychecks.

"Anne," Terry called just before Anne disappeared into the night.

"Yes," Anne said waiting at the door for Terry to catch up.

"I just wanted to say congratulations on your first week. You're doing a great job. Keep up the good work."

"Thanks, Terry." Anne sighed. "How does Mr. Clark think I'm doing?"

"Oh, he doesn't pay attention until something goes wrong. So if you don't hear from him, don't worry. It means things are going well." Terry laughed. "Let's walk outside together." She put on her coat and gloves.

"Terry, I think the man hates me." Anne cringed. "I don't think he would have hired me if it weren't for your recommendation, right?"

"Nonsense. He's just aloof, that's all, so don't worry," Terry said, shaking her head.

"I took your advice, you know," Anne said.

"What advice?"

"About confidence...remember?" Anne nodded. "Confidence is denial of the negative possibility."

"Yes, I do remember." Terry blushed.

"How did you ever think that one up?"

"Well, whenever I'm scared, I just deny that things can fail and then I try to do them without thinking about the bad stuff," Terry said.

"What kind of things?"

"What kind of things--what?"

"What kinds of things are you afraid of doing that you do anyway?"

"Oh, everything, I guess. I don't know. Everything. Like starting a new job, or getting married, or having kids, or taking a class, or whatever. I don't know. Everything," she said.

"Well, it's a great saying, and it helped me a lot!" Anne turned to hug Terry.

"What's that for?" Terry asked shocked.

"Oh, for having faith in me and for helping me keep my job. Thanks." Anne's eyes filled with tears.

"No problem. Remember, I told you everyone deserves her first break, after that she's on her own. Now, you can repay me by continuing to do a good job."

"I will," Anne said. "I certainly will. If there's ever a time I can help you, please let me return the favor."

Terry shrugged. "No problem."

Anne couldn't wait to get home. *Imagine! My very first paycheck.* Within fifteen minutes, she pulled into her driveway.

Not bothering to open the garage, she grabbed her purse and raced to open the front door, picking up the mail when she entered. Moving into the kitchen, she put the mail and her paycheck on the table, deciding to make a cup of tea before opening her prize.

Getting a teacup from the cabinet, she filled it with water and a tea bag from the canister next to the sink. These went into the microwave, it's time set for two minutes. While waiting, Anne opened the mail first, tantalizing herself to make the big moment even more exciting.

The microwave announced that the tea was done, and she retrieved it and placed it on a trivet while she took milk from the fridge to add along with a packet of sugar substitute.

With this accomplished, Anne strolled over to the table and set down her tea. Ever so slowly, she opened the check. Her heart raced when she scanned the unfamiliar stub. She didn't understand all the words or columns, but when her eyes fell on Pay to the Bearer line, she gasped.

"Oh, my God! $300.00! Is that it?" Her breath caught in her throat. "Something's wrong here," she said aloud. "Something's very wrong. I was supposed to get $10.00 an hour, which comes out to $400.00 per week, not $300.00. There's a mistake, here. I have to get this straightened out, now!" she cried, her breath coming in short, little pants, and tears close behind.

"Please, yes, I need the number for Terry Woods. Yes, that's right. Yes, I think her husband's name is Mack. Please, hurry." She could barely speak. "Yes, I have it. Thank you," she said.

Anne dialed the number. It seemed to ring forever.

"Yeah!" a man answered gruffly.

"Oh, excuse me." Anne was caught off guard.

"What do you want?"

"Um, is this Terry Wood's home?" She rushed to get the words out.

"Who's asking?" he asked.

"This is Anne Craig. I work with Terry."

"Yeah, Terry lives here. What do you want?"

"I'm sorry to bother you, but is Terry home?"

"No."

"Then, can you ask her to call me at 555-1442 when she gets in? It's very important."

"Yeah, sure." He hung up.

Anne reached for her teacup but her hand shook. She set it down again.

What's going on? That's a lot less money than I had planned on, and if that amount is right, I may as well starve outright, as to starve by degrees! That money won't pay the bills, much less, food. I'll lose my house! There has to be some mistake. How can I live on that?

Terry drove home sorting things out in her mind. Both Gary and Anne had complimented her today, and though the compliments made her uneasy, even embarrassing her, somehow they also thrilled her. She felt a little smug.

Imagine, Gary thinks I'm bright and that I could actually have a career. And then, Anne gave me credit for her being hired and trained. Maybe I can do something right after all. Thank you, God. Terry laughed out loud. *I asked you to show me the way, and I guess you have. See, I helped a poor widow and you helped me by sending encouragement.*

Despite the cold air, she opened the window and sang along with the radio, her heart full of thanksgiving.

Her mother's house came into view, and she pulled up in front of it, beeping to announce her arrival. The kids burst out of the front door, running for the car. Terry saw her mother's figure in the doorway, beckoning her.

"Grandma wants to talk to you, Mom," Cara said.

"I don't have time right now."

"She said you better, Mom. You know how she gets."

Terry laughed at the old head on her young daughter's shoulders. "Okay, honey." She closed the window and turned on the heat for the kids. She put the car in park and reminded them, "Now, stay in the back seat and don't touch anything up here, all right? I'll be right back."

Grabbing her purse, she walked to her mother's front door. A sour smell assaulted her.

"Hi, Ma. What's up?"

"Today is payday, right?" Her mother extended her hand.

"Yes, today was payday." Terry sighed, pulling two twenties from her wallet. "Here, you go. Thanks for watching the kids."

"Yeah, sure," mother said, grabbing the bills, dismissing the thank you. "I need a raise."

"What?"

"Are you deaf? I said I need a raise. Food costs plenty, you know."

"But, Ma, they're only here two or three hours a day after school. How much can they eat? And they always eat dinner when they get home."

"You callin' me a liar?" her mother bellowed, slurring her words. The reek of alcohol stung Terry's face. "Those goddamn kids eat me out of house and home. If you won't give me a goddamn raise, you'd better find another sucker to take care of them. You're just like your goddamn father. You want a piece of me, but you aren't willing to pay for it." Mother's head wagged out of control, spit flying back into her own face.

"For crissakes, Ma, wipe your face," Terry said, digging a tissue from her purse, and handing it to mother. "I'll see what I can do next payday, okay? Thanks for watching the kids." Terry spun around, and walked back to the car, her head shaking from side to side.

I knew I shouldn't have stopped today. I just knew it. Terry cursed, getting back into the car. The kids reached across the seat trying to hug Terry.

"Don't worry, Mom," Cara said. "We can take care of ourselves. Honest."

"You're only babies, sweetie." Terry maneuvered the car onto the road. "I can't leave you alone."

"Then why do you leave us with Grandma?" Cara asked. "That's like being alone, Mom. She's mostly asleep."

Terry looked at her young daughter in the rear-view mirror, thanking God for the help he sent through her child. "Do you really think you'd be alright at home, alone?" Terry asked through welling tears.

"Of course, Mom. It's only a little while until you get home, and besides, Dad's home after school, anyway."

"I know, honey, but he needs to sleep, Cara, you can't disturb him."

"That's okay with me!" Cara said. "I can watch Tommy. We'll be fine, I promise."

"We'll see, honey. I don't know what to do. I can't afford to pay Grandma any more money if I'm going to pay bills."

"We can take care of ourselves. Then you won't have to pay Grandma anything."

"Oh, I'll still have to pay her something, honey, but I won't have to pay her twice."

"Twice?"

"Yeah, once with my money and once with my sanity."

"Why do you have to pay her anything, if she's not going to watch us?"

"Because she's a poor old woman whose husband left her without any money."

"Why can't she get a job like you? You go to work, why can't she?

"I don't know, honey. I honestly don't." Terry's smugness and surety were gone. She was back to square one.

When they pulled into the driveway, Terry knew something was wrong. The kitchen light was on. Mack must be awake.

"Okay, kids, it looks like Dad is awake, so please let's not upset him. Be as quiet as you can, all right? Please?"

"Yup," they answered in unison, looking at each other. Tommy squished his face into a hideous lump and crossed his eyes. Using her thumbs, Cara pulled her lips far apart, then pulled up her nostrils with her index fingers, making her look like a pig.

"Oink, oink, oink," Tommy whispered, laughing and they poked each other.

"Oink, oink, oink," said one, then the other. "Oink, oink, oink."

"Don't start, you two, please! Not now!" Terry snapped. The kids stopped their noises and funny faces. They sat up straight and looked straight ahead.

When Terry opened the front door, Mack yelled, "Look at the goddamn time."

Running to him, Terry said, "What's the matter, Mack? What about the time?"

"When do I get up?" he asked, the words forced through gritted teeth.

"Nine o'clock, honey. Why?"

"What time is it now?"

"Six-thirty."

"Why do you suppose I'm up now?" He leered at her.

"I don't know, Mack! Why?"

"Because some freaking broad named Anne Craig called and woke me up. That's why."

"I'm sorry, Mack. Really! She's the new receptionist, I don't..."

"I don't give a good goddamn who she is or why she's calling here. You know I need to sleep."

"I'm sorry, honey." Terry apologized again. "I'll call her back and tell her that you work nights so she won't call in the early evening again, okay?"

"She better not call here again or there...will...be...hell...to pay. You understand me?"

Terry shuddered. "I do, honey, I'm sorry. Did she leave her number so I can call her back?"

"What am I? Your freaking secretary?" He brushed past, knocking her aside. "I'm going back to bed, and nothing better wake me up until it's time for me to go to work. Do you understand me?"

"Yes, Mack, I understand. I'm sorry, honey."

He stalked from the room.

Great. Now what's wrong with Anne? Terry threw her purse onto the table and motioned the kids into the kitchen. She wanted to scream, but first things first. "You kids look starved."

"Yeah, we're hungry."

Terry reached into a bottom cabinet for a saucepan and placed it on the stove. "Okay, you kids sit at the table and start your homework while I fix supper."

She took a measuring cup from a cabinet above the sink, filled it with water, and poured it into the pan. Pulling a package of instant potatoes from a third cabinet, Terry tore the top off with her teeth and dumped them into the water. From the refrigerator, she took out butter and a package of hot dogs, she walked back to the stove and poured milk into the spuds.

Terry broke off a chunk of the butter and dropped it and the hot dogs into a skillet she pulled from a bottom cabinet. Soon, the smell of wieners blackening in the sizzling butter filled the kitchen just as the potatoes began to bubble. Opening a can of green beans, Terry put them into a small saucepan then onto the stove. Within minutes, the food was ready.

"Okay, kids, supper." Terry tried to sound happy, but her heart wasn't in it. Sweets were always a good substitute for sincerity. "How about some ice cream after you finish?"

"Sure, Mom," they said without enthusiasm.

"What's the matter? You love ice cream?"

"Yup...that's good." Their hearts were not in it either.

She wanted to cheer them up, but she was lacking in cheer, just like the memory of sunshine could not brighten a dark day, she had forgotten her earlier brightness. The three sat in silence through the rest of the meal.

It was almost 8:00 pm. before Terry had a chance to get Anne's number through the phone company. Despite Terry's fear of more bad news, she might as well get it over with today. Maybe, then, tomorrow will have a better chance of being okay.

The phone rang four times before Anne picked it up.

"Hello," Anne answered.

"Hi, Anne, this is Terry. My husband said you called? Is

everything alright?"

"No. There's something wrong with my paycheck, Terry. You need to fix it. I got only $300.00! You said that I would be paid $10.00 an hour. Well, that comes out to $400.00, not $300.00." Anne took in a huge breath.

Terry didn't know what to say. Her heart was breaking.

"Terry? Are you there?"

"Anne, listen, why don't we meet tomorrow afternoon? I'll take a look at the paycheck and see what's going on, okay?"

Anne voice brightened. "Okay, Terry. Thank you."

"Alright, then. Where shall we meet? How about at the mall at, say 3:00 pm. The ice-cream kiosk?" Terry tried to sound cheerful.

"Perfect. And thanks, again, Terry. I knew you'd take care of it." Terry heard the smile in Anne's voice. *Oh God, What am I going to say to her tomorrow? Why didn't I just tell her now? I'd better tell her face to face, the poor thing.*

Terry hung up the phone, heading back toward the kitchen, tears streaming down her cheeks. *Thank you, God that I'm not alone and have to depend on only my measly paycheck.*

She headed to make supper and feed the real breadwinner in the family.

Mack had calmed down and fallen back to sleep. Now, the aroma of food eased his waking. He swung his muscular legs over the side of the bed, moved to the dresser for underwear and socks. He pulled on his jeans and tee shirt, and headed for the kitchen.

"Something smells good in here," he said.

"It'll be ready in a minute. You're up quick tonight."

"Yeah. Just don't take all night with that food, huh?" he said.

"Okay, okay—be right there." She hustled the vegetables from the strainer into the bowl.

"Here, start dishing these out for yourself while I get the lamb chops from the oven," she set the vegetables down in front of him.

"I just woke up for crissakes, and you want me to fix my own dinner?"

"All right," Terry said.

She pulled on the oven mitts, carefully removing the pan of chops from the rack to lay them on the stovetop. He watched her remove two juicy, aromatic hunks of meat and put them on his dinner plate.

"Okay, now...let's put some veggies on here," Terry said, walking to the table. "Okay, you're all set." She put the veggies on the plate.

"Where's the applesauce? You don't eat chops without applesauce."

"That's pork chops, Mack. You don't eat pork chops without applesauce," she said losing patience.

The vein in his forehead pulsed. "I don't give a frig what chops go with applesauce! I want some."

"All right." Terry stomped to the refrigerator, and pulled out a half-empty jar of amber substance. She gave it a quick shake and put it in down front of him.

"Here," she said.

"Good, now leave me alone. Let me eat this shit." He motioned for her to leave. She did.

"Okay, kids, let's get ready for bed, huh?"

"But Mom, it's Friday night. Can I stay up tonight?" Cara pleaded.

"Well, get ready for bed first, and we'll see."

"Okay. Come on, Tommy, I'll help you," Cara said. The kids passed through the kitchen. Cara called out in her sweetest voice, "Goodnight, Dad."

"Umph." He groaned, waving them on without missing a beat in the upward swing of his arm and the downward swallow of his gullet. "Yeah, g'nite," he finally managed gulping for air between chews.

Terry watched her beautiful little girl sleep on the couch. "God, please watch over her. Don't let her be hurt or helpless like me." Terry prayed aloud. The sound of her voice disturbed the child, who nestled deeper into the couch.

"Cara, honey," Terry called. "Come on, it's time for bed." Rising from her chair, Terry walked over to her sleeping beauty, and gently touched her shoulder. "Come on, honey, beddy-bye."

Sleepy eyes opened and a smile spread across Cara's face. "Hi Mom," she said. "Thanks for letting me stay up late."

Terry smiled back. "Come on, let's get you to bed." Terry shut off the television, and taking Cara's hand, they made their way upstairs.

Once Cara was tucked into bed, and Terry had kissed her on the forehead, she headed for her own room. She undressed, an anxious knot inside her, aching to be let loose. Looking over her shoulder, and listening, she decided all was quiet. She was alone.

From between the mattress and box spring, Terry took out the journal and brought it into bed with her. The knot unwound.

Dear Diary:

I can't take much more of this. First my mother wanting more money, then Anne's problem, and Mack not even helping dish out his vegetables. For crissakes (sorry, Lord), how much can I do? I feel like I'm trapped in a well, and everybody is calling down saying: as soon as you're free, I need you for such and such, and oh, by the way, could you hurry it up? I feel like there isn't a single person in all the world who's grateful for anything I do! Except maybe Gar....

She stopped short. What the hell was she saying? Worse, what was she writing? That kind of slip could get her killed. She gouged a heavy line over the last sentence, until both the line and the paper were gone, leaving a gaping hole. Tears erupted.

That's how I feel — like I have a big gaping hole inside me! She threw the damaged journal across the room and smashed her fists into her pillows — hard. The rage still driving her, Terry jumped out of bed and moved to her bureau. With a single sweep of her arm, she knocked everything from its top and watched as each piece smashed onto the floor. Broken bottles, picture frames, knick-knacks.

What hadn't broken, Terry reached down to pick up, then threw it against a wall, scattering glass and plastic throughout the room. Jagged pieces lay scattered about like shrapnel. *Am I losing my mind?*

She tore out of the room, down the stairs and out into the frigid night. The heat of her anger forged through her as she stood crying and gasping, until the temperatures reversed — the night absorbing her heat, her body taking its cold. Shivering, she gave her insanity to the darkness and went back inside.

Terry slumped at the kitchen table and thought about making a cup of tea. She had to find the courage to go back upstairs and clean the room. If she got it done tonight he'd never know there had been a problem. And she knew, from past experience, that it was better when he didn't know because usually he only added to it.

Chapter 10

By morning the bedroom was immaculate, and the journal hidden, but Terry's anger had returned, bringing a feeling of incredible viciousness. She still wanted to hit something, or someone.

Despite having no sleep, she left the room, and stormed downstairs. She thrashed around in the kitchen, putting dishes away and straightening up before Mack got home. It was easier to work when he wasn't around, and given the mood she was in, she knew if she didn't work it off, she would fight with him. Never a good thing.

She made a sweep of the living room and dining room, accidently knocking one of the chairs into the adjacent radiator, gouging the chair's frame. She dropped what she was holding and slumped onto the floor next to the battered chair. *It's ruined! And I just fixed these!* She sat cradling the wounded chair, crying. *I just refinished this poor chair, now look what I've done. I can never have anything nice for very long.*

The set was an antique that belonged to her great aunt. When Auntie became too old and sick to use it anymore, she offered it to Terry who was delighted to have it. Not only because of its functionality but it was familial — something good from her past that could be carried into the future — something saved from a family of loss.

But, Mack had been furious. "It's nothing but shit," he screamed when she brought it home. "Why doesn't she give us something good instead on dumping this shit on us? She only wanted to get rid of it without feeling guilty, so she passes it on to you as a freaking heirloom. And you, you dumb bitch — you take it. This isn't anything but shit, and you're a freaking shithead. Now get rid of it!" he demanded.

"Please, Mack, this is an antique. It just needs to be refinished — I'll do it myself. It'll be beautiful, I promise. Please let me keep it, Mack," she had pleaded.

"I said get rid of it! It's not staying in my house!"

"Why can't we keep it? We don't have a dining room set?" She knew immediately she had made a mistake.

"Well, isn't that nice, Mrs. Mouth? We don't have one anyway." He mocked her whining. "I suppose you told that old bitch that we didn't have one, right? Tell the whole world that we don't have stuff, so everyone can donate their shit to us. What are you trying to do, shame us?" he bellowed, each word building on the anger of the previous one until his rage exploded, consuming everything in his path. His arms flew from his sides, as he swept away the invading chairs, then he struck out at Terry, catching her face and chest with a blow that knocked her off her feet.

He reached down to catch her by the blouse and pull her up. His free hand plowed across her face. "Don't ever tell anyone our business, do you hear me?" he screamed. "No one!"

He threw her to the floor and walked away. "Stupid bitch. You don't tell nobody nothing."

For months, down in the cellar Terry refinished the furniture. Working on it made her tense. She wasn't afraid of getting caught, he never went down to the cellar anyway, but she was afraid of the time she was stealing from him and his needs.

What if he yelled for her and she didn't hear, or the kids annoyed him and he started in on them?

She planned each cellar visit to coincide with either his sleeping or his working hours. Still, she ran up and down the stairs between the cellar and the kitchen to check on things.

Sometimes, she enlisted the kids' help, when Mack wasn't home. She loved to have them with her, but each time she swore them to secrecy about the project. Still, it was fun to teach them how to do things, like how to sand the wood, pointing out its texture and grain.

Once the furniture was restored, Cara helped Terry sneak it up into the dining room while Mack was at work one night. Every day, Terry worried and waited for Mack to say something about the set, but he never did. He acted like it had always been there.

Terry looked at the damaged chair in her arms, again. *What's the use? Nothing ever works out. No matter how hard I try, nothing ever lasts for very long!* Her throat ached, and she wanted to cry again, but the tears were too deep. *What good does it do trying to make things work? They only get destroyed in the end, and you never make progress. As soon as you fix one thing, two more break. Then you start fixing the second and third things, and the first one breaks again, anyway. I just can't win.*

Terry thought about taking the chair down to the cellar and fixing it, but defeat snuffed out her enthusiasm. From discouragement, it was a quick hop to blame. *Maybe I'm being punished for keeping the furniture in the first place. It is his house, too, and he didn't want it. Okay, so we didn't have a set, but maybe he would have bought one eventually. What right did I have keeping it? I probably hurt his feelings by taking hand-me-downs, like maybe I didn't have faith in him, or something. Why do I always insist on having my own way? My mother warned me about that.*

She sobbed — guilt required penance and a contrite heart. She moved up, off the floor and righted the chair. It wouldn't be refinished, again. It would remain a sentinel, reminding her of pride's folly.

She continued through the house, half-heartedly picking up clothes and other displaced objects, her anger stolen by discouragement.

In the kitchen, Cara intercepted her. "Mom, can I help?" Cara reached out to claim some of what Terry was carrying.

"Thanks honey," Terry sighed. "Put these things in the rubbish, and try not to leave your clothes around, okay?"

Terry knew it wasn't the kids' fault that they weren't neat. She couldn't be with them all the time and kids learned good habits through consistent training. If Mack ignored or failed to remind the kids to be neat, that wasn't their fault.

And Terry knew better than to ask Mack to reinforce the training because his emphasis was on the force, not the lesson. He knew only one way to overcome resistance — eliminate it. Kids needed instruction, not destruction. Terry knew that her lessons alone would have to suffice, even if they were given only part of the time. She only hoped that some of it stuck, or that she didn't get too tired making up the difference.

"Did your father come in just now, Cara?" Terry asked.

"I don't know, Mom."

"I have to go food shopping this morning. I wonder if I should take you kids with me, or if I should wait and ask your father to watch you," Terry said half to herself.

"Mom, Sarah asked me to come over today, remember?" Cara whined.

"I forgot, honey," Terry said, shaking her head. "What about Tommy? Is he going with you, too?"

"He can't come with me! My friends will laugh at me! Please don't make me take him."

"Okay, I can take him with me, then." Terry sighed. "Go call him for me, please, while I finish picking up the house. But do it quietly in case your father is home and asleep."

Terry's momentum returned as her duty list loomed. She put the dishes to soak, and swept the kitchen floor. The vacuuming would have to wait until later, and there were at least five tubs of wash to do, which would also have to wait. If she tried to collect dirty laundry from the bedroom now, and Mack was home, she'd disturb him. *Let sleeping dogs lie.*

That was fine, but Terry knew that an early reprieve meant a late execution — saving tasks for later in the day when her energy was lower, meant that the tasks would be more difficult and she'd be more tired. *Save the neck now, expend the body later. What a choice!*

She hated Saturday. It was the worst day of the week. After the workweek, her other fulltime job began on Saturday. House cleaning, grocery shopping, clothes washing, fixing things around the house like the damn toilet seat that came loose every now and then; errands to run, kids to cart to activities — everything that couldn't be done during the regular work week.

On the weekends, there was never a moment of rest or relaxation, only frenetic activity that left her more exhausted than working the job did. She couldn't enjoy a minute of her weekends, because each task crowded into the next, and the next. Everything needed completion without consideration. How could she enjoy something if she couldn't consider it? *Maybe that's why memories are so precious. They're recalled and recreated in leisure.*

Terry went upstairs to shower, feeling like she'd already done a day's work. *Oh no! Work,* she thought in a panic. *I forgot. I'm supposed to meet Anne this afternoon. Damn. Now I'll really have to hurry.*

She snuck into her bedroom for clean underwear. Luckily, Mack was asleep.

Somehow he'd come home, and gone straight to bed without announcing his arrival, which angered her. What if she'd said something she shouldn't have, thinking he wasn't in the house? She hated it when people snuck up on her — a favorite tactic of his. Well, today she was just as glad he didn't see her or speak with her; she might have fought back given her earlier mood.

She gathered up her things quietly, and headed for the shower.

The bathroom, too, was a mess. Makeup spills, soap rings in the tub, hair in the sink. The hamper overflowed, and the mirror was so encrusted with scum that it was opaque. Terry could barely see her reflection in it.

Even the floor felt gritty under her feet. *Another job.* She sighed, dropping her nightclothes on the floor, stepping into the shower. Within minutes, the warm water washed over her, beating her stiff neck and shoulders, then flowing past her breasts, back, stomach and buttocks, and finally caressing her feet. She stood there for a long time, letting the water massage her, bringing blood and life back into her.

Within a few minutes she felt better. She stepped out of the tub and into the steamy, cozy room. She massaged her shoulders and torso with a clean, fluffy towel she'd retrieved from her room, where she'd hidden it. *Sometimes you need to put a little something away for yourself, no matter who else needs or wants it.* She gloried in the towel's clean luxury and fragrance. "Thank you, God, for such a wonderful gift," she said aloud. She finished drying herself, put on deodorant, and just a dab of perfume for fun. She put on the panties and bra she'd taken from her bureau, followed by the slacks and sweater. She was ready to meet the day again.

Tommy was already up and dressed and finishing his cereal when Terry came back downstairs into the kitchen.

"Morning, honey." She nuzzled his neck. "You almost ready to go shopping with me?" she asked.

"Is Cara going, too?"

"Nope. Just you and me today."

"Yeah!" He jumped up and threw his arms around Terry's neck.

Terry knew he loved it when they were together, without anyone else to butt in. He told her all the time that she was the best person in the whole world and there was no one he wanted to be with more.

"I'm all ready now, Mom," he said, heading for the door.

"Just a minute, young man," she called after him. "Come back here. Put your dish in the sink!" she said without reprimand.

"Oh, yeah, I forgot," he giggled, running back to grab the dish. *He's such a good child. And Cara...my reasons for living.*

Terry smiled. He ran past her again, headed for the door. She took her purse from the countertop, lifted the car keys from the hook on the wall, and pulled open the door. Mack stomped down the stairs, brushing past her.

"Coffee!" he shouted, moving toward the living room.

Within seconds, the television started up mid-sentence, like a robot halfway through a word. Terry put her purse and keys back on the countertop, sighing. Taking a coffee cup from the cabinet, she poured the hours-old coffee into it and put it in the microwave to reheat. She drummed her fingers on the countertop, waiting for the dark liquid to warm.

Terry jumped when the buzzer went off, not realizing that she had been holding her breath. She took the steaming cup from the microwave, picked up her purse and keys in her free hand and walked into the living room. Without saying a word, she put the coffee on the coffee table in front of Mack, smiled and headed for the door.

"Hey, where you going?"

"Shopping," she said trying to sound cheerful.

"Hey, wait a minute," he yelled, jumping off the couch, running over to her. "Come back here. Who else is going?"

"Tommy," she said, edging toward the door.

"Is that perfume I smell?" He stepped in front of the doorway to block her exit. "You don't get all dolled-up just for your son." Mack's eyes narrowed, his mouth hardening into a thin line.

"I'm going shopping with Tommy, for heaven's sake, Mack. Come on now, please get out of the way," she said, trying to nudge him from the door.

"You aren't going anywhere!" he said, pushing her back into the living room.

"I'm going shopping, now get out of my way," she said, tapping into the earlier rage.

He grabbed her coat and swung her around, his open hand catching her jaw with a thud.

"I said you're not going anywhere. Do you want to make something of it?" he said, challenging her, his fist held in front of her face.

"No." Tears streamed down her cheeks. "I don't want to make something of it," Terry said, pretending to turn back toward the living room. From the corner of her eye she saw him move away from the door. She bolted for the exit, but he leapt back and caught her by the throat, hurling her into the adjacent wall.

"Now I know you're meeting someone, you sneaky bitch!" His hand tightened around her throat.

"Okay," she pleaded hoarsely, "I won't go shopping."

He wasn't appeased. He leered at her, mocking her words. "I'm only going shopping," he whined, "with Tommy." His voice dropped off to a whisper. "Do you know what you sound like? Huh? A squealing rat." His lips curled back, his eyes unfocused. "A freakin' squealing rat."

"Mack, please let me go. Mack…please!" she cried, but Mack's eyes went blank.

For Mack, the room dissolved into a memory —

"You're gonna do what?" my girlfriend cried.

"Hey, man, you freakin' nuts…whatta you wanna shoot rats for anyways? Them suckers bite you and you die!" my friend said.

I shrugged off their remarks. I don't know why I like shooting rats, only that it scares me and I sure like pitting myself against them in the middle of the dump in the dark. I love waiting until I heard the rats coming, and feeling them running between my legs. I always wait an extra second then I switch on the flashlight I taped to my rifle and start shooting.

I love it when they don't die right away. They squeal in pain, making me want to squash them underfoot. But I never move because I might lose my footing and fall. I don't like to think about falling.

It was a ritual. I retrieve my girlfriend from school every Friday afternoon, then leave her at the corner with my buddies. She protests my desertion, and sometimes her whining flatters me. Other times she is like a squealing rat that I want to squash. She bitches and moans until I find one of my buddies to take her somewhere, then she's satisfied.

Just like a rat. They squeal and cry so you give them another bullet and they shut up. It's all the same — girls or rats, they're all the same. They run in herds in the dark toward the unknown and are satisfied with whatever stops the pain. Me or the next guy — what difference does it make? Any guy could make my girlfriend squeal with pain or delight. She isn't fooling anyone. She's just looking for a painkiller, just like them all — just like my mother.

"I know you've been screwing around again. You're a goddamned slut." I heard my father screaming, his words followed by a slap that knocked my mother into view.

"I swear I haven't been outside the house."

"Goddamned liar." I watched his huge hand hit her again, sending her across the room. "Even the neighbors look at me funny, 'cause they know what's going on around here, you pig."

"No, no, no, please believe me..." She is running back to him, her arms outstretched. Smack...her face caught another blow.

My breath stopped with every word, every smack, every second. I couldn't see them now, but I could feel their hot breath and raspy voices pulsating toward me. I was afraid to look, but more afraid not to.

I looked into the brightly lit kitchen, half-hoping they would come closer so I could jump up and stop their fighting, but two gleaming black eyes stared back at me from the kitchen table, instead.

"Oh, God, no!" my voice stuck in my throat. I wanted to shut my eyes so the light wouldn't betray my presence but I was afraid that if I closed them, even for a second, the thing would be upon me. I wanted to scream for help but what good would it do? They wouldn't hear me. I could only lay there in the dark waiting for the rat to come for me.

"Mack...please...Mack!" Terry gasped, trying to break through his vacant stare. "Mack, you're killing me," she screamed, trying to wrestle his hands from her throat. "Let go!"

"Mommy," Tommy ran into the room, and punched his father. "Mommy!"

Mack shook his head, and dropped his hands from Terry's throat.

She doubled over, gasping for air.

"Mommy, are you okay?" Tommy cried, tears running down his face. "Mommy!" He yelled when Terry didn't answer.

Frightened, Mack cried too. "Oh, baby, I'm sorry. I'm so sorry. Please be okay. Terry...*Terry*!" He put his hands on her shoulders and tried to shake air into her.

Tommy pushed his father away and clung to his mother. "Mommy!"

"Terry, baby?"

"I'm okay," she whispered, pushing them both away, needing air more than care. When she straightened up, they closed in on her again, so she threw her arms out, limiting their approach.

Tommy being small stepped in beneath her arms, glaring at his father.

"Please, honey, just let me breathe for a few minutes, okay," she said. "I'm okay, really." The child wouldn't give up his claim.

Mack cried even harder. "Terry, I'm sorry...honest to God...I just lost my temper. I'm sorry, honey. You know I never hit you before. Please forgive me...." he wailed.

Terry's heart broke to see Mack cry. He'd never done that before. She tried to reach for him, but Tommy wouldn't let her go.

"Tommy, I'm okay honey, honest." She tried to soothe him and loosen his grip.

He squeezed harder.

"Tommy, I'm okay!" Terry tried again to free herself. She managed to break his grip and push him away.

He stood there, tears gushing down his face, sobbing hiccups from his mouth.

"Tommy, honey, please. I'm okay, now let Daddy and I talk, okay?" she said, reaching out to stroke Mack's head while shushing Tommy's pleas. "We'll go shopping later, okay?"

He reached for her again, but she rebuffed him, raising her voice. "I said I'm alright, Tommy, now go upstairs and let us talk."

Terry didn't want to lose this precious moment with her husband and she knew that Tommy could wait. He was only a little boy. She could soothe him later, but if she lost this chance to break through Mack's shell, there was no telling when she'd get another one.

She saw Tommy shoot his father a hateful look, but he moved away as instructed. Twice, Terry saw him look back over his shoulder before leaving the room, still sobbing.

Chapter 11

Anne hated weekends. There was no one to get up for, and nothing of consequence to do once she got up. On weekdays, her job left her few choices—get up, get dressed, get fed, go.

The job lasted eight hours a day, but it took at least two to get ready and another hour to drive to and from. This left her less empty time to survive each day.

On weekends, without the expectations and activities that work created, life became leisurely. Anne realized that leisure was valuable only when one's life was constrained by, and obligated to, others' expectations and needs. Then, whatever free time could be gleaned was precious and meaningful. Without duties, leisure bred lethargy and emptiness.

Saturdays were the worst. Aside from the laundry, and the few other chores that living alone required, there was little else to do. Anne sat in her kitchen, alone and empty, wondering again why she continued to live. Why and how the beauty of Saturdays past could be gone.

"Come on, woman, it's Saturday. Get out of that bed, you lazy bones!" Joe set the coffee tray on the nightstand beside her. *"Rise*

and shine." He reached over to pull the covers off and tickled her.

"No!" she screeched. "I'm up, I'm up!"

"Okay," he said, releasing her. As soon as he let go, she stuck out her tongue at him and jumped beneath the covers, giggling.

"You little monkey," he laughed, pulling the covers down again, and locking his arms around her to pull her from the bed. She threw her arms around his neck and a leg around his middle, pulling him onto bed. They rolled over to face each other.

"Umm," she moaned, snuggling her form into the contours of his body.

"Are you trying to tell me you don't want to get up?" he said, with a smirk on his face.

"Uh-huh." She teased him by rubbing her body against his.

"Umm." He embraced her, stroking her back and buttocks.

She lifted her face to his and kissed him while his hand caressed the hollow of her back. She stroked him, too, though her reach was shorter than his. Her fingers ended at the little tuft of hair at the base of his back, which she twirled round and round.

He pulled his arm away from her back and slid it down to her hip and onto her belly. His hand pressed her triangle. She shuddered and broke off the kiss. He reached for her breasts and took one gently into the warmth of his mouth, sucking and releasing her nipple, while his other hand found her valley and entered it.

She cried out when he mounted her, sharing the moment until both were brought to convulsion. Shivering, he rolled off and they lay together.

"Coffee's getting cold," he whispered.

Anne smiled. "Umm."

Joe stepped onto the floor. "Come on, girl, we've got a full day ahead of us. Let's get rolling."

She slithered up against the pillows, and gave him a lazy smile.

"I love you, you know."

"You better!" he answered. "I've got a lot invested in you, lady."

How can that love, that passion, those years be gone? Anne wiped the tears from her face, feeling like her heart would break.

She pushed herself away from the table, dumped out the remaining coffee in her cup, and forced herself into action. Sometimes remembering just hurt too much.

The sun streamed in through the opening in the heavy drapes, like a slice of lemon in a rum and coke. Gary opened his eyes, but the brightness bore into his brain. *God, my head hurts. What time is it? Ah, who gives a damn?*

He thought about staying in bed, until his stomach lurched. *Oh Christ. Great reason to get out of bed…to heave my guts out.* Anger pushed the bile from his stomach up into his throat. He shot from the bed. Tilting his head backward, he ran, trying to close off his throat so the bile wouldn't overflow into his mouth. Instead, his quick movement made his head rush. He became dizzy and unbalanced, making the flight even harder and he barely reached the toilet before his head shot forward, his throat pitching the poison from his esophagus, over his teeth, and spewing out through his distended lips.

Retching, he gagged until his stomach emptied, pulling his innards forward. He pitched and swayed, his body growing weaker, his head lighter. He slumped down onto the floor to regain strength, but the movement brought him closer to the toilet. The stench made him gag again though there was nothing left to hurl.

He struggled to his feet and staggered toward the bed, barely clearing the edge before flinging himself face down.

For a full ten minutes Gary laid there until his head and stomach ended their rhythmic dance and he pulled himself fully onto the bed to roll over. The slice of light again invaded his view and sent his brain back into visible waves of pain. He lifted his heavy arm and dropped it over his eyes, feeling shriveled up and empty. He was neither remorseful nor angry. He was just plain sick.

The parking lot was mobbed. Anne drove around for quite a while before finding a space at the back of the mall perimeter. She looked at her watch — 2:45 pm. *Good. I've got fifteen minutes before meeting Terry.*

Locking her car, Anne headed for the entrance, looking at the people coming and going through the doors. *Where are these people coming from?* It annoyed her to dodge young women with gaggles of kids, and oldsters with walkers and portable oxygen tanks. A young man, tall and covered with tattoos nearly knocked her over, pushing past her, gyrating to some weird music escaping from things in his ears.

Anne shook her head recalling the newsman's comments, "Record sales are reported at retail outlets as shoppers live off plastic money."

Credit cards didn't make sense to Anne. *If you don't have money for something, you do without it. Simple. But, with Joe gone, I don't have a back-up resource. What if I get into a financial bind and need something? Maybe having a credit card, just for emergencies, might be a good idea. After all, I know how to stretch money and besides, I'm working now.* She decided to look into it after Terry straightened out her paycheck.

Arriving at the ice cream shop at 3:02 am, Anne walked in expecting to find Terry waiting, but she wasn't there. When a table cleared, Anne took it, deciding to wait the few minutes before ordering so that she and Terry could order together.

By the time the waitress approached a third time, Anne felt obliged to order, choosing a hot-fudge sundae. When it arrived, she picked at it, watching the ice-cream turn to mush.

Anne drew dirty looks from a couple waiting nearby with screaming kids.

What am I going to do now? Should I wait outside, or try to call her house? Anne felt nervous about calling there after the reception she received last night, but it was already 3:40 and Terry hadn't shown. Anne still needed her paycheck fixed. She'd have to make the call.

Mack cried for a long time with Terry holding and rocking him. Without warning, he'd had enough and pushed her away. He huddled into the corner of the sofa, looking like he slept.

Terry's heart ached for him. *Guilt is a terrible thing. It can crush you and grind you into the ground. I should know. I'm always guilty…guilty for the trouble I cause everyone, guilty for going to work and not being here where I belong…guilty for spending money I wouldn't need to spend if I didn't go to work…guilty for leaving my kids with my alcoholic mother, and guilty for burdening my mother with their care. I'm guilty for not keeping a clean house, or a happy house, or a happy family. And, I'm especially guilty for getting Mack so upset that he's forced to hit me. Look at him, feeling guilty, now when it was all my fault.*

She looked away. Seeing him like this wrenched her insides…like looking into a mirror, watching blood pour down her face, while being inside that face, feeling the pain.

For a long while, Terry sat there, afraid to move, afraid to lose the tender break-through that had happened between them.

The front door burst open, flooding the room with sunlight and noise. "Hi, Mom. Did you go shopping?" Cara yelled.

Terry's eyes flew open. She cringed and shot a quick look at her husband. Had the spell been broken?

Terry saw Cara wince. "I'm sorry, Mom," she whispered, pulling her shoulders up to her ears. She tiptoed to her mother's side.

"I'm sorry, Mom," she repeated. "I didn't know he was in here."

Terry shook her head and lifted her finger to her lips. "Shhhh."

Mack hadn't stirred, thank God, but no sense pushing her luck. Whispering, Terry said, "No, I haven't gone shopping yet, honey. Would you check on your brother for me?"

"Sure, Mom. Should I send him down?"

"No, no, not yet," she said. "I have to take care of Dad first."

"Right," Cara said under her breath, leaving the room.

Later, Terry heard Tommy answer the upstairs phone.

"MOOMMMMMMMMMMMMMM!" he yelled.

"Tommy!" Cara said in a harsh whisper. "Mom doesn't want to be disturbed."

"MOOMMMMMMMMMMMMM!"

Terry pulled herself out from under Mack's head. Moving up the stairs, she whispered, "Tommy, what is it?"

He whimpered. "Cara hit me."

"Terry!" A voice shouted from the receiver.

"What are you doing, Cara?" Terry yelled, too, now. "I asked you to check on him, not hit him."

"Fine." Cara stormed off to her room.

Noticing he still held the phone, Terry asked, "Who's on the phone, honey?"

"I don't know. Who's this?" Tommy asked.

"Anne Craig."

"It's Anne Leg, Mom." Terry reached into her pocket and withdrew a tissue, wiping Tommy's wet face.

"Oh, my God, I forgot." Terry took the phone. "Anne?"

"Did you forget about me?" Anne asked.

"No, no I didn't. I'm so sorry, I didn't forget. It's just that things got...well, hectic. I'm really sorry. Can we still meet?"

"I guess so." Anne said with a stiff voice.

"Okay, Anne, just give me a little while to finish things up here, and I can meet you. Shall we still meet at the mall?"

Anne thought for a minute. There were some things she could pick up while waiting, and there was that credit card to apply for. "Yes, I'll be here. What time?" she said.

"What about 5:00? Will that be okay?"

"Okay, 5:00, but I've already had my ice cream. Meet me in front of Linley's Department Store."

"Okay, fine. See you then." Terry had put the lid on one problem, now she hoped to contain another.

"What was that all about?" Mack asked, awake on the couch, when Terry walked down the stairs.

She sighed, walking to the couch to join him. Wiggling in next to him, she shifted him until his head cradled in her lap. "That was the widow I work with. Remember? I told you about her." Her words tumbled from her mouth.

"No," he said, rising from her lap.

"Sure you do, honey. I told you. Her name is Anne, the woman who took the job on the switchboard a couple of weeks ago. Remember? Anyway, the poor thing got her first paycheck yesterday and is all upset because she doesn't understand it. She asked me to meet her at the mall to straighten it out." She hurried through her explanation, hoping she'd gotten it all in before he closed his mind.

"So what are you now, her social worker?"

Terry felt his muscles tense against her body. "No, honey, but I am her supervisor. I feel responsible for her." She inclined her head toward his.

"What about your responsibilities here? What about taking care of me first?" he raised his head and kissed her, sucking her lips between his teeth and biting her.

"Owwww!" Terry cried, trying to pull her mouth away from his. When she couldn't, she reached down and pinched his nostrils, forcing him to open his mouth for air.

"What's the big idea?" he pushed off her. "I was only trying to get you horny," he said in a small, hurt voice. "I'm trying to show you I'm sorry for this morning." He hesitated, his face taking on a boyish grin. "Thought maybe I could get you upstairs." He giggled. "Watta you say? You wanna play?" He reached an arm around her shoulder and cupped a breast with his free hand, squeezing her hard. "Come on, you forgive me, don't you? Please. I'm sorry, I tell you. I'm sorry for this morning. Now show me you love me!"

She giggled at his antics, not because they were funny, but because that's what he expected, and because she couldn't be in two places at once. Right now, she needed to meet Anne.

"Okay, when I get back, okay? I'll really show you how much I love you, okay?" She pushed him further away and rose from the sofa.

Once free, she backed toward the coat rack, not making any sudden movements that could arouse him. She lifted her coat from the rack, retrieved her purse and keys from the floor where they had fallen earlier, and slipped out the door.

◆◇◇◇◇◇◇◇◇◇◇◇◇◇◇◇◇◇◇◇◇◇◇◆

Gary's head finally stopped spinning and his empty stomach stopped pitching long enough for him to get out of bed and collapse into the tub. He let the water from the showerhead run over him like the booze had run through his body last night. It had been stupid...getting drunk again. The third time this week.

What the hell is wrong with me? I'm not a lush, so why am I getting crocked every night? Because I'm lonely and at least there's people there who want to talk and connect. Who else has made an effort to be friendly? The guys at work? Cutthroat bastards, all of them. That asshole, Clark? All he wants to do is get into Terry's pants. He paused, shaking his head. *Yeah, Terry...now there's someone nice.*

Right from the start, Gary was attracted to her, which didn't surprise him. She was a good-looking woman, but there was something more...a kind of mellowness or a safeness about her, that put him at ease. Maybe he felt an affinity of some kind with her. He just knew that he wanted to be near her more and more.

She's married. But at least I see her and talk with her during the week, and that gives me an outlet. But what does that leave me on weeknights? The barroom? Who can blame me for finding comfort where I can? I don't take anything from anybody, and it's sure not costing anybody anything, so what the hell.

He felt better. The shower calmed his shakes, like his thoughts calmed his mind. With body and soul back together, he toweled dry and dressed.

Christ, look at the time. I've got to get to the mall before it closes. I need razors and a couple of new shirts in case I don't get to the Laundromat." A happier face stared back from the mirror. *I think I'll get something for Terry, too. Just a little something for making my weekdays so nice. I also need to call the motel office. This place smells like hell.*

Terry drove straight to the mall without noticing the beautiful day or the crisp, cold air around her. She didn't need externals to feel happy today. She was already grateful enough. *Imagine, after all these years, I finally found a way through his armor and now he's sorry. I've finally made him see and now everything will be fine.* Not even her worry about meeting Anne took away from the larger scope of relief her life just experienced.

The mall crowds were thinning. Anne found a bench that made it easier to watch for Terry. She laid her purchases down and waited.

She was actually quite pleased with herself. The store approved her credit instantly, telling her that she would receive her permanent card in a few weeks. In the meantime, they could approve a small charge up to $50.00 from which they would also deduct 10% for her first purchase.

A charge card and 10% off? Anne couldn't resist, and besides, she hadn't had a store-bought blouse or skirt in years. She chose a beige silk blouse and a mauve print skirt for $65.00. That was a little steep, but she was working now. Once Terry straightened out her paycheck, it would be fine. She felt quite accomplished and even a little smug, learning and testing new skills, which constantly amazed and pleased her.

"Hi Anne. I'm sorry for keeping you so long," Terry said, jolting Anne from her thoughts.

"Oh, Terry, hi." Anne felt the heat of blushing in her cheeks. "I'm sorry if I sounded harsh on the phone. I think I have worklag."

Terry laughed. "What's worklag?"

"Oh, that's what I call Saturdays. It's the residual exhaustion I get from rushing and working all week. Then it takes me until Sunday to feel like I'm free of work. So, Sunday is my weekend. Saturday is my worklag."

"That's pretty good. I like that." Terry laughed out loud.

"I kept wondering," Anne said, "why it felt like I only had one day off a week. Then, I realized that all day Saturday I finish up those things I can't get done during the week. So, between catching up and keeping up, I had only one day for rest and relaxation. Sunday."

"Isn't that the truth?" Terry said, thinking back over her day.

Anne mulled over how lucky Terry was, but brought her attention back to the issue. "Where do you want to go to discuss my paycheck?"

"Well, I haven't eaten yet," Terry said.

"What? Lunch or dinner?"

"Either."

"Well, we'll take care of that right now," Anne said, taking Terry by the arm. "There's a great little Italian place in here, and we can get a nice glass of wine with dinner.

Uh, oh." Anne laughed. "No wine for you if you haven't eaten all day. You'll get drunk and then your husband will be angry with me."

Seeing Terry's frown, Anne laid her hand on Terry's arm. "Terry, I was only teasing. I didn't mean anything by it."

Terry smiled. "Oh, I know that. I was just thinking of something else. No, an Italian dinner and wine, sound wonderful!" Terry said. "Which way to the wine?"

"Follow me, madam," Anne said, bending down to pick up her packages without losing her grip on Terry's arm.

Terry felt like she had stepped outdoors into a real vineyard when she entered the restaurant. It was a cozy little place with old Chianti bottles hanging from the ceiling and plastic grapes strung between each bottle. Murals of the Mediterranean coast adorned the plaster walls alongside vineyards with people carrying produce and grapes. Small bistro tables and chairs, decorated with black grapes and leaves, sat strategically placed throughout the small room.

"I like this place, Anne. It's so cheerful and I love the paintings."

Anne sighed. "It was one of our favorite places, Terry."

"Then, thanks, for sharing it with me." Terry whispered.

The waitress brought menus and the wine lists, and they spent extra time looking over their choices.

Terry ordered spaghetti with meatballs, while Anne chose chicken parmesan with rigatoni. They picked Chianti to complement the dishes and then made small talk.

"So, how are your children?" Anne asked.

"They're fine, thanks." Terry smiled.

"And, your husband?"

Terry laughed. "He's fine, too."

"You know, I'm sorry I woke him last night," Anne said, picking up a breadstick and breaking it in half. "He works nights, right?"

"Yup. Has for years. I used to hate it, but now I like the time alone with the kids."

"I'd love to meet them someday. Why don't you come over and visit with me some Sunday?" Anne took a bite off the torn end of the breadstick.

"That's a great idea. I'll talk with Mack and see when we're free."

The waitress brought the wine and then Terry made a toast. "To work and co-workers."

"To work, indeed." Anne laughed.

The Chianti loosened Terry's tension. Her shoulders relaxed and her midriff expanded. She took another sip of the wine.

"Listen, Terry," Anne said, "I'm sorry to burden you with this stupid problem about my paycheck, today, but I'm really at a loss."

"Did you bring it with you?" Terry hoped she hadn't.

"I have it right here." Anne dug into her handbag. "Here we go."

Terry took the offered pay stub and studied it. "Umm, I see." Her head nodded with less control than normal. "I think I know what the problem is." *How can I say this without hurting her.* "Anne, I, uh...I know I told you that you'd get ten dollars an hour, or four hundred dollars a week, right?"

Anne leaned forward, wide-eyed, her head bobbing. "Yes, but this check isn't right."

Terry hesitated. "Well." She swallowed hard, her throat dry. "What I failed to tell you was that the company deducts taxes for the government from that money." She went on without looking up. "Some people are exempt from taxes, like retirees working part-time, or welfare recipients in a training program. But if our accountants believe the government will require taxes on the earnings, they automatically withhold that money from the check. If you think that you should be exempt from taxes, then we could..."

"Stop." Anne's voice sounded thready.

Terry looked up to see Anne weeping.

"I have to leave." Tears spilled down Anne's face. "I'm sorry for being so stupid and dragging you away from your family today."

Anne gathered her things and placed $20.00 on the table. "Please, finish your drink, Terry. That's the least I can do to repay you." She rushed from the restaurant.

"Damn!" Terry said aloud, slumping in her chair. "I handled that well, didn't I?" She wished she could fall face first into those vineyards and never get up. "Miss." she called to the passing waitress. "Another glass of wine here, please."

Gary saw Anne running from the restaurant and tried to catch her. "Anne, hello." His call went unanswered. "Anne, wait up."

He caught up to her just before the exit and placed himself between her and the door.

"Hi there." He stopped to catch his breath. "Boy, you walk fast." He laughed. "It's nice to see a familiar face. Are you shopping?"

"I'm just heading home." She forced a smile.

"Can I buy you a cup of coffee, then?"

"Oh, no, thank you," she said. "I really must go. I'm sorry, Gary."

His smile faded. "That's okay, Anne." He shrugged. "Maybe another time."

"Oh! Do you know who is here, though?"

"Who?"

"Terry," Anne said. "I just saw her in the Italian restaurant."

"You're kidding. Terry's here?" Excitement pushed his voice higher.

Anne nodded.

"Great." He hugged her, but looked distracted. "Thanks,

a lot. See you Monday," he called back, rushing toward the restaurant.

Terry surrendered to the soothing warmth of the wine, her tension gone. "Miss," she called. "Another glass of wine, please," she said, enjoying the sensuous prickling of her mouth.

"Where's the other lady?" asked the waitress.

"Oh." A wave of sadness hit Terry. "She left."

"Hey, there!" Gary stood next to the waitress, out of breath, but smiling.

The waitress looked up. "He with you, too?"

Terry pulled back in her chair and raised her brows in confusion. "Gary! Watta you doing here?" She struggled to bring his face into focus.

"I just ran into Anne. She said you were here. Can I join you?" he asked, pointing to Anne's vacated seat.

"Is he with you?" the waitress asked a second time.

"Looks like he is," Terry said and waved her hand toward the other chair. "Get him some wine, too, please."

"I hate Saturdays." The waitress cursed and stormed off.

"Thanks." Gary settled his big frame onto the tiny round bistro seat. "So, tell me. Why are you here alone?"

Terry blushed, unwilling to throw Anne under the bus.

"I had shopping to do and…" Her hand flailed and her head tilted to the side. "…and I didn't eat all day so…what the hell," she said, her hand flying up again.

Gary laughed. "How much wine have you had?"

"Why? You think I'm drunk?"

"Don't worry about it. Eat some of that food. It will absorb the alcohol. You'll be fine."

Terry's eyes flew open. "Oh, my God, I can't go home like this." She foresaw Mack's newfound openness going out the window. "Oh, God," she wailed. "I've got to get sober." She tried to sit up straighter, but tipped a bit to the left. She raised her head, getting her bearings.

"Here, start with this." He offered her some bread and then pulled it back. "Do you want it buttered?"

"What?" Her face fell into a frown. "What did you say?"

He laughed. "Do you want some butter?"

She shook her head. "No." She grabbed a piece and took a large bite.

"Hey, don't panic. Slow down. You'll be fine, honest. So you had a little wine. It's no big deal," he said.

A lump formed in Terry's throat. She wasn't sure if it came from the half-chewed bread or the novelty of someone worrying about her for a change.

"I'm sorry." She choked on an air bubble that made its way past the swallowed bread. When the hiccups came, they brought tears with them.

"Terry, it's no big deal. Come on." He reached over and covered her hand with his. "You'll be okay, I promise."

The lump in her throat grew bigger until she felt her whole chest about to explode. She dropped her chin to her chest, feeling bad…confused…out of control. Tears threatened to spill.

"What's wrong, Terry?" He squeezed the hand under his. "Are you okay?"

"Umhwmumn." It came out on a sob.

"Okay, I didn't understand a word of that," he laughed. "We'll eat something and you'll be fine." He called the waitress over. "Two cups of coffee and I'm ready to order now."

The server grunted, took his order, and left.

Chapter 12

"How stupid can I be, Joe?" Anne cried to her empty car. "I didn't think about taxes!" She leaned against the steering wheel, her arm cushioning her head. *You were so good to me and took such good care of everything. I'm like an idiot. I don't know anything.*

She beat her fist on the dashboard under the waves of despair that shook her. *How could you let me be so helpless? How could you leave me not knowing anything? How am I going to live? My pay after taxes isn't enough to live on, much less buy food, or gas for the car, or...*

Anne saw the packages on the other seat—clothing she'd bought with the plastic money. She remembered one of her early job interviews. *Maybe that man was right, work is an entrapment: you have to keep working to pay for what you have to buy to keep working.* Forever, that blouse and skirt would be the harbingers of her imprisonment, reminding her that she had unwittingly strolled into a cell and taken her place among the millions of Joes and Janes who need to work for a living, and who have to spend what they earn to live.

She would never wear those hated clothes.

"Feeling better?" Gary asked.

"Yes, thanks," she answered, slumping against her chair. "I'm sorry for…panicking a while ago." She avoided his glance.

"No problem." He smiled. "I can see why you don't want to go home drunk when you're supposed to be out shopping."

Terry burst out laughing at Gary's mock reprimand. "Yeah, I can just see my husband now." She cackled. "And where have you been?" she asked, her voice deep with an authorial tone, her hands on her hips.

"Is he really that bad?" he laughed, tears running down his face.

"Oh, no," she stopped laughing, shaking her head vehemently. "No, he's really a nice guy." Or at least she planned for that after today's breakthrough with Mack. She smiled. "I actually think you'd like each other."

"Maybe," Gary said.

Terry felt her face flush. "What?"

"Nothing." He laughed again. "And, I think it's pretty safe to let you go home now, don't you think?" He teased her, scrutinizing her with a sidelong look.

"I think so, Dad." She laughed at his dramatics, part of her response to his care.

"Thanks, Gary," she said, squeezing his hand, and standing up. She pulled three, ten-dollar bills from her wallet, placed them on the table and turned to walk away.

"Just a moment, young lady!" he called out in mock horror. Everyone in the restaurant turned their heads to listen. "You forgot your money," he said, rising and extending the bills toward her.

Terry rushed back to the table. "But that's for Anne's wine and my food and wine," she whispered.

"I would *never* let a young lady pay for a drink," he

said in a loud, theatrical voice.

Her face heated up.

"Here now." Bowing ceremoniously, he forced the money into her hand. "It's my pleasure of course."

People sat staring at them, and Terry felt their collective breath suspend, waiting for her response.

"Why, thank you sir," she faked her most charming voice, and giving a little bow, she took the money and bolted from the restaurant.

Gary smiled.

Mack was asleep when she got home. Terry felt enormous relief. Despite now being mostly sober, the smell of wine still hung on her breath, and she didn't want to arouse suspicion or distrust.

The unease of self-consciousness stole over her along with her sobriety. She couldn't believe that she and Gary had practically had a date this afternoon. A hot prickly uneasiness filled her stomach.

Oh God, it's just not right to be with Gary, or to get drunk on a Saturday afternoon, or laugh and joke with a man who isn't my husband.

Still, they had enjoyed each other's company, aside from her worry about being drunk, but she knew she treaded on dangerous ground...even getting downright brazen. *God, I better cut it out, because if Mack ever finds out, he'll kick me out, or kill me. And can I blame him? No, it's flagrant flirtatiousness, and I'm just asking for trouble.*

Terry shuddered. *It's only by Your grace, God, that Mack is sleeping. I swear I'll never compromise myself or my marriage like that again.*

She decided never to speak to Gary again, at least not in that way. Sure, she had to work with him, but the friendly stuff would stop.

I'm a good woman, and Mack is a good husband, or at least he's trying to be. And I have a chance to help him now that he's opened up. I'd be a fool to throw it all away on a guy I hardly know. No more Saturday interludes. That's it.

"Mom, where have you been?" Tommy asked, his lips pouting.

"I was meeting with Anne, honey. Remember, the woman from work?" she asked.

"You were supposed to take me," he whispered, his lower lip quivering and his eyes filling with tears. "And you forgot me."

"I'm sorry, honey, but I had to help Anne with her paycheck. You understand, don't you?" she asked, embracing him. "Don't you?"

"I wanted to go with you." He sobbed, his little face, with its swollen eyes and leaking tears looked up at her.

Terry's throat constricted. "We'll go out together after church, tomorrow, okay?" she promised.

Big tears ran down his face, and Terry's heart broke thinking about having spent the better part of an afternoon flirting with a guy from work, while her poor son sat home waiting for her to keep a promise. Terry's eyes filled with tears, too.

"How about making pizza together for dinner?" she asked.

He couldn't resist. "Okay," he squirmed from her embrace. "I'll get the pan and you get the other stuff."

God love him...so easily distracted from his pain. Terry shook her head, knowing that this time the pain would go away. She knew this only too well that when new ones were added, they'd eventually accumulate and lodge somewhere dark, festering.

Mack went out every Saturday night. It was his time to unwind and he didn't give a damn if Terry liked it or not. After all, he worked all week, brought his paycheck home, or at least most of it, and he did his sexual duty, what did she have to bitch about?

He walked into the long, dark barroom with its familiar row of ancient metal stools bolted to the floor on the left, fronting the century-old black mahogany bar with its divots and dents from years of use and abuse.

A few old guys sat chugging their suds at the bar and looked up at Mack's entrance. They nodded in his direction, though none spoke.

Mack nodded back, and walked between the bar and the high-backed wooden booths to his left until he reached the last booth in the row where a young couple sat sipping drinks and cuddling.

"Hey," Mack said motioning for them to get up and leave the booth.

"No problem," the young guy said, pulling his girl up and out of the enclosure.

"Don't forget your drinks," Mack told them.

"Thanks." The former occupant dropped his girl's arm, picked up the two drinks and motioned for her to move to another booth way up front.

"But, we were there first," the girl protested.

"Shut up," her date said, pushing her shoulder with his, propelling her forward.

"Jeez, my hero." She moved away from the table.

Mack took the seat on the wall side of the booth so he could watch the whole bar.

Within minutes the waitress came over to Mack's booth. "Hey baby, how you doin' tonight?" She giggled.

"Where you been, Kitty?" he teased her. "I've been sitting

here for hours just waiting for you."

She did a little shimmy. "Oh Mack, you're so cute." She scrunched up her face and lips and leaned into him, giving him a little buss on the lips. "What'll you have tonight, baby?"

"Anything you're giving…"

"I mean to drink, silly."

"Get me a Bud."

"You got it," she sighed as she walked away.

At that moment, two guys walked into the bar, and again the old guys looked up in unison. They nodded at the familiar faces.

"Where's Mack?" he heard them ask.

One of the regulars jerked his head toward the back of the room. "Same as always."

The men walked back to Mack's booth and slid in on the opposite side.

Mack nodded to them. "Hey Tank, Weasel."

"Hey Mack, been here long?"

"Nah, just got here."

"What's going on?"

"Nothing."

Kitty returned with the Budweiser and a huge smile. "Here you go, baby." She placed the drink on the table where Mack had placed a ten-dollar bill.

When he nodded for her to take the money, she rummaged through the pile of bills and coins on her tray. She laid down the change on the table, still smiling.

Mack's left arm swung out and encircled her hips. "C'mere," he said, drawing her in close.

"What?" she giggled.

He dropped his arm and used his left hand to pull on the front waistband of her shorts. Then he took a five-dollar bill from the table and brought it to the gap between Kitty's flesh and her shorts.

Kitty laughed when Mack slid the fiver down her belly, stopping just north of her Bermuda Triangle.

"That tickles." She squealed.

The two guys in the booth smirked.

"Why don't you put some powder on it and meet me outside?" Mack smiled.

"I'm working right now, silly," but her wink suggested that she wasn't working all night.

The barroom door opened again, but this time when the old men looked at the new person, their heads snapped back toward Mack.

"Hey," Mack yelled. In a single movement, Mack pulled his hand from Kitty's pants, shoved her aside and jumped to his feet heading for the wide open door.

"Hey you fucker, get back here," he screamed and tore through the door.

Mack's friends jumped up and followed him out. They arrived in time to hop into the back of Mack's pickup truck before he peeled out of the parking lot racing toward the fleeing guy.

"You mother-fucker, I said get back here!" Gaining as much distance as he could before the guy fled down an alley, Mack slammed the stick shift into park, reached under his seat and grabbed the first tool he found and ran after the retreating figure.

Mack's friends followed him into the alley, and arrived just as Mack took a flying leap onto his prey. Mack jumped up and motioned for Tank to help.

On cue, Tank straddled the prostrated figure at ankle level, reached down and wrapped his massive arms under the guy's armpits and raised him up.

With all the grace of a brutal ballet, Tank locked his hands behind the guy's head and pushed it down onto his chest. Tank crisscrossed his legs in front of their prey's legs pinning him in place.

Mack stepped in front of the captive. "Where's my money, you fucker?"

"Mphnfddhfff,"

Mack motioned to Tank to let up on the neck pressure so the guy could speak.

"I'm sorry, Mack, I don't have it."

"Why'd you run, you piece of chicken shit?"

The man trembled. "I'm sorry, Mack, I just—"

Mack held out the wrench and nodded at Tank again. Tank reapplied the pressure so the guy couldn't speak.

"The way I see it, you owe me $50.00 bucks, so I'm going to give you a reminder, okay? You know how you tie a string on your finger to remember something? Well, this is going to be like that." Mack laughed.

He motioned to Weasel to join the group. "Hold out his hand."

While Weasel bent the guy's right hand down, Tank continued the chokehold.

Mack twisted the wrench's wheel until it looked right. He placed it on the man's thumb. He turned the wheel slowly.

"Ahhhhhh," the guy screamed.

Mack shot Tank a look, who applied more pressure until only garbled gasps escaped from the blocked wind-pipe.

"Okay, now that was for the first ten dollars you owe me. Man-up bro' you got four more to go," Mack, Weasel and Tank laughed at the joke.

By the fifth reminder, the guy had messed himself and passed out.

"God damn, you fucking wuss," Mack said, cursing. He motioned for Tank to let up on the neck pressure again. Within minutes the man came around again.

He started screaming again and once again Mack nodded to Tank.

"Okay, fucker, now I just gave you a string for each finger so you'll remember you owe me fifty bucks, right?"

The guy expelled a muffled response.

"Good, but you know what? You were late, weren't you? You got to pay interest, right?"

"Ahgggssgggg..."

Mack nodded to Weasel to straighten the man's other hand. He placed the wrench on its thumb. "This little piggy went to market and paid for his bill..."

They all laughed except for the guy with the broken fingers.

Chapter 13

Terry found herself humming on her drive to work. With things going well at home, and spring making an early debut, all was well. She put down the car window, and drew in a huge breath of the fragrant air with its smells of earth and grass. Life once again entered the natural world.

That's how I feel…like I've pushed through mounds of winter debris, and have shaken off the remaining crust.

No matter the cost or the scars, she was happy to put the pain behind her. This single step up obliterated the memories and the anger, and relegated her battles to solitary skirmishes, instead of a momentum toward war. None of those battles mattered now. It had all been worth it. Life was good.

The sky, turning from early morning gray to bright blue, awoke too from its long winter nap and threw off its woolen blanket. Everywhere, trees delivered their first born buds, and younger siblings followed close behind.

Happiness rose inside Terry like a song waiting to be sung. Little giggles flew up from some forgotten place deep inside her and she warbled, *How Great Thou Art*. Her voice sounded awful but her spirit flew high. She wanted to kiss someone, or hug someone. Or maybe leap through the air, happy to be alive.

The euphoria carried her all the way to work and into her office without her ever touching ground. Even the doors opened by magic, her hands never straining or guiding her key to unlock them. She dropped into her chair spinning round and round in joyful exuberance. She whirled, a bright red kaleidoscope of color encircling her movements.

She slowed the spinning to claim a better view of the colorful ribbon. There, in front of her on the desk sat a huge red zinnia, its hundreds of arms raised in unison praise to the glory of the day. Her breath caught in her throat and her eyes moistened in agreement.

"Oh, yes, Lord, praise you and your glorious day. Your handiwork is seen throughout the firmament," she proclaimed aloud.

"That's how it made me feel, too," he said just above a whisper.

Terry nearly jumped out of her chair. "Gary!"

He smiled. "I didn't mean to startle you,"

"I was just...ah, I mean...I was feeling so...ah..." she stammered.

"It's okay." He laughed. "I'm glad you like it." He motioned to the zinnia.

"Did you put that there?" Her face tingled.

"I saw it and thought of you."

"Well, that was very nice of you...but...really...I can't imagine why you'd do...such a thing." She couldn't look into his eyes.

"I wanted to," he said, leaning toward her. "I'll be leaving for Bangor, soon, and you've been so—"

"That's very nice of you...but, please...there's no reason for you to buy me gifts." She didn't know how to respond. She didn't like surprises, they made her tense.

"Listen, you've done a lot to help me, and I really enjoyed sharing that meal with you on Saturday. Can I at least buy you dinner before I go?" A grin spread over his face.

Terry kept her voice light. "No, Gary, it's my job to train you and, about lunch on Saturday..." sweat trickled down her face. "Lunch was very nice, but please don't mention it again. I mean, not that it was bad, or wrong or anything, but, I mean…but it wouldn't look right to some people, you know?" Her face burned, and her words came out so fast that they ran into each other, despite her quick pauses to swallow her fear.

Oh, God, that's all I need…for word to get out that I am running around. My life…my marriage would be over. I can just see Mack smashing my head into a wall and grinding it into the beams…then he'd go after Gary…Oh my God….

Besides, it wasn't Gary's fault. All he'd done was bump into her at lunch. Terry felt sick. Such attention could get him killed.

"Gary, I'm sorry. I really like the flower, but there's no need to buy me things or take me to dinner. And, please, don't mention the lunch again, okay?" she tried to sound calm and matter-of-fact.

He shrugged his shoulders, "Okay, if that's what you want. But, honestly, you don't know how much you've done for me," he left her office.

Damn it. Now I've hurt his feelings and ensnared him in a secret. Why didn't I just accept the damn flower…why did I make such a big deal of the lunch? I blew the whole thing way out of proportion.

Terry gulped against her rising guilt, realizing why she'd reacted that way. Even Mack's new attitude wouldn't preclude rage for Terry's infidelity. Her heart sank below the earth's crust again. So much for spring.

Terry looked at the clock when Anne arrived at 8:00 am. She watched her go directly to her console, pick up the headset and look up. Anne stared at Terry who watched her from her office. She nodded to Anne, but didn't speak.

With a heavy heart, Terry turned back to her desk, closing the door behind her. She sorted through the mounds of paperwork left from Friday, realizing that Anne was probably angry with her, and with good reason. After all, it was Terry's fault for not mentioning the tax deductions. Anne probably felt like Terry had set her up, though she hadn't. *I'd better let her stand up and brush herself off first, before I offer her a hand.* She knew that when you knock someone down, you have to let him retrieve his dignity before he'd let you near him again, even to help him up. *And maybe that's why Mack gets so mad at me, too. Maybe I don't really help him after all. Maybe I just stick his face in his mistakes and make him feel worse. Maybe I'm just a ball buster like mother says.*

"But, Mama, why are you and Daddy friends, again?" I cried. "He hurt you yesterday."

"What are you trying to do? Start trouble? You know damn right well your father wants to make up with me, so don't start your shit." My mother's fetid breath enshrouded me.

"Mama, you said he hurt you."

"He made a freaking mistake, so what? You gonna crucify him forever for one mistake?" In her rage, mother pushed me to the floor. "You're nothing but a goddamned ball-busting bitch — I tell you, someday you'll get yours." Mother towered over me. "Now you mind your own goddamned business and keep that freaking mouth of yours shut. Do you understand me?" She emphasized her words with a flailing fist that caught me on the side of my head.

I curled into a tight, little ball on the floor.

A ball-busting bitch — mother's right. That's all I am. I don't know how Mack has put up with me for this long. Terry wept.

The rest of the day dragged on like purgatory, her sins ever before her, penance beyond her reach. Neither Anne nor Gary had spoken to her since this morning, and the day felt like a week.

As five o'clock came, people filed out of their offices and

into the foyer toward the door. Terry waited in her office, though she had opened her door hours earlier. She hoped that Anne and Gary would be gone before she left, but after waiting for five minutes, she saw them talking together in the reception hall. Terry's face burned, sure they were talking about how awful she was.

A lump came to her throat as she stood up from her desk. She walked to the door and closed it, again, wanting to cry in private. *No wonder so few people love me...all I do is hurt others. Especially Mack. I'm so quick to remind him of his faults in order to make him see the error of his ways, but are they really errors, or just things I don't like? Is he so bad, or am I so bitchy?*

Terry understood now that Mack was the only person on her side, the only one to stick by her. She was so stupid to alienate him. He was the only one who had ever put up with her ball-busting ways and unreasonable demands. He hadn't abandoned her and would never talk about her like Anne and Gary were doing outside now.

Sure, sometimes Mack gave her a tough time, but he never betrayed her. He was always there for her, both physically and emotionally, if she would only open up and stop shutting him down. His bad behavior only happened when she demanded her own way or she wanted to break loose. No wonder he got ugly, then. She was no prize. She had to get home to him — get home to the only adult in her life who put up with her shit and didn't flush her away.

Terry pulled on her coat and flung open the door. Without a moment's hesitation, she sped past the two gossipers and ran through the doors toward home.

Gary and Anne, standing side-by-side, called out to Terry, but she pretended not to hear them.

Chapter 14

Anne couldn't believe she'd been working for nearly two months all ready. The days were productive and busy, but the nights remained brutal. Since the funeral, she had lost fifteen pounds despite forcing herself to eat. Nothing could fill the emptiness inside, not even food. When she did manage to eat, her body rebelled and gave her indigestion. She became dependent on antacids and laxatives.

Her body grieved, too, and without help, her physical ailments would only become worse. She read about widows who developed serious illnesses within two years of their husbands' deaths, some widows dying themselves. Doctors said these widows died of broken hearts, yet Anne knew it had nothing to do with the physical heart but the spiritual heart. Such deaths were a form of passive suicide where one wills death by not taking care to preserve one's life. Despite knowing these things, she found herself powerless to stop her fasting or her desire to slip away.

Besides, who really gave a damn if she lived or died anyway? Yeah, sure, her job was pleasant enough, and though odd at times, her supervisor seemed interested in her, but where were her real friends? They'd all abandoned her. Even the minister who'd visited once or twice after Joe's funeral didn't come around once Anne refused to go back to church.

How could she go back to church? Every time she went in that building, she saw Joe's casket at the front of the sanctuary, and it took all her strength not to collapse. How could she relive that terrible memory every week? How could she worship a god who let her husband die when so many rotten people still lived and wreaked havoc in the world? Her husband had been a good man and he was loved, yet God took that love out of her life, and she couldn't love such a god in return.

At least during the day, her job occupied and focused her, and with some creative scrounging she found ways to meet her bills. It wasn't a bad job, either. In fact, it was often more like a revolving soap opera than work, and Anne had learned a lot about the company, its people and its secrets.

She knew who cavorted with whom in the company, who came in on time and who left early. She was wise to those trying to become her friend with flowers and candy in exchange for tidbits of information. She enjoyed letting the goodies come to her desk, but they never went to her heart.

Terry was not one of the brown-nosers, nor, had she changed toward Anne from their first meeting. She was just as supportive now as in the beginning, and had never called in payment for intervening on Anne's behalf. Terry was just too sweet to be wholesome, but she hadn't given Anne any reason to doubt her. Still, she couldn't shake the feeling that Terry was dynamite wrapped in velvet. She interacted with others with a soft and gentle touch, but with a certain passion beneath the surface.

Gary was an interesting character too. Always trailing behind Terry like a puppy, or in her office, or walking toward it, or staring moonstruck at Terry.

"Good morning, Anne," Mr. Clark said without warmth, breaking into Anne's thoughts.

"Good morning, Mr. Clark," she said. She didn't like him and never would. He had been insensitive and thoughtless at their first meeting and had never shown the least guilt or remorse ever since.

Sometimes Anne wanted to tell him what she thought of him, though she resisted, remembering what Joe had taught her, *'when anger looks for an acknowledgement or an apology and gets neither, it becomes addicted to its source.'* That was one thing she certainly didn't want to do...become addicted to Clark and spend her whole life trying to make him confess and apologize. No, he was just one of those horrible people that God let live instead of Joe. What a waste.

"Has Terry come in yet?" Mr. Clark asked.

"I...ah...haven't seen her." Anne's scalp tingled. She hoped her conversation had been held inside her head and not out of her mouth. "Shall I call you when she comes in?"

"Don't bother," he said stomping away.

Soon, others were filing into work and the phones started ringing.

Dear Diary:

I was too sick to go to work today. I have a headache and I feel like I'm going to throw up. I hope the medicine works soon. I don't know how I got the kids off to school but now my head's killing me so bad I can't get up. I just have to get this off my chest. Oh, God, I'm beginning to hate Mack. Why do I keep going through this shit over and over again? For three weeks he was as good as gold, never complaining or starting a fight, and then all of a sudden, the roast wasn't cooked enough and he went crazy, again. First he threw the meat on the floor and then he smashed the plates. I grabbed the kids and we headed out. Then, he said we weren't going anywhere. Oh, God, I am sick of this shit. And poor Tommy. He wouldn't let go of me this morning, so when the school bus came I had to yell at him to get on it. Poor Cara never said a word, but I know she was upset, too. Uh-oh, I'm going to be sick.

She ran to the bathroom just in time.

She must have fallen asleep. It was 3:00 pm. when she awoke to the sound of the doorbell. She stumbled down the stairs to find Cara and a little friend at the door.

"Hi, Mom. I forgot my key. Can I go play at Gail's?"

"I'm sick today, honey, so why don't you play here instead?"

"Where's Dad?" Cara asked looking around her.

"He's not home. He's probably working overtime. Just play quietly, okay because I have a headache." she said, motioning to her daughter to take her friend into the living room. "I'll get you girls some cookies and milk, alright?"

"Yeah," they both said, moving into the other room.

Tommy came up the walk, but had no friends with him. "You sick, Mommy?" he asked, giving her a hug.

"Just a little, honey, but I'm getting cookies and milk for the girls. Do you want some, too?"

"Okay." He smiled up at her.

"Since Cara has a friend over, would you like to invite someone over, too? We haven't done that in a long time." Terry raised her eyebrows trying to assuage her guilt for having no time for the kids, or to entertain their friends. There was always cleaning, cooking, shopping, running errands, and of course, working.

Work...oh God. I never called into work. Mr. Clark will be furious. The last thing she remembered that morning was writing in her diary and then getting sick. Luckily she'd put the journal away before going back to bed, but she'd forgotten to call work. *Now I'm in big trouble. Why does everything go badly at once? If only I hadn't screwed up yesterday and started the fight with Mack. No point calling work now, either. It's too late. I'll go in tomorrow and apologize for sleeping the day away and not calling. I hope Mr. Clark understands.*

"Terry must have been very sick not to call in," Anne said when she and Gary left the building. "She'll probably call or come in tomorrow." She brushed away her worry with a wave of her hand.

"I hope so," Gary said.

Anne shot him a quizzical look. "Why?"

"Well, I have to go to Bangor next week and I've still got a lot to learn. She was going to show me the production line formulas, today."

"Oh." Anne shrugged, smiling. "She's pretty smart, isn't she?"

"Sure is. She could run this terminal if she wasn't a girl," he said.

"A girl?" Anne was horrified, now understanding why Terry insisted on saying woman.

"Yeah. You must have noticed that the company doesn't let girls run things. Besides, it takes a man to calm the drivers when they get out of line."

"Why would the drivers get out of line?" Anne found the chink in his armor.

"Well, guys are always blowing off steam and a girl is no match for a guy, right?"

"Hmmm." She decided never to call her gender *girls* again. "See you tomorrow, Gary." Anne called out, leaving his side and walking to her car.

"Okay," he said.

He opened his car door and sat inside thinking for a long while.

Now what am I going to do? I haven't been going to the barroom except on Friday and Saturday nights because I can't function when

I drink every night. And you can't very well sit with drunks if you're not drinking. Makes them paranoid. And I'm sick of watching TV in that motel room. That only fills the airwaves. I wish I had someone to talk to...someone sober. Like Terry.

He didn't expect that thought. Sure, she was nice, and really cute, but she was married. Not that an inconvenient thing like that had stopped him in the past, but, somehow, this time was different. She seemed interested in him, too. And she was smart. No matter what topics he mentioned, sports, science, politics, she knew something about it and commented on it.

Actually, she was the smartest girl he'd ever met, and he really missed her today. Without seeing her, he knew his night would be that much longer and lonelier.

Maybe I should call her and see what happened. Wait a minute. I can't do that, for Christ's sake. What if her husband answers? Wait! I'll buy her some flowers — flowers are ok when someone is sick, right? Sure, she'd gotten a little miffed a few weeks ago when I brought her that red flower, but she let me spend some of my coffee breaks with her after a while.

He revved up his car engine and sped from the lot, happy to have something to do now.

Anne turned the corner, hoping she left the driveway light on this morning. Despite the lengthening days, it was still near dusk by the time she got home.

"Whew, the light is on," she said aloud, backing the car into the driveway so the trunk sat close to the garage doors. She shut off the engine and stepped out to unlock the trunk.

At lunch, she bought peat moss and seeds and wanted to place them beside the garage. Garden supplies were an expense she could barely afford, but it was a rite of spring she and Joe had always observed. She wasn't giving it up no matter what it cost.

She gathered up the packages of seeds that had fallen from the large bag. *I wish I could start these tomorrow, but I have to wait until the weekend. God, I hate working.*

She managed to close the trunk, and carry the bundle up the flagstone path beside the garage. It was not well lit back here and she tripped on a jagged piece of stone that had risen up during the winter. She nearly lost her balance.

"Damn it," she cursed aloud. A terrible thought came to her. *What if I fell? I could be here for days before someone found me, and then only if the mailman happened onto the side of the house, or if a kid came into my yard chasing a ball.* "I could have died out here!" she yelled to the darkening sky.

Feeling sorry for herself, Anne realized that despite all the advances she had made in the last few months, she still lived alone. No one knew if she came home safely, or if she ate dinner, or if she needed help or worse, if she became sick or injured and needed help. Once again, she wanted to give up. Angry tears shot from her eyes.

"Mrs. Craig?"

"Ahhh...." She screamed.

"I'm sorry to scare you, Mrs. Craig."

"Who's there?" Anne asked in the dwindling light.

"It me, Daniel, your paperboy. You owe me for two weeks," he said. "Can you pay me now?"

"Oh, of course, Daniel. I'm sorry, I didn't know you were there." she said, her heart pounding. "I forgot to put out the envelope, didn't I?" she said, putting down the bag, and reaching into her purse.

"Yup, you forgot."

"I'm, sorry. How much do I owe you?"

"Five dollars," he reminded her. "I got a flashlight if you need it," he said, turning it on and directing it on her wallet.

"Thank you," she said, pulling out six, one dollar bills. "Here you go, Daniel" she said, smiling, "with interest."

Daniel beamed. "Thanks, Mrs. Craig. See you next week."

"Thanks, Daniel, and I'll be sure to put out the envelope." she smiled into the dark. *At least, I can live for the paperboy, that's something.*

Chapter 15

Mack hadn't come home yet and Terry paced the floor. Her head still hurt, but she dragged herself through a shower and got dressed to get ready for his return.

It was fun sitting and watching television with Tommy, while the girls played up in Cara's room. Terry loved being a mother when she could stay home for the day and be with her kids. Unfortunately, it was a luxury beyond their means. And she still worried about the kids coming home alone. What if one of them missed the bus or Cara forgot about waiting for Tommy and he had to find his way home alone? Or Mack woke in a rage and gave them a hard time?

Terry could still use her mother, of course, and she continued to pay her a stipend to keep the door open. In the long run that was cheaper than paying twice, once with the money and once with her kids being with a drunk all the time.

I know it's not her fault. She's had a hard life. A brutal childhood with two alcoholic parents of her own, adolescence spent during wartime when her father was off fighting somewhere, and finally marrying a violent drunk, herself. At least it was not that bad for me growing up. Oh, sure I was embarrassed, having the whole town know about my parents' alcoholism, and knowing kids whose parents wouldn't let them be friends with me, but I can understand that.

Thank you, God, that at least I didn't marry a drunk. Everything else is do-able. Even our fights. I just have to learn to say and do the right things and Mack and I will be golden.

Terry woke up in a panic, fear soaked the sheets engulfing her. Something terrible was going to happen. She could feel it. Maybe someone was in the house. Maybe he was going to kill her. She strained, listening for footsteps, but her own rapid breathing drowned out all other sounds. Her heart raced and sweat poured from her. Another wave of dizziness and nausea swept over her.

Oh, please, dear God, help me. Her heart beat so loud, she was sure the noise would lead an intruder right to her. *Let him kill me, and get it over with, just don't let him rape me.* She sobbed, fear rising in her throat, choking her. The shadows in the room grew larger each time she looked around. *God, I can't stand it. Let me die.* Becoming hysterical, the memories charged back.

"When that drunken father of yours comes home, don't let him in, do you hear me?" Mother screamed from her bedroom. "The son-of-a-bitch will probably have his filthy buddies with him and I'm not putting up with them coming into my house, making demands... goddamned drunken bastards. All they're good for is boozing and balling...if you let them in, you'll have to entertain them, not me — do you hear me? And you won't like it, either, sister. You think balling is fun? A woman has to just lie there and take their shit. She has no say in it, then they knock you up, and you think that's fun? Well, believe me kiddo, it's no fun. That baby starts coming and you want to shoot yourself. You've never had pain like that, believe me." On and on mother raved, slipping back into her personal hell, leaving me to grieve her pain and protect the house from the goddamned drunks.

"Mom, who are you yelling at?" Cara called out in a sleepy voice from the next room.

In less than a second, Terry jumped to her feet raced to her daughter's bed. "It's alright, honey, don't worry. I was dreaming, that's all," she answered, now wide awake. "What time is it?"

"I don't know, Mom. Do you want to sleep with me?" Cara reached out to embrace Terry.

"No, sweetie," she answered, a lump in her throat. "I'm okay now. It was just a bad dream. Go back to sleep." *God, how I love these kids. They are the only ones in the whole world who have never hurt me.*

The alarm went off at 6:00 am and Terry lay in the bed, exhausted. She'd fallen back to sleep, but it was a fitful, troubled sleep. Maybe she should have slept with Cara. After all, she seemed upset, and maybe sleeping with her might have comforted them both.

Why do I always upset people? First Mack and now Cara. Why can't I be normal like other people and have a good life? Why is everything so hard? Why does everything always get so screwed up and complicated? Why can't I be at peace like that woman Anne at work? Look at her. She's lost a husband and everything, but she isn't a mental case. And she always smiles at people. Even though she cried a lot in the beginning, she's doing fine now. And what kind of problems do I have that compares with the death of one's husband? Sure, Mack can be a pain, but what would I do if he died or left me? I can't even face the nights alone now while he works, never mind trying to raise two kids alone. How can I work and still take care of them if he isn't here to help? True, he doesn't help very much, but at least he brings home his paycheck and sometimes watches the kids. What more could a woman ask for? Sometimes he's even good with the kids, like when he cut out letters and hung them on the porch to teach them the alphabet. They loved it. No, it's just that he's so tired all the time that sometimes he loses his patience with them. Maybe I should ask Anne what's her secret.

Terry finished dressing.

Once the kids were on the school bus, Terry headed toward her car. The other mothers chatted together, ignoring her.

"Hey, where ya going?" Mack called from the driveway, startling her.

"Where have you been? I was worried," she answered.

"Well, thas' none of ya goddamn business. C'mere and gimme a kiss," he said, staggering over to her and pulling her into a bear hug.

"Mack, please, people are watching," she whispered, seeing the other mothers stopping to listen. She tried to push him away. "Honey, I just put on my lipstick," she said, trying to make light of the request.

"Oh, you can't look good for me, but for work you hafta be perfect, huh?" When he squeezed her harder, she struggled to get loose.

Terry felt him swaying against her. *He's drunk.* "No, honey, I just meant that I'll be late for work if I don't hurry."

"Well, that's too freaking bad if you're late, ain't it? I want a kiss now," he said, pushing his mouth down on hers, and pulling her tighter.

"Let...let me go! I'll be late for work, Mack," she said. Breathless, she struggled to free herself.

"Oh, and why is it so freaking important for you to get to work today? Who you meeting there?" He pulled her head back by the hair, without letting her out of the bear hug.

"No one, for crissakes. Please, let me go." She panicked, pushing him away, but he was too strong.

"Well, if you can give at the office, I think you can give to me first," he said, dragging her toward the house.

"No," she yelled, drawing open-mouthed stares from the young mothers still watching from the bus stop.

"Let me go!" She pulled against his grip trying to wrestle free. She knew if he got her into the house she didn't have a chance of getting out to work. "Please, Mack, I have to go to work today. I was out sick yesterday. Do you want me to lose my job?"

His grip loosened when her words registered.

Terry saw the young mothers watching them from the corner. "Listen, I promise to wake you up early when I get home tonight, and then we can fool around, okay?" She hoped he'd take the bargain. "Okay, Mack?"

"Alright, but you freaking well better wake me up, you understan' me?" he whispered. "'Cause if you don't those goddamned kids of yours won't be too happy when you get home."

"Okay, I'll wake you up, I promise. Now let me go," she said. She pulled herself free, ran to her car and jumped inside. She rolled down the window to get air and heard the young mothers talking.

"Look, they're at it again." One of them snickered.

"Well, maybe if she stayed home more, he wouldn't get so mad." Another one sniffed. They turned back toward the bus stop.

"He seems like a nice man," a third one said, defending Mack.

"He is a nice man," a fourth said. "My husband talked with him a couple of times and said he was always nice."

"She's a bitch," the first one said. "You ever notice how she doesn't talk with us? Or attend any of the school functions? She's a real stuck-up bitch, I tell you."

"Sometimes she says hello to me, and her kids are very polite and quiet," ventured one of the mothers, who was assaulted into silence with hateful looks.

"Big deal, so she's nice to you once in a while. She's still a bitch, I tell you." The first woman glanced over her shoulder.

"I guess you're right. I don't know her that well," the defender said.

"Well, I still think things would be alright if she weren't so independent. She's the type who makes it bad for all of us. My husband started teasing me that I'll be just like her and want to go to work, too," the sniffing one said. "God, can you imagine," she laughed, "wanting to go to work when we have so much to do at home? She must be nuts!"

"I certainly don't want to run off to work every day and leave my husband high and dry. My place is at home and that's where I'm staying! Let her be the career girl, and see what it gets her," another said.

With heads bobbing up and down in agreement, the crowd dispersed.

With her hands shaking, it took three tries for Terry to start the car. She wished she could drive it into those busybodies and squish them, but instead pulled onto the street. She sped off, leaving tire tracks in the roadway. *Maybe I should just run this car into a tree, instead.* She cried, the pain in her head so bad she thought it would crack her skull and her brains would explode. Stomach acid churned and bubbled up into her throat like lava.

Terry turned the radio on full blast, and screamed with all her might. "Why can't you just let me die, God?" she cried. "Mack would never hurt the kids if I weren't there to aggravate him. Please, just let this car crash and let me die."

Great strangled sobs came from the depths of her despair, blurring her vision, and she almost hit another car.

Oh, God, I can't kill someone else. That was a close call. They don't deserve to die. Only I do. She pulled the car over to the curb, collapsing against the steering wheel, sobbing.

Some cars slowed down and looked at her, but no one stopped. When the grief abated, it was only resignation that made her to go on. She was very late for work. *Not only was I absent yesterday without calling, now I'm late today.*

Terry shook her head and reached up to wipe away the tears. If she hurried, she would be at work in ten minutes. She drove on, exhausted already.

"Terry's not in yet?" Clark asked.

"No, Mr. Clark," Anne said.

"Call her house and see if she's coming in today." He stalked off to his office.

"Yes, sir," she said, pulling the employee roster out from under her desk. Her finger scanned the rows until it landed on Terry's name. "Here it is," she said under her breath, dialing the number. She didn't like checking up on people. It made her uncomfortable, and she sure didn't want to talk to Terry's husband, again. Unfortunately, he answered.

"What?"

"Oh," Anne said. *Not again.* "This is Hollicorp calling. Uh, is Terry at home?"

"No, she isn't! She left for work, and I was sleeping."

"I'm sorry, I didn't mean to wake you."

"Yeah."

Click.

The connection broken. Anne said thank you to the dial tone. *What a nasty man. I'll never get used to his rudeness.* She looked up from the console to see Terry entering the building.

"Terry. Are you alright? We've been worried about you and Mr...What happened to you?" Anne whispered, distressed at Terry's swollen face. "Did you have an accident or something?"

"Yeah, I had something alright." Terry looked disheveled, leaking at the seams.

"Come into the lounge...wash your face," Anne said, pushing her way past the console and taking Terry by the arm.

"What about the phones?" Terry asked.

"The hell with the phones." Anne reached over and switched the console to automatic.

Once they entered the lounge, Terry lost control again. "Sometimes I hate him, Anne. Honest to God, I hate him. No matter what I do, it's never right. If I stay home, he's mad because I'm not working and helping to pay the bills, but when I work he's mad because I'm not home taking care of him and cleaning the house. If I go shopping, he gets mad, and if there's no food in the house he gets mad. If the kids come home from school and wake him up he's mad, and if they don't come right home he's mad because no one knows where they are. I just can't stand it anymore." She sobbed through the river of rage gasping for oxygen.

Anne reached out to take Terry's hand. She didn't say a word, just waited for Terry to stop crying. What else could she do? She barely knew this woman, and besides, when people gave away information about themselves they usually regretted it later. Unless, of course, you were a trusted friend who would bury the troubles deep in your heart. Unlike acquaintances who held your secrets close to the surface like a shallow grave, where they could be exposed with the slightest digging.

Anne was hardly Terry's trusted friend...their interactions had all been work-related — hardly deep enough to receive this kind of information.

Terry's eyes were more swollen than before, but her tears had stopped.

"Terry, your eyes look terrible. Do you think you should work today? Don't you think you should tell Mr. Clark you're still sick and go home?"

"No! I don't want to go home. Not now. Not after all the trouble I had getting here."

"What trouble getting here?" Anne asked.

"My husband." She spat out her words. "He was mad because I came into work today."

"Why was he mad? Did he think you were still sick and should stay home and rest?" Anne asked.

"Rest. Ha!" Terry snickered, glaring at Anne. "Rest indeed. No, he wanted me to rest with him."

"What do you mean, rest with him?"

"Of for God's sake, Anne, he wanted me to make love with him?"

"Make love with him? When? Before you got ready for work?" Anne asked.

"Not before I got ready for work," Terry said, "after I was all dressed and ready to leave. He wanted me to come back into the house and make love with him."

"What?" Anne asked. "Was he only teasing?"

"No, he wasn't kidding, Anne," Terry said. "In my house we don't make love, I make payments. You know, a fuck a day keeps the anger at bay."

"Oh, my God, Terry. How long has this been going on?" Anne's throat closed and tears threatened to explode.

"I don't know, Anne. Please, help me get back to work now." She struggled to stand up. "Oh, my God, my head is killing me." She fell back onto the couch.

"You're not going anywhere just now," Anne said. "I'm going to tell Clark that you're still sick and need to rest in here for a while. Maybe, just maybe, you'll be alright to work later on today."

"Please, Anne, I have to focus. I'll be alright. Working helps. And, please, promise me you won't say anything to anyone about what I've told you," Terry said. "Promise!"

"On my husband's grave, Terry, I swear," Anne said through the lump in her throat. She wouldn't tell a soul, but one thing was for sure. She wouldn't leave Terry in that shallow grave, either. Anne decided to become Terry's friend and help her get out of that hole.

"Okay, if you insist on going back to work, let's get your face calmed down," Anne said, going into the lavatory and coming back with a cold cloth. "Put this over your eyes. I'll let Clark know you're in here and will be out in a while. Okay?"

"You're a real friend, Anne, thank you." Terry sighed. "I'll be out in a minute."

Anne wished Terry could fix the rest of her life as easily as wiping away her tears. She suspected that it would take a lot more than a crying towel to fix it at this point.

Twenty minutes passed before Terry left the lounge, and though her eyes and lips were still red and swollen, she walked into Mr. Clark's office to apologize for not calling in the day before. She tried to smile, but her lips, twice their normal size, wouldn't respond to movement.

"Are you sure you're all right, Terry?" he said, his eyes flew around the room. "I mean, are you sure you can work today?"

"Yes, sir, I'm fine. I'm just a little woozy, that's all."

"I'll drive you home myself, if you need to leave."

"No, sir, I don't need to go home," Terry said. "I'll be fine. Honest."

"You sure?" Mr. Clark's eyes narrowed.

"I'm fine. I'll be one hundred percent by tomorrow. Thank you, sir."

"If you say so." Changing the subject, Clark kept Terry in his office for another ten minutes, reviewing the previous day's events.

When Mr. Clark finally dismissed her, Terry left his office, looking down at her toes, with him right behind her like a shadow.

"Now I mean it, Terry. If you can't work today, I'll manage without you," he said one last time.

"I can work, Mr. Clark, honestly," Terry said. "I'll be okay if I take it slow. Thanks."

"If you think so," he said, shrugging his shoulders.

Anne watched Terry, looking for signs of collapse or aftershock. *How could a man be so hateful and cruel to his wife? Mack must be a fruitcake.*

The final piece fell into place, like an iceberg into the ocean. *Terry's a battered wife! No wonder it seemed like something was missing, why she always held back. Obviously she's walking on eggshells all the time. That explains why she is so conciliatory, trying to help people. No wonder she hates conflict and disagreement. And, she never gets personal calls or speaks about her family. Had Mack beaten her yesterday? Is that why she didn't call in sick? If he beat her, why did Terry allow it? She's obviously a smart woman. She can work and make a living. Good God, I don't know how to help her.*

Terry sat at her desk in a kind of limbo. Her head still pounding, she felt a numbness of neither fear nor ease, just a suspension between their polarities. She wondered how long it would be before life geared up again, and she was pulled into rage or surrender.

"There you are!" Gary said from the doorway.

Terry's head snapped up. "Hi."

A startled look crossed his face. "Are you all right?"

"Yes, thanks. Not one hundred percent though," she said.

"Do you like them?" He smiled, motioning to the huge bouquet of flowers on the credenza.

"Wow! I didn't see them." Terry stared at the beautiful arrangement.

"I wanted to cheer you up. Did it work?"

"They're beautiful, Gary. I don't know what to say."

"Thank you is fine." He laughed.

"Of course, thank you." She felt heat rise up her neck. "They're beautiful."

"Like their recipient."

"Please, Gary. Why do you keep doing this? I've asked you not to buy me things." She sighed, feeling too tired for the usual claustrophobia.

"Terry, how many times do I need to tell you how much I appreciate your helping me with my training, and uh…" He hesitated. "I…like you Terry," he said, throwing out the words as though they were hot in his mouth.

"Well, I appreciate your um…" She wouldn't look him in the face. "…appreciation," she said and the silliness made them laugh.

Gary turned and closed the office door and spun around to face her.

"Terry, I like you. I like you a lot...you've helped me, and taught me, and been a friend to me. Can't I thank a friend with a few flowers?"

"Yes, but..." She searched for the right words. "I'm just doing my job, Gary, that's all." She looked down at her feet. "And I...I like you, too." Her throat closed off, preventing the tears from reaching her eyes.

Gary walked over to her, and she cringed. He lifted her from the chair. His arms encircled her, pulling her close to him. She felt herself stiffen when he bent down and kissed her.

Terry pulled her head away, "Gary, please, I can't..."

"I know." He dropped his arms and walked away. Before he reached the door, he turned back to face her. "I really missed you yesterday. I didn't expect to feel this way, Terry. I'm sorry."

"I don't know what to say."

"Thank you will do." He forced a laugh. "Talk with you later. Feel better, please."

Oh, God. It had happened so fast that it took her breath away. She inhaled deeply, and shook her head. *What am I supposed to do now?*

Within minutes, Anne stood in the door frame, their coats in her arms. "Lunch time, Terry. My treat today." She motioned for Terry to get up.

Still in shock, Terry sat for a moment, staring past Anne. Getting her wind back, she rose, "I have to tell Mr. Clark we're going out."

Anne scrutinized her. "Okay, I'll wait outside."

Terry moved past Anne and walked to Mr. Clark's office. "Mr. Clark, Anne and I are going to lunch now," Terry said, peeking her head into his office. "Do you want anything before I go?"

"Come in here," he said, motioning for her to close the door. "Why don't you let me take you to lunch? I'll even pay." He smiled.

"Very funny, Mr. Clark. I'll be back in an hour or so," she said, turning to leave.

"Wait a minute. I just want to keep an eye on you because you're not feeling well."

"Thank you sir, but we have errands to run, and I'll be with Anne, so don't worry about me," she said. "See you in an hour." She opened the door and hurried through it.

"I was about to give you up for lost," Anne said teasing. They walked away from the building toward Anne's car.

Once inside, Terry shrugged and rolled her eyes upward, shaking her head. "I swear to God, I get them all, Anne."

"You certainly do." Anne laughed. "You certainly do!"

"Well, I'll gladly give you one of them."

"No thanks! A tyrant I don't need, and an idiot I don't want!"

Terry laughed with Anne as they left the parking lot. She rolled down the windows and inhaled the beauty and freedom of their time away from work. It was a beautiful spring day and the little green fingers of nature were peeking out from under their brown winter coat, the air promising a mild, glorious day. Spring always makes me believe in the innate goodness and righteousness of life, and of love and second chances. "No, seriously, Anne. Forget about Mack and Mr. Clark. What if a nice man, a really nice man came along, wouldn't you be a little interested?"

"I would not." Anne's face tightened. "I had the best man ever made, so why would I settle for less?" she said with less sting. "Look, I am neither desperate nor despondent, nor am I randy or unhappy. I'm fine the way I am, thank you."

"I would think that having loved a good man already, you could love again? I mean there are many kinds of love…why would it have to be the ultimate one again? Why couldn't it just be a companionable love?" Terry asked.

"Look, Terry, a good man is your fantasy, not mine. I think your wish for me is really your hope for yourself," she said.

Terry winced.

"I'm sorry, Terry. I shouldn't have said that. You're asking me to compromise my feelings for Joe. I still love him. And I'll tell you something else. Compromise in politics is necessary, but in love it's a cheap concession. If a man can't or won't return as much love as I'm giving him, then there's nothing to exchange, and I'll start pouring my love down a bottomless well. I'll give him more and more of myself, hoping in some way, to prime the pump until all I've got left is my self-love. And when I've finally given him that, too, I'll have nothing left. I won't have the strength to fight the long way back to self-esteem. I'll be a doormat that he'll wipe his feet on and throw away when he's done. It's not worth it, Terry. It's like dying by degrees. Joe loved me. No one else can do that so well."

"Anne, I wish I had a love like yours, but..." She couldn't finish through the flood of tears.

※※※※※※※※※※※※※※※

It took their entire lunch hour for Terry to cry it out while Anne drove around the area. There was no time left to eat, but Anne wasn't hungry anyway.

Anne remembered Joe saying solace for the soul is often more nourishment than people get in a lifetime. Now, she understood what he meant. It amazed her how her appreciation for his wisdom had grown since his death. She felt like she wanted to cry, but their arrival at the company parking lot prevented it.

"Anne, I'm sorry I wasted our lunch hour," Terry said sniffing.

"What are you saying? You've given me more than a lunch hour, Terry. You've given me something I lost when Joe died," Anne said.

"What?"

"You've given me a friend again. Now go wash your face before Clark thinks I beat you up. He already hates me. I don't want him to fire me as well." she chuckled.

Terry laughed. "Thank you Anne. I can't tell you all that I am thinking. Maybe someday I'll find the words. But for today, I'll just say thank you."

Chapter 16

All afternoon, Terry thought about Anne's self-esteem. Maybe Anne had a sense of worth and value from being loved by others. She just has some innate sense of worth and value. She had been happy in her marriage and her life until Joe's passing. Not like Terry, for whom happiness was the concessions she could make to the wills of other people, or the fantasies she lived in instead of a future — banking on other's intentions rather than benefiting from real actions. *I have never been loved or valued and I've spent my whole life waiting for someone to say I was worthy. God, I'm so confused.*

Terry hadn't left her office that afternoon, staying within the safety of its four walls, but she couldn't contain her raging thoughts. *Why did Gary kiss me this morning? Had I led him on? Did he think I was easy? Could we still be friends? Where could it go? What was it anyway? It felt so nice to be attractive. What am I saying — a man steals a kiss in my office and suddenly I expect it to mean something. For God's sake, he's a lonely man, who kissed a lonely woman. Now I feel privileged and expectant, like it meant something. It was nothing.* She started to cry. *But it felt like everything.*

Confused, she wished with all her heart that Gary really liked her. *But what good could it do anyway? I'm married and death is the only way Mack will ever let me go. I'm not a free agent...I have kids. Who would take someone else's kids? It's bad enough raising them with their own father, never mind a stepfather. So what could come of it? Sex? Even sex without the dirty socks is still no bargain, because I could end up paying with my life, or with those of my kids. Wait a minute! What am I thinking? The poor bastard only kissed me, and already I have him balling, bankrolling, and burying me. I'm a sick puppy. It was just a kiss, and it meant nothing.*

She continued to cry because it meant nothing, and because it meant everything.

"Hey, anybody in there...quitting time..."

Terry opened the door and peeked around the edge. "What did you say?" she asked, sure that her adulterous thoughts showed on her face.

"Come on, boss lady," Anne said. "Quitting time. Let's get out of here."

"I lost track of the time." Terry gathered her handbag and jacket. "Let's get out of here."

"Yeah." Anne locked arms with Terry and pulled her from the office. "It's Friday night and I just got paid." Anne started to sing the old fifties' ditty.

Terry gave a side-long glance at Anne's sudden exuberance.

"Don't try to save...." Anne continued singing. "Buy those lunches every day...."

Terry burst out laughing. "I don't think those are the lyrics I remember." She hee-hawed and they both doubled over with laughter, pulling each other forward until they reached Anne's car.

Terry stood with Anne letting the late afternoon absorb their laughter, taking with it all the tensions of the day and the week.

"Terry?"

"What?" Terry said, still chuckling.

"If things are bad this weekend, you can call me, you know."

"Anne, please. Everything will be fine," Terry said. "Really."

"Will you promise to call me?" Anne pulled out a pen, wrote down her phone number and address, and handed it to Terry.

"Okay." Terry sighed, tucking the note into her purse. "I promise. But honestly, it'll be fine. I think he went out drinking after work last night, that's all."

"Drinking may explain, but does not excuse bad behavior. Anne pulled Terry into a hug. "Now, don't forget. You call me if anything is wrong, alright?"

"Okay, I promise, Anne...and thanks."

Anne drove home still worried about Terry, but the day's other activities crowded out the young woman's predicament.

The afternoon lasted forever with the phones ringing constantly. *Every caller was either rude or impatient, too. But a little dinner and a hot bath ought to take care of all that.*

Once inside her house, Anne picked up the mail, hung up her coat in the closet, and headed for the kitchen. She pulled a TV dinner from the freezer, having come to terms with eating alone, and looked at her choice.

"Hmmm...turkey with stuffing. That's as good as anything, I guess," she said to the empty room. Putting the dinner in the microwave and selecting the temperature and time, Anne headed for the bathroom to wash up.

She thought about Terry again and how different her own experience had been. *How he spoiled me. Anything I wanted he gave me. He loved me and I loved him.* Anne wept. *We had a partnership, but were we so unique? Were we so different from all the other lovers on this earth? People who want to please because they have been pleased and who give because they have been given to? We worshipped one another, instead of worshipping the unholy trinity of me, myself, and I. Were we really so different?*

Different or not, Anne had only had one man in her life, and when he left, her life went tumbling after him. There'd be no more men or love for her. She knew it.

Her appetite gone, she returned to the kitchen and took the dinner from the microwave and put it into the refrigerator. Going back to the bathroom, she undressed, turned on the water, and entered the tub. She lay there without thinking, the water rising around her, soothing the aches and pains of her day. A warm, tingle started in her breasts and flowed down to her navel, pulsing through her flesh until it came to rest in her pelvis. She shuddered, squeezing her legs tightly together, arching her back to meet the pulsing, internal rhythm.

Oh, my God. She bolted up, squashing the mood. *Not once have I longed for sex since Joe died. I know I would have given my paycheck for the touch of another person, but I never looked for or wanted sex!* She cried, angry at her body's betrayal.

Joe had been the only man she'd ever known intimately. Surely she didn't want or need sex outside her marriage—it was just a matter of willpower. *It was probably all that man talk with Terry today.* Getting out of the tub, she grabbed a towel. *I just need some exercise. I'm going start that garden tomorrow and get rid of this extra energy.*

Chapter 17

Terry pulled into the driveway and saw her neighbor peek out her front window. Her heart sank and she hurried the kids and the groceries out of the car. That's when she heard him, too.

"How come it's so late? Terry! Terry, goddamn you, where are you?" He screamed.

No wonder the neighbors stare at me. He's in there bellowing like a cow needing to be milked. Of course! That's the problem. He needs to be milked.

Terry's face tightened. Anger pushed fear out of the way. *Every night I leave work, go food shopping, feed the kids, and cook for him. Now he's braying because I didn't screw him before I left.* She slammed the trunk and hustled the kids into the house.

"Is that you?" he yelled turning the corner and knocking her off her feet. She lay sprawled on the floor, the groceries scattered across the room. The kids stood there dumbfounded. "Where the fuck have you been?" He didn't move to pick her up or gather the scattered groceries.

"We went shopping, Daddy," Tommy said, picking up the food nearest him.

"Who asked you, Mr. Mouth?" He sneered at the child. "Just shut the fuck up and pick up the food. And you..." He spun around and yelled at Cara. "Help your goddamned mother up from the floor. I got to get to work and I'm waiting for my supper." He stormed out of the room.

"I hate him, Mom," Cara whispered.

"Me, too," Tommy said.

"Shhhh, kids, please. We don't want to get him started." Terry's head throbbed. She picked herself off the floor. "Let's just get these things put away so I can make supper, okay?" She smiled a weak smile at the kids.

"I still hate him," Cara mumbled under her breath.

Tears streamed down Tommy's cheeks. "Me, too."

"Please don't cry, honey," Terry said, reaching out and hugging her boy. "It'll be alright, I promise. After he leaves we'll have some ice cream, okay? Now let's just be quiet and not give him anything else to get mad about."

They finished picking up the groceries and Terry rushed to put them away. She opened a can of beans and dumped them into a saucepan and put them on the stove to heat. Taking hamburger from the fridge, and making five patties, Terry plopped the meet into a cast-iron frying pan on the stove. She felt him staring at her back and a shiver ran down her spine. She turned to find him standing behind her, dressed for work.

"Well, how come it's so late?"

"How come what's so late?" she asked, afraid.

"It's late!" he screamed in her face.

"I don't know what you mean? The time? You mean the time?" Her throat went dry and she swallowed hard trying to bring moisture to her mouth.

He shot her a dirty look.

"I can get your supper done in time," she said, her voice quivering. "Don't get upset…it'll be done in a minute." She cowered beside the stove, her hands shaking. The grease spit at her.

"You think I care about the freaking swill you cook? There's better food at the bar," he moved beside her and hovered. "You weren't here and I overslept. What if I hadn't gotten up?

Then what? I'd lose my freaking job and then who'd take care of you and your freaking kids?"

His mouth moved so fast spit flew into her face and his foul breath overwhelmed her. When she didn't answer him he grabbed her and threw her to the floor, kicking her in the ribs. "You make sure you're here to wake me up, you understand?"

"Leave her alone!" Cara yelled from the doorway. "Leave my mother alone!" Her fists swinging in huge arcs, Cara lunged at her father.

Like a bull distracted by a rodeo clown, he turned and caught her mid-air. "I'll teach you to mind your own business, you little bitch." Swinging her, he bounced her head off the door frame with a resounding crack and blood spurted from her temple running down the woodwork.

Cara screamed.

"No!" Tommy darted into the melee, trying to push the great hulk away from his sister. "Leave her alone!"

With his free hand, Mack swept the boy from his feet and catapulted him across the room into the opposite wall.

The kids' screams brought Terry off the floor in a rush. Grabbing the frying pan from the stove and sending hamburgers and grease flying, she swung the heavy skillet into the side of Mack's head. His skull split open and blood gushed out, spraying everywhere. He fell to the floor with a groan.

"Oh, my God," she moaned, standing over his lifeless body watching the blood make bigger and bigger circles around his head and face on the floor. "Oh, my God, I've killed him." She rocked back and forth. "Oh, my God."

"Mom, help me." Cara pulled her hand away from her head and stared at the blood. "Mom! I'm bleeding."

Cara's voice broke through the cell of terror holding Terry captive. Once free, she took command. "Oh, my God, Cara, look at your head!" Terry grabbed a dish towel from the counter and pressed it to Cara's temple. "You've got to get stitches. Hold this tightly."

Looking around, Terry spotted her son lying on the floor across the room sobbing and rushed to his side. "Let me look at you!" She turned him over and checked him front to back. "Thank God, you're not bleeding. Are you hurt?"

"A little," Tommy answered.

"Come on kids, quick. Let's get out of here."

Terry grabbed her purse and car keys from the table and wrapped her arms around them. Stopping, she glanced back at the bloody and unmoving body of her jailer. She hoped he was dead, but God help her if he was. She shuddered and pulled her kids close. They ran from the house.

At the hospital Terry concocted a story about Cara slipping in the mud and striking her head on a stone while they carried in the groceries. She hoped they wouldn't suspect the blood on Terry's clothes might be different from Cara's, or that Terry's nervous pacing was different from that of any other hysterical mother whose child was hurt. Even Terry's furtive glances toward the door each time it opened didn't raise suspicion.

What if he's alive? What if he comes looking for us? He'll kill us for sure. She was more worried now about his revenge than his death. *What am I going to do? I can't go home, and I don't have any money because I just spent my whole paycheck on groceries. Where can we go? A shelter? I'd have to answer a lot of questions and they'd find out what I've done. But where?*

Cara came out of the cubicle, smiling and sucking on a lollipop, a second one in her hand for Tommy.

"She is a brave little girl, Mrs. Woods," the doctor said, winking at Terry and smiling back at Cara. "She didn't cry once."

"She never cries," Terry said.

"We gave her a mild sedative before we stitched," the doctor told her. "So get her home and into bed as soon as possible." The doctor turned and smiled at Cara. "Bye, Cara, and watch where you walk next time, okay?" He strode away.

"Thank you, Doctor," Terry called after him, forcing a smile. Home and into bed...what home...what bed? She never felt more alone in all her life. *I'm the mother and I'm responsible for these kids, but what am I going to do? Where am I going to take them?*

The jailer she knew seemed better than the exile she didn't. She wished she could go back home, but she couldn't. At least, not yet. He might be dead, or worse, he might be alive, and she had let his rage spillover onto the kids. She had failed to protect them, and she needed to let him cool off. But if they couldn't go home right away where could they go? Not to her mother's, that was for sure. Not only would Mack look for them there, but it was as bad there as at home. The filth, the stench, the fighting...as a matter of fact, she was surprised that the police hadn't already called to say that her father, who still visited from time to time, had been killed by her mother, or vice versa.

Anger welled inside her. *You've really improved your life, haven't you?* For the first time since her marriage, she realized what she'd done. She'd traded rings...not wedding rings, but boxing rings. She'd left the ring in her parents' home only to create a new one with her husband.

Did everyone do the same? Fight so viciously? If so, what was the point in living, or in loving, if loving only meant fighting?

Anne's words came back to her. 'If your man can't or won't return as much love to you as you're giving to him, then there's nothing to exchange'.

Is that why we always fight? Is Mack exchanging his hate for my love? Some of it's my fault, I know, but I try to be a good wife, yet it never seems to satisfy him. I can never do enough...there's always one more thing I have to do before I get it right or make him happy or make it work. But I can never find that one more thing.

She held back her tears, still torn between her feelings of frustration and the fantasy that everything was up to her.

Didn't he want to make it work? I've tried everything but it feels like the rules keep changing.

"Mom? I'm tired." Cara's looked up at her with unfocused eyes and tugged on Terry's sleeve.

Cara brought Terry back to the moment. *I have no place to go to, no money, and two injured kids. What am I going to do?* She guided the kids out of the hospital and into the car, hoping to buy some time by driving around for a while.

Hours later, the heat turned up full blast to keep the children warm she noticed the gas gauge close to empty. "Oh no! No money, no gas, and now there'll be no heat, either."

The kids had fallen asleep as soon as they'd left the hospital, but now without heat they couldn't stay in the car. Terry's rage and frustration peaked, and she pounded the dashboard. *What am I going to do, God? I can't go home even if I wanted to, but where can I bring these kids?*

She gulped huge breaths of air and tried to keep her eyes on the road through the torrent of tears. *Please help us.*

Anne's voice sounded in Terry's head, 'If things are bad this weekend, call me, okay?'

Of course! That's the only solution. Thank you, God!

Terry fished Anne's paper from her purse, and headed toward Anne's address. *Will she help us, really? Would she call the police? Would she be an accomplice if Mack were dead?*

She had no time for discussion or debate. She hoped she wouldn't run out of gas before she made it to Anne's.

Chapter 18

It was nine in the morning, the kids were still sleeping in the guest room and Terry slept in Anne's den.

Anne had been awake all night after Terry and the children arrived. Never had she seen such frightened people or heard a more tragic tale than the one Terry related.

"If he's not dead, I'd like to kill him myself." Anne remembered fighting down her rage. "But if he is alive, I'm calling the police and having him arrested."

"No, please don't do that, Anne," Terry had said, grabbing Anne's arm.

"What are you going to do, then?"

Terry shook her head. "I don't know, but I don't want to go to jail if he's dead. Who'll take care of my kids?"

Anne handed Terry the tissue box. "All right, I won't call the police."

But that was last night. This morning she dialed her lawyer to make him aware of the situation. *If Mack were dead, the lawyer could argue for self-defense.*

The poor woman. She's so worried about involving me, but what have I got to lose now? I've already lost everything worth having so I don't care if I am an accessory. I'm standing by her!

◊◊◊◊◊◊◊◊◊◊◊◊◊◊◊◊◊◊◊◊◊◊◊◊◊◊◊◊

"Gregory and Hansen," the operator said.

"Who?" Anne hadn't recognized the second name.

"Gregory and Hansen, ma'am. They're lawyers. Do you want to speak to a lawyer?" The operator asked.

"Yes, I want to speak to Mr. Gregory, my lawyer, please." Anne didn't like surprises.

"I'm sorry, Mr. Gregory is away on vacation, but Mr. Hansen is available. Would you like to speak with him?"

"I guess I must, then." The operator put her on hold. *Just what we need — a stranger at a time like this. He's probably some kid just out of law school without any experience. Maybe I should wait for Sam to get back.*

Anne hated that the world was growing up beneath her feet, pushing her and her peers off the streets and into pine rockers, or worse, pine boxes.

"Steve Hansen here."

His voice disrupted her thoughts. "Mr. Hansen, this is Mrs. Craig calling. I'm a lifelong client of Mr. Gregory's…and I, that is we, have a little problem that I must discuss with Mr. Gregory right away. Is there any way I can reach him?

"No, I'm sorry, Mrs. Craig," he said. "Mr. Gregory's at a cabin in the woods with no phone. But he'll be back in two weeks, if you'd like to wait."

"No, this can't wait."

"Well, in that case, maybe I can help you. I'm Mr. Gregory's partner, and I could see you today if it's that urgent," he said.

"Well…" She hesitated. "I guess I better see *someone* today."

"Fine. Then, why don't you come in at two, Mrs. Craig."

"Two p.m.?" she asked. "Since when do lawyers work until two p.m. on a Saturday?"

"When they need to, Mrs. Craig." He laughed.

"Well, thank you, Mr…ah…"

"Hansen..." He chuckled. "Steve Hansen."

"Yes, Mr. Hansen, we'll be there at two o'clock then. Thank you."

Why was I so rude and impatient? Maybe I'm becoming a crotchety old widow. Well, it doesn't matter...there are more important things to do right now than to worry about my first impression on some new lawyer.

The first thing she needed was to buy food for her guests before they awoke. She had nothing on hand to give them, not even an egg. She never ate breakfast at home anymore because it was just too lonesome.

Great homemaker you turned out to be, but then this isn't a home anymore, anyway. It's just a way-station, but now you have guests.

Anne chided herself into action. *Okay, get going before they wake up.* She hurried out, being as quiet as she could.

At the store, she fought through other stressed and sleepy workers also out shopping. People trying to make up for a lack of time during the week. They crowded into the busy store, pushing through the aisles like race car drivers. Each shopper acting anxious to be out enjoying their weekend. More than once Anne had to make a second or third sweep up an aisle because of the flow of people behind her. One persistent woman kept pushing her cart into Anne's legs whenever Anne stopped. Anne spun around and said, "If you push that carriage into me one more time, you'll be wearing the largest set of braces on your teeth the world has ever seen." The woman backed off, muttering under her breath about a 'crazy lady' being loose in the store.

Anne hadn't done any appreciable grocery shopping since Joe's death. It surprised her to see the strain it put on people who had to shop only on weekends. If Terry and the children didn't need food right now, she'd have abandoned the cart where it was, half full, and left this insanity to those who had no choice.

She finished shopping, her anger rising with every minute, until she realized she was acting like the other hassled shoppers—rude and impatient. She hurried to get out of there. Within half an hour, she headed back home.

Anne opened the kitchen door, startling the children sitting in the kitchen table.

"Hi," she said, seeing their frightened faces. "My name's Anne, and I work with your mother."

"Hi," they said, huddling together.

"How is your head this morning, Cara?" Anne asked.

"Who told you about my head?" Cara mumbled.

"Your mother did, last night. Is that okay?"

"I guess so." Cara shrugged, looking at her brother. "Where's my mom, now?"

"She's sleeping. Can I fix you some breakfast?" Anne smiled at the silent children. "Aren't you hungry?" She got more shrugs in reply.

"What's this about breakfast?" Terry asked from the doorway.

"Hi there," Anne said, her words drowned out by the children's voices.

"Mommy," they shouted running to Terry and clinging to her frame.

"How did we get here?" Cara asked. "Who is that lady?" she whispered into Terry's ear, motioning toward Anne.

"Cara, Tommy, this is Anne Craig, my good friend..." Terry choked up. "Anne, these are my children."

They straightened up and smiled at Anne, at least for a second. Then, they were all over Terry again.

"Ouch! Honey, please be careful." Terry winced when Tommy squeezed her ribs. "I'm still sore, and I can hardly walk."

"Then, we'll have to carry you to the table!" Cara laughed, bending down to grab hold of Terry's legs.

"No...No...stop, Cara, I'm too heavy, please." Terry laughed at their effort, but the action catapulted her back to the past.

"Mommy, please help me...I don't feel...gooooood..." I cried out. "Mommy...please...help me. Mommy..."

"Wha' izzit, for crissakes, Terry?" Mother called from the bottom of the stairs, her words slurring.

"Mommy, I'm sick...please help me..."

"Oh, for crissakes...I'll be there in a minute..." mother yelled back, fighting to negotiate the stairs. She stumbled, cursing, "This goddamn house...these stairs aren't worth shit...oh, he's gonna fix 'em up, alright. Like hell...maybe when the cows come home, he'll get around to it...the son-of-a-bitch..." She pitched into a wall.

"Mommy, hurry...I'm gonna be sick..." I sputtered, trying to hold back the vomit, but it gushed out anyway – all over the bed. I sobbed. "Mommy. I'm going to be sick again..."

"For crissakes, I'm coming...I'm coming...hold your horses," she said, reaching the top of the stairs, stopping mid-stride when she saw me. "Look at that freaking mess!" she screamed, her eyes narrowing, trying to get a steady view of the sight.

"I'm sorry, Mommy," I whimpered. "I couldn't help it. It just came out."

"Well, get out of the freaking bed then!" Mother yelled, lunging toward me, grabbing me by the arm. "Don't just lie in it." Mother pulled me from the slop.

"Owwww...for crissakes, you're burning up!" Mother yelled, shaking her hand in an exaggerated flutter. "What the hell's the matter with you anyway?" she said. "You're going to the hospital."

"No, please, I'll be alright...please...don't take me there...please," I begged.

"Don't be such a crybaby. You're sick and you need to see a doctor. Now, c'mon, we've got to go downstairs. Naturally, your goddamn father isn't around when I need him. Now, I'll have to ask that old bastard next door to take us." With one mighty swoop of her right arm, Mother raised me off the floor into her arms, and weaved toward the stairs.

"No, Mommy, please...put me down...I can walk...please...I'm too heavy for you, Mommy. Please put me down...I'm too heavy."

Mother tightened her grip, constricting my chest—hurting me. Still, she wouldn't let me go, but continued down the stairs, weaving and pitching with every step.

Each time mother's arms began to droop. I was sure she would drop me.

The old man next door arrived with his sickly wife who stayed with my brother and sister.

"Your child has pneumonia, I'm afraid. She'll have to stay here," the doctor said.

"No, please don't leave me, Mommy!" My screams echoed throughout the emergency room.

For a brief moment, Mother looked into my eyes, her own welling with tears. "Gotta be done, Terry. I'm sorry." With that, Mother and our neighbor left the hospital.

I cried myself to sleep that night inside the oxygen tent, separated from the other children in the ward by plastic sheeting. For two weeks, I wept every night because I had no visitors. I would never let someone pick me up and carry me off again. Ever!

"Hello, Terry." Anne laughed. "Did you fall back to sleep standing there?"

"No, just remembering something," Terry reached down to hug her children.

Anne watched their loving interaction. "Okay, now, get yourselves cleaned up while I get breakfast ready," Anne said, shooing them away with a sweep of her hand.

She pulled a frying pan from a lower cabinet, lifting the utensils she needed from the rack on the wall.

"Go ahead," she said when the children still clung to Terry. "There's fresh towels and soap in the hall closet. By the time you're done your breakfast will be ready.

The children looked at Terry who nodded and the three of them moved down the hallway.

Anne's heart ached as she watched them disappear. *Why would anyone want to hurt this young woman and her children?*

In the bathroom, Terry cleaned up the children as best as she could, trying not to hurt Cara's head while washing her face and neck. Tommy, eager to be touched, threw his arms around her neck when she lifted him onto the toilet seat for better access.

"I love you, Mommy." The sentiment gushed from him.

"I love you too, big boy." Terry pushed her words past the lump in her throat. For a long time, she stared at the kids.

"Are you okay, Mommy?" Cara asked, bringing Terry around.

"I'm fine, sweetie. I love you, Cara."

"Me, too," Cara said.

Anne smiled when Terry led the kids back to the kitchen. Everyone ate the huge breakfast of bacon, eggs, muffins, and juice she had prepared. It was nearly one o'clock by the time they finished.

"Children, go wash up. Then, you can watch television so your mommy and I can talk, okay?" Anne said.

"Okay," they said, racing to the bathroom.

"Let's watch wrestling, Tommy," Cara said.

Terry winced. "You'd think they'd seen enough of that!"

"Terry," Anne said. "That's the whole point. Don't you think they've seen enough violence? Don't you think it's time you shut off the live-TV in your house?"

"Anne, I may already have." Terry hung her head and tears dripped from her eyes onto her lap.

"I know, you told me last night."

"I don't know what I would have done if you hadn't let us in last night." She reached her hand across the table grabbing Anne's.

"Terry, I'm glad you came here." She squeezed Terry's hand, fighting back her own tears. "You once said everyone deserves a first break, and you gave me mine by hiring me. Now I can repay you. Besides, you're like my family." She was glad she said it, though it scared her some. "Listen, we're going to see my lawyer this afternoon."

"But, what if – "

"I've already called him. We have an appointment at two o'clock, so no buts about it."

"I'm scared…What if I killed him? I'll go to jail. But if I didn't kill him, he'll come looking for me and kill…all of us." She sobbed, taking in great gulps of air.

"Terry, if you did kill him, then good riddance to bad rubbish. If you didn't, then we'll lock him up so fast he won't know what happened. Trust me. No one has to put up with that business. Not now, not ever. I'll help you. I promise."

Anne had nothing to lose. She had only herself to worry about. She couldn't hurt, stigmatize or slander anyone else that mattered now. Nor could she be blackmailed or browbeaten, for there was no one left in her life that enemies could hurt or harass. There was only her, and that made for the best kind of crusader – a free one.

"Anne, I'm still scared."

"I know…I know." Anne squeezed Terry's hand tighter. "Let's get the children ready to go."

"Okay," Terry whispered, pulling herself to her feet moving to the door. "Cara, Tommy, do you have your shoes on?" she called into the living room.

"Yes, Mommy."

"Then, get your jackets, please."

Within minutes they left the house. Once outside, Terry's head ached and the sunlight made her squint. "Cara, how is your head, now? Do you have a headache, honey?"

"A little, but it's okay." She, too, squinted in the bright sunlight, tilting her head to avoid the light.

"I feel like I've got a hangover," Terry said to Anne with a laugh stopping short of her lips.

"If that's the case, the drink was poison." Anne said.

"Aren't they all poison?" Terry asked.

"Oh, no, Terry. They're not all poison. Joe wasn't poison."

"What are you talking about?" Terry asked.

"Your…husband…" Anne whispered in Terry's ear so the children wouldn't hear her.

"Oh! I meant that booze was poison!" Terry said.

They both laughed.

Chapter 19

The front office was empty when they walked in. This is nice, Anne thought, unaccustomed to such informality.

"Hello," she called out.

"Hello, Mrs. Craig?" a deep masculine voice called out from another room.

"Yes," she said, annoyed at not knowing whether to follow the voice into the other room or remain in the reception area. *What kind of confidence will this informality and lack of protocol give Terry, for heaven's sake?* Anne scowled.

"Hi, I'm Steve Hanson," he said from the doorway, looking straight at her and smiling. He walked over to them and extended his hand.

Anne's mouth dropped and her eyes flew open. The most handsome man she'd ever seen stopped in front of her. He stood over six feet tall, with graying hair, a gorgeous tan, and a smile that melted her anger.

"Oh, Mr....ah..." Anne stammered, reaching out to return his handshake.

"Hansen, Mrs. Craig," he reminded her.

"Yes, Mr. Handsome," she said, then realizing her mistake, pulled her hand back. "Ah...I mean, Hansen," she said, her face feeling hot.

"Hi, I'm Terry Woods. I'm the cause of all this."

"Hello. Why don't we all go into my office then, and talk," he said, leading the way.

The spacious, well-decorated office had pictures of gentle seascapes and fluffy clouds adorning the walls and a heavy oak desk in the center. Behind the desk, bookcases, filled with books of all sizes and colors, spanned the walls from ceiling to floor. Sculptures, and two large geodes, whose crystal interiors radiated beautiful color from within their craggy exteriors, sat on shelves.

"Oh, wow, look at the rocks!" Tommy said, pointing to them.

"Would you like to see them up close?" Mr. Hansen asked, moving toward the bookcase.

"Oh, yes!" the boy said, delighted.

"Be my guest." He handed the geodes to Tommy and smiled.

"Mr. Hansen," Anne said, getting things back on track. "My friend has a serious problem we need to discuss. Can we begin?" She tried to regain her lead.

"Of course. Do you think the children should stay?" he asked.

"Yes, they've been hurt too, and should be heard," Terry said tears already flowing.

"Why don't you tell me what's going on, then?" He took the seat behind his desk and inclined his head toward her.

For the next hour, Mr. Hanson listened to Terry describe the events of the previous night, and the previous years. At times, Terry cried so hard that he had to wait for her to go on.

He noticed too, that the children didn't move or speak. They hung their heads and cried along with Terry like a tragic chorus.

People don't give children enough credit. They're smarter than we think, and whichever comes first in their young lives, love or fear, is what they'll look for ever after. I've seen it a million times. I only hope it's not too late for these little ones to expect a better life.

Anne cried too, and he suspected that this was the first time she'd heard much of this.

Twice he passed a box of tissues among them, and when Terry finished, he spoke. "All right, Mrs. Woods, the first thing we need to do is find out if your husband is…ah…alive." Mr. Hansen reached for his rolodex. "So—.

"No, please, don't call the police…please…"

"We don't have to do that just yet," he said, giving her his best, compassionate smile. "Wait here for a minute, I'll be right back." he said, stretching his tall frame up from his chair and walking away from the desk, he left the room.

"Oh, Anne, I'm afraid…" Terry sobbed. "Do you think he'll help me?"

"Well, he'd better or I'll know why not. Sam Gregory has been our…I mean…my lawyer for a long time. He helped me when my parents died, and when I married Joe…and then, when I had to bury him, too. Sam knows more about my life than my husband did. And if this man works for him, then you can bet he'll help us, too. Don't worry, Terry. We'll all help you, so don't be afraid."

Leaving the women in his office, Steve walked to the phone booth on the ground floor. It was an antique but at least when closed up tight it was soundproof, and that's just what he needed for this call.

"Hi, Eddie, this is Steve. I want you to check out someone for me. Name's Mack Woods, 2349 Winter Street. See if he's receiving any visitors. Yeah…Good. Call me at the office without names…Yeah…Thanks." He left the phone booth and walked back upstairs.

"Alright, Mrs. Woods, why don't we discuss your options."

He looked at the fragile woman in front of his desk. *How could anyone want to hurt her?* "Once we've established that your husband is still alive, we need to make sure he doesn't have another opportunity to hurt you. We don't want him near you or the children without supervision. Our first step will be to get a restraining order. Did you tell the hospital what really happened?"

"No, I was afraid, to." She sunk into the chair and wiped at the tears moistening her cheeks.

"I know this is difficult, Mrs. Woods," he said handing her the box of tissues, but Terry didn't look up.

He nodded at Anne who reached out and took the tissues, handing them to Terry a few at a time. Steve wondered about her relationship with the young woman.

"I'll need a copy of the medical records. Will you sign a release of information?"

"I don't know. I lied to them. Will I get into trouble? Will the police arrest me for Cara being hurt?"

"No, not at all, I'm sure they've treated lots of battered women in the past."

Terry's eyes flew open. "I'm not a battered woman! Mack was just angry with me." She shook her head, glancing between Steve and Anne.

"I'll have my secretary type a release for you to sign on Monday," Steve continued. Now, I'll have to petition for a restraining order through the police because it's Saturday and the court is closed." He looked at her though hooded eyes. "Of course, if we don't need the order, then…we'll worry about that later."

"But what if I want to go back there and try to work things out?"

"What!" Anne said. "You mean you'd go back there?"

"I didn't say that, Anne. But I am his wife, and wives are supposed to help their husbands, no matter what. What if he's really hurt and he needs me?" Tears poured down Terry's face. "He was just angry with me, that's all."

"The only reason he needs you is to hurt you again, Terry. And he's going to keep hurting you if you don't get away from him, right, Mr. Hansen?"

"Terry, he might have been angry with you, but he hurt your daughter, too. This behavior won't stop and it won't get better. Trust me. Battering husbands seldom stop hurting their families without professional help," Steve said.

Terry looked up into his eyes. "Professional help! I'll tell you what kind of professional help he'll get. He'll get a professional contract put out on me and the kids! He'll kill me for bringing in outsiders."

"Terry," Mr. Hanson said, "that's not something you should worry about at this point. There are legal ways of preventing him from harming you and your children."

"You think the laws of man will stop him, when the laws of God haven't?" Terry's words became a rant.

"What do you mean?"

"Don't you think I've been praying for years for us to stop fighting, but it's only gotten worse." She sobbed.

"I'm sure God doesn't intend for your husband to get away with this behavior," he said.

"Then why hasn't God stopped him!"

"Maybe God was waiting for us to be his hands and feet in stopping your husband's violence."

"But God can do everything."

"Yes, and he can do more with our help, or, at least with our agreement. What do you say? Will you help God help you?" He hated it when religion forced people to stay in bad relationships. If that wasn't hell, nothing was.

"I...I guess so..." Terry became even smaller in the chair.

Steve nodded to Anne. "Why don't you go home with Mrs. Craig, now and I'll call you when I know what's going on." He rose from his seat, walked to the door and held it open for them.

"Thank you, Mr. Hansen," Terry unfolded herself from the chair, sniffling. She and the children, huddling together, walked out en-masse.

Anne hung back. "Thank you, Mr. Hansen...I didn't mean to...be...rude this morning."

"Steve," he said.

"What?"

"Please call me Steve." He smiled.

"Thank you for seeing my friend, Mr. Hansen." She brushed past him and collected her wards on the other side of the doorway. "Come on, Terry, we're going home."

He watched Anne square her shoulders and lead the troop toward the elevator. He wanted to laugh at her cockiness. He liked her already.

This thing with Mrs. Woods, though, wasn't something to laugh at. He hoped Eddie would call soon with good news. He'd much rather represent Terry at a divorce hearing than a murder trial. Divorce could be a killer, but easier to live through than a murder.

On the ride home, Terry listened to Anne chatter on and on. While Anne talked it out, Terry and the children shut down.

"Shall I fix something to eat when we get home?" Anne asked.

"I'm not hungry," Terry mumbled. "How 'bout you guys? Hungry?" she asked, half turning in her seat to look at the children.

"No, we're not hungry, Mom," Cara answered for them both.

"Shall we go shopping, then?" Anne said.

"I don't want to, but you can if you have things to do."

She felt bad for involving Anne in all of this. She hated herself for going to the lawyer, and hitting Mack, and disrupting their lives, and for just about everything. If she hadn't made so much about it, the children would have been out playing in their own backyard right now, she would have been doing the wash, and Mack would have been watching television relaxing like he always did on a Saturday.

What have I started — what have I ruined? What are we going to do for clothes? Or money? How am I going to pay this lawyer? We already have so many bills that we barely manage to pay. What about the cost of the food we're eating at Anne's, or the cost of the hot water and heat we're soaking up? What about work on Monday? How can I go to work without clothes? Or the kids go to school? It's at least five miles to their school from Anne's house, and I can't keep them out of school for long without the authorities asking questions.

What if they take the kids away if I can't get them to school? And what about the kids? What about their needs? Do they still love their father? Who am I to take them away from him? If I really leave Mack, or worse, divorce him, he'd never come to see them again. What right do I have to do that to them, or to disrupt the whole family and destroy everything we've worked so hard for?

We'll probably have to sell the house and split the bills, and there'd be an ugly fight, if it gets that far. He'll probably kill me or have me killed before it goes that far, anyway. Then, what happens to the kids? Who will care for them, or make sure Mack doesn't hurt them? The kids have years before they can take off on their own and be safe. There is just no way out. No matter what I do or what happens from this point, I've ruined it — ruined it all. I brought outsiders into our private lives, outsiders who don't understand what we've worked so hard for. What about the shame of misrepresenting him and over-dramatizing our problems? I've destroyed everything, that is if I haven't already killed him outright.

Chapter 20

A dark gray van with its magnetic Carpet Cleaners sign pulled into the driveway, stopping behind the old car already parked there. When the driver climbed out and approached the house, he listened for activity that would tell him if someone was at home. Hearing none, he approached the front door, surveying the house for any unusual things like a porch light left on, or doors and windows left open or even blood trails. He rang the bell and waited. No response. He rang it a second time.

"Hold your goddam horses!" a voice roared from inside. Within minutes an angry face appeared. "Yeah, what is it?" the man growled, pulling the door open wide. He wore a towel wrapped around his head with dried blood caked under his right temple. He breathed hard from behind glazed eyes.

"Hi, I'm with Carpet Cleaners," Eddie said a cheerful voice. "We're doing work in your neighborhood this month and wondered if you could use our services, too."

"No. I don't want no carpets cleaned," Mack barked, slamming the door in Eddie's face.

"That's all I wanted to know, pal," Eddie said under his breath, walking back to his van. He pulled out his cell phone, anxious to report his findings. The phone rang only once before Steve picked it up.

"Steve, Eddie, here. Yeah. He's receiving visitors all right. He looks pretty rough. Yeah, a real asshole. I wouldn't want to visit him again."

"Mrs. Craig, this is Steve Hansen."

"Yes?" she said, holding her breath.

"Good news. Someone spoke with Mr. Woods at home today. Everything is fine."

"Oh, thank God." She sighed. "I mean, I think that's good, right."

"Well, it's easier…I don't know about…better."

"Right. I've been worried about Terry saying that he'd get a contract out on her and have her killed," Anne said.

"Mrs. Craig, I've seen a lot of these cases before. Believe me, it is rare when these threats are carried out. Usually, they're only a means of frightening and keeping the woman hostage. Don't worry. I doubt that Mr. Woods has any connections, as they say. Now, can I speak with Mrs. Woods, please?"

Anne called Terry in from the den. She smiled and passed the phone to her. She saw Terry's hand shaking and the beads of sweat trickling down her forehead.

"Hello," Terry said. "Oh, God," she slumped to the floor, bursting into tears and dropping the phone.

Anne scooped up the phone. "Mr. Hansen," she said. "Terry is very upset. What did you say to her?"

"I told her that we talked to her husband and that I want her to call him."

"Why in the name of God do you want her to do that?"

"So, we can be sure it's him at the house. Do you think you can get Terry to call him, and then call me back?"

"I'll try, but it may take some time. Terry's pretty upset right now." She looked at the sobbing woman slumped on the floor beneath her feet. "What time are you leaving the office today?"

"Soon. If you can't reach me here, I'll be at home. Call me there." He gave her his number. "Be sure to call me no matter what time it is."

"Yes." Having someone else in charge again reassured her.

"I'll wait to hear from you," he said.

She hung up the phone and turned to Terry. "Come on, we'll have a nice hot cup of tea." She pulled at Terry, who wouldn't budge. "Come on, Terry, please," Anne's tears joined her friends.

Joe, help me. I've never helped someone before. You always did the rescuing, the solving, the thinking, the planning. Now you're not here and I don't know what to do.

"Terry, please, honey…come on…let's get some tea and talk about this," Anne said, one more time.

Terry's eyes were red and swollen, her mouth quivering. She tried to say something, but no words came. She grabbed onto Anne for support, and finally rose from the floor.

"Oh, Anne," Terry whispered, "He's not dead…" she cried. "He's not dead…"

They moved to the kitchen table, where they collapsed onto chairs.

"Terry, please. You must call him. Mr. Hansen said Mack is all right. Please call him and make sure it's him at the house. Mr. Hansen said he'd wait for our call, Terry."

"I can't, Anne. What if he comes to find me here?"

"He doesn't know where I live. Don't worry he can't get to you or your children here. Please call him."

For over an hour Anne tried to convince Terry to call her husband. Finally, Anne gave up. "All right, if you don't want to call him, I guess I'll have to," Anne said, heading for the phone. "I remember what the nasty bastard's voice sounds like."

Terry sprang to her feet and stood in front of the phone before Anne could reach for it. "No, please, don't call him." She cried, blocking the phone with her body. "I don't want him to know where we are. Not yet, please."

"Terry, I won't tell him where you are, for heaven's sake, and you won't either! I just want to know if he's alive so we can get the restraining order. Look, you're safe here because he doesn't know me or where I live. And I'm certainly not about to tell him where you are," she said.

"Okay, just give me a few more minutes. Then I'll call him, okay?" Terry whispered.

"Okay," Anne said, going back to the table. "Come finish your tea. I'm going to ask the children if they want a sandwich. They must be starved by now."

Anne left the kitchen and Terry walked back to the phone. She picked up the receiver. Her heartbeat pounded in her ears—her breath coming in shallow, little puffs. A wave of dizziness hit her and she leaned against the wall for support. She dialed and heard the phone ring once, twice, then three times.

"What!" he yelled into the receiver.

"Mack?" she whispered. "Is that you?"

"Who the fuck do you think it is?" He let out a growl. "Where are you?"

"Mack, are you all right?"

"Where are you?"

"I'm at a friend's house, Mack," she said. "Are you okay?"

"What the fuck are you doing there? Why aren't you here where you belong?"

"Mack, I was worried that I killed you." She sobbed into the phone.

"Well, you didn't. Get the fuck home where you belong."

"I'm scared, Mack."

"Scared of what?"

"You hurt Cara last night, Mack. Do you remember that?"

"What the fuck are you talking about?"

"Cara...I took her to the ER and they had to stitch her

head last night after you knocked her into the wall," Terry sobbed again.

"What are you saying—after I hit her into the wall?" he said. "I was only protecting myself from you people. All of you yelling at me and making me nervous. You got them kids turned against me, Terry, and you know it. I can't even talk with my own wife without them coming between us. You know that's true. Whatta you doing over there? Bringing outsiders into our business? Did you tell your friend you nearly killed me?" He raved on, sobbing at the same time, barely taking a breath. "Oh, sure, you took Cara for stitches, but watta 'bout me? What the fuck did you do for me? Were you hoping I'd die? Leaving me here all by myself bleeding to death?"

Terry couldn't answer...she only saw him lying in a pool of blood, life slipping away, no one to help him. She was bad. Real bad.

"And now watta you doing? Making more trouble for us with this friend of yours? Who is he? Does he lay you real good? Is that it? I go to freaking work and you get someone to take care of you when I'm out busting my hump? Or maybe that wasn't good enough for you? Now you was hoping I was dead so you could have him all the time instead 'a me? Huh?" He went on, not waiting for her answer. "Well, you hurt me, Terry, you hurt me real bad and now my freaking head is bad. I'm dizzy and I can't see nothing...I keep banging into walls Terry, you hear me? You hurt me real bad."

He cried now, and she knew he was right. She'd been so preoccupied with a stupid kiss yesterday that she'd gone off shopping with the kids, and hadn't given Mack a thought. And men could tell when you weren't thinking of them. Then, when she came home, she had escalated his rage. She was a bad person. Real bad.

"Terry?" he shouted. "You still there, Terry?"

"Yes, Mack, I'm here," she whispered, too exhausted to speak.

"Why don't you come home and we can talk about it? You never did talk to me about your problems, did you? No, you just started hollering and carrying on and turning the kids against me, right? Then you go running to outsiders and tell 'em all your freaking troubles. Why don'cha give me a chance to be a good husband, instead 'a bringing outsiders in ta our business. Are you trying ta shame me, Terry? Well, you don't gotta do that. Hey, if you want out, just say so...but don't freaking railroad me out...just give me a freaking chance, will you?" He gasped. "You know I never hurt you or the kids before this, right? I never hurt you before, Terry? You know that, don't you? Answer me, Terry."

"Mack, I'm sorry..." she wiped at her tears. "Really sorry. I didn't mean to hurt you...and I didn't mean to turn the kids against you, either...but I just can't come home right now. Please try to understand...I'm scared. Maybe I'll come home tomorrow, Mack."

"Go ahead an' spoil everythin' now." He wept. "Everythin' we've worked for...all the years we was together...and just remember all the times I stuck by you, too...and I'm the father of them kids, and no one's gonna love 'em like I did."

"I know that, Mack, but I can't come home just yet..."

Click. Anne cut off the connection.

"What are you doing, Terry? You can't be thinking about going home, can you? Not after all that's happened!"

"But, Anne, you don't understand. He didn't mean it!" Terry sobbed. "He didn't mean it."

"The only thing that man didn't mean was for you to get away!" Anne said, raising her voice. "Look at what a single conversation with him has done to you? It's made you blame yourself again. For God's sake, Terry! You're not at fault here." She stood with her hands on her hips, shooting the words at Terry like bullets. "The man's no good, Terry. Please believe me!"

"But you don't understand, Anne. If I can only make him see what he's doing wrong, I know he'll change. I know I can make him stop. I just haven't found the right words yet."

"There are no right words to say to a man like that, Terry, except maybe goodbye!"

"You're wrong," Terry yelled back. "We can fix our relationship if I just work harder at it." She started sobbing again.

"Relationship? There isn't any relationship, because you're the only one relating. And you're relating all his deficiencies to some excusable, temporary condition that will improve with the aspirin of patience." She threw her hands in the air. "Don't you see? He's not only letting you make up for everything he won't do, but he's also got you convinced it's your job. Please, Terry, consider what you're doing to yourself in comparison to what you're doing for him! The scale is way out of balance."

Anne stopped to catch her breath. "Terry, you're such a beautiful girl. Why don't you love yourself half as much as you love him? Maybe that's it!" Anne said. "Maybe you hate yourself, and Mack's your executioner…that's it, isn't it? Death by degrees, except that it's a perpetual death…one where you're never extinguished, only executed over and over again.

She paused and paced the floor. "Terry, please try to see that one person cannot make a marriage. It takes two, and you're the only one working at this one."

Anne stopped, exhausted and out of breath.

"But you don't understand…if I could only make him hear me," Terry said again.

Gary drove past Terry's house and noticed that her car wasn't in the driveway. *Good, maybe she's at the mall.* He headed in that direction. *Maybe I can find her and we can have lunch together again.* Thinking he might meet her some place other than work made him happy. He knew he shouldn't be so attached to her, he would be leaving for Bangor, soon. What would he do then?

The mall was crowded with people getting ready for Easter, and he barely saw more than three feet in front of him through the crowd. At this rate, if he didn't physically bump into her, the chances of finding her were nil. Yet he spent the next two hours being pushed, bumped, and crushed in a futile effort looking. He finally left the mall and drove by her house again. "Damn, she's not here yet!" he cursed, heading back to the motel, debating whether to stay in and watch television or head for the bar. He was tired of being alone, so the bar won.

"But what about the kids? I can't take them to school now, it's too late, and I don't want to leave them here alone. They might get scared."

"I have a neighbor whose daughter is a college student. I think she's home on spring break right now. I'll call and see if she's available to babysit," Anne said, picking up the phone and dialing information.

"Hi. Greenridge, please. The number for Berger, yes…fine; thank you." She jotted the number on a message pad adjacent to the phone.

"Hello, Emma? This is Anne Craig. Fine, thanks, but I have a problem. I'm working now, you know…yes, I had to go to work…well, thank you. Yes, I miss him, too. Well, thanks…I'll be seeing you as soon as the weather warms up and we're all outside again. Yes, thanks…Listen, the reason I'm calling is I have a guest whose kids need a sitter for the rest of the week after school, and I wondered if Sara's at home? Oh, great! Would she like to earn some extra money? Fine, have her come over now if she can, and I'll introduce her to the kids."

"Thanks, Emma. You, too. Bye." Anne hung up the receiver. "Well, the kids have a sitter. Now you get to work before we're both fired."

"How am I going to pay for a sitter, Anne?" Terry asked.

"I don't even have enough money right now to pay for the food we've eaten this weekend, never mind the clothes you bought us."

"We'll worry about that later." Anne dismissed the young woman's worries. She had tapped into her *Joe Fund* and somehow felt a whole lot richer than she had before.

Chapter 21

"Terry!" Mr. Clark bellowed. "Where have you been? This place can't run itself, you know!"

"I'm sorry, Mr. Clark, but the kids were sick this morning and I did my best to get in as soon as possible."

Gary looked up from his desk and winked at her when she walked past.

"Now, about this Craig woman. She's not in yet, either!" Mr. Clark said.

"Oh? Did she call in sick?" she asked.

"Well, no, she said she'd be late, too."

"I don't think she has any kids, though, sir," she said, leading him away from the front desk.

"Well, what do you suppose she's doing then?" he asked, frowning.

"I don't know sir, but I'll ask as soon as she comes in."

"Good. We can't have goldbrickers in here, you know."

"Absolutely not, sir," she said in mock agreement.

"Now, about Flora."

"Flora? Is she late, too?" Terry asked in mock horror.

"No, no, she's here, but she was complaining to me this morning about Mrs. Craig's, ah…shall we say, inabilities."

"Well, she never spoke with me about any concerns, sir." Terry knew Clark didn't like anyone jumping the chain of command.

"You supervise them both, don't you?" he asked.

"Yes, sir, but I can't help her if she doesn't tell me there's a problem."

"But it's your business to know what's going on, Terry."

"Yes, sir, but if she goes behind my back..." she paused, "to *my* superior...then what can I do? It's hard to play team sports if one of the members plays outside the game." She put on a pouty face.

"Damn it, you're right," Clark said, his cheeks getting red. "She tried to use me. Well, we'll have no more of her little tricks, will we?" He faced Terry. "Keep up the good work, and watch the two of them, will you?" he growled without baring his teeth.

"Yes, sir." She smiled, leaving the room.

Gary stood outside the door, taking his time pouring a cup of coffee. "Good work," he whispered when she passed. Her face turned red, but she kept walking. "Terry, can we meet later this morning?" he called after her in a most professional tone of voice.

"Certainly, Gary. Give me ten minutes to put my desk in order and then come on in." She tried to sound confident, but her voice shook a little.

"Great," he said.

<hr />

Anne introduced the kids to Sara and gave the babysitter the phone number where she and Terry could be reached.

"The kids may be going back to school tomorrow," Anne said, "and I wonder if you'd like to pick them up and stay with them until we get home each day?"

"Sure, Mrs. Craig. I'd be glad to," Sara said, smiling at the kids.

"Fine, it's settled." She grinned, handing Sara some money. "This should cover it then?"

"Oh, Mrs. Craig, that's too much money!" the young woman protested.

"Well, let's see if you feel that way by the end of the week," she said.

"What?" Sara said, frowning at the kids.

"Oh, nothing." Anne laughed. "The kids are angels, Sara. I only meant that running back and forth from here to school could be a hassle. That's all."

"Oh, okay." Sara smiled at the kids. "Do you want to go to the playground for now?" she asked and received a rousing vote of approval. "Mrs. Craig, may I have a house key so we can get back in?"

"Absolutely," Anne smiled. She liked this girl—always had, ever since Sara was a baby when her family moved here. A lovely girl and a smart one. If Mack showed up at school, Sara would know what to do, without having to be made aware now the situation, and that was a lucky break.

"Thanks for seeing me this morning, Terry." He closed the office door behind him.

"Well, we have to go over the OS&D systems again anyway, don't we," she said, her face flushing. She was still embarrassed by what had happened last week and she hoped he wouldn't bring it up. She had enough problems right now.

"Yes, that's right," he said. He looked as nervous as she felt. "Why were you late this morning? Nothing serious with the kids, I hope."

"No, they're fine. Let's get started with 'Overages,' then we'll move to 'Shortages' and finally, we should finish up with 'Damages' this afternoon. Now," she said, pulling a manual from the shelf above her desk.

"Speaking of damages…" he reached up, taking the manual from her hands and placing it on the desk, "did I damage our friendship by ah…kissing you last week?" he asked in a rush.

"Gary, please, I have to teach you all this stuff and we've

got to get started on it, so please..." She ignored his question, and picked up the manual again.

"Terry, tell me if I hurt our friendship. I'm sorry if I upset you," he said.

"Gary, you didn't hurt our friendship, but we have to learn *all* this," she said pointing at the huge manual.

"Then we're still friends?" His eyes brightened.

"Yes, we're still friends." She laughed. "Now, to work..."

"Terry, I'm sorry but I have to say something to you," he said, pulling the manual away from her again. "You are one of the most wonderful people I have ever known," he snatched up her free hand, "and I feel very strongly about you. I know you're a married woman and all, but I can't help myself."

"Gary, please." She tried to pull her hand away.

"No, listen to me." He hung onto her hand. "You've given me a reason to come to work each day, and a bright spot in that work whenever I see you. We talk together like no two people I've ever known and we share the same goals, and like the same things. I'm leaving for Bangor in two weeks! What am I going to do when I leave? I can't stop seeing you, Terry." He squeezed her hand until she yelped. "I'm sorry Terry, but I can't let you go. I think I...ah...oh, I don't know what I think."

Terry stood there, her mouth open but her mind unable to take it in. Her fantasy was being spoken, but in someone else's voice, and it scared her.

"Gary, I can't deal with this right now." She pulled her hand out of his and drew it back to her side. "I can't even think right now, so please get out of my office." She started to cry, unable to look at him. "Please go," she said, getting up and opening the door.

He rose. "I'm sorry, Terry. I didn't mean to insult or embarrass you," he said, his voice barely audible. "I won't bother you again."

"I'm sorry, Gary, really." She closed the door and fell

against it, sobbing. A huge vacuum sprang up inside her and the pain in her head echoed throughout that empty space, pulsating and reverberating so that she hurt in every part of her body. Her mind throbbed from holding back the explosion. She bit the inside of her mouth and tasted blood. She bit even harder. She wanted to claw her face and go screaming through the world, but she couldn't. She pulled out a piece of paper and wrote instead.

> *Dear God, I'm writing this because it is quieter than screaming, and it lasts longer. But my pen can't dig deep enough into the paper without destroying it, unlike my anger, which now threatens to drive me into the ground. There's no way out. I can never go home again...but where, then, do my kids and I go?*

She paused. Gouging the paper, she tried to move beyond the question.

> *"And he says it's all my fault. Mine!!! Like I'm insatiable or unreasonable, but what about him? Doesn't Mack have to try, too? Now this man, Gary, comes to me and says he's worried that I'm mad at him, for God's sake! And he blames me for nothing! And still likes me! Can I be both blameless and blasted? Can I be both bad and good? Can I mean so much to one and be the death of another?*

She dug the pen into the paper with heavy black slashes over the rest of the page. She sliced into the heart of the enemy, dismembering her demons. She threw the pen down and fell upon the carnage, sobbing and inconsolable.

Somewhere I did a bad thing, whatever it was. And there is no rescue or relief for me from the fracas.

Anne arrived about an hour after Terry and took her place at the console. Flora, who covered the reception desk, sneered and threw the pad of paper she'd written messages on at Anne. "Now maybe I can get back to my own work," she sniffed, and turned on her heel heading for the secretarial pool.

"Do you work here?" Anne asked with a smug smile.

"I'll have you know I'm very responsible!" the flame yelled, blasting back over her shoulder in anger.

"Responsible for making trouble maybe, but that's all," Anne said.

Flora growled. "Screw you." She turned and stomped off.

Anne shouldn't have started an argument with Flora, but today was special. There was too much pain and aggravation in the world to let Flora off without a fight. And, it felt good.

Once settled, Anne looked around the office, which seemed unduly quiet. She noticed almost all the office doors closed, so very few eyes peered at her. The sales manager's door was also closed. *Oh, but he's on vacation. Just as soon as I can I'll check on Terry, and let her know the kids are okay.*

Just then Gary opened his door and walked toward her. "Hi, Anne," he said, his eyes downcast.

"Well, hello. Did you have a nice weekend?"

"It was okay," he said with little enthusiasm. "And yours?"

"Fine." She hated lying to him.

"Listen, Anne, would you do me a favor?"

"Sure, what is it," she smiled.

"I'm concerned about Terry this morning. Could you sort of…ah…check on her?"

"Sure. What's the matter with her," Anne asked.

"Well, I think she's under a lot of stress, and I sense that she needs a friend."

"Oh, sure." "I'll talk with her during our coffee break, okay?"

"Great. And thanks!" He smiled.
"Anytime, Gary."

Soon, everyone left their desks and headed for the lounge, but Terry had not yet opened her door. Anne walked over to it and knocked.

"Yes," Terry called out.

"Terry, it's Anne. Let me in," Anne whispered.

"I'm going to take my coffee break in here this morning. I'll talk with you later," Terry said without opening the door.

"Terry, open this door, now!"

Anne watched the door open a tiny crack. She saw Terry's red face and swollen eyes.

Anne gasped. "Terry, what's the matter?"

"Come inside before everyone sees me, Anne." Terry opened the door just enough for Anne to squeeze through and closed it behind her.

"What is it? Are you still upset about this morning?"

"I don't know what I'm upset about, Anne." Tears fell from her swollen eyes.

"Terry, is it Gary?" Anne asked.

"What about Gary?"

"You tell me. All I know is that he asked me to look in on you. Did you tell him about your home situation?"

"Of course not!"

"Then why would he be asking me to check on you—" Anne stopped short. "Has he been bothering you?"

"In a way, yes." She wept openly now.

"Why that louse…" Anne started to sputter.

"No, Anne, you don't understand…he likes me…."

"What do you mean 'he likes you'?" Anne was confused.

"He was nice to me." Terry sobbed now.

"Terry, what are you talking about? You're not making any sense.

"He likes me, Anne, and he...he...kissed me, last week."

"Oh, for heaven's sake! Is that all?" she sighed, relieved that it wasn't serious. "So he likes you, and he kissed you once. So what." She dismissed it.

Terry kept on crying.

"You don't understand," Terry said. "He likes me."

"So he likes you," Anne said, throwing her hands in the air. "What does that mean?" she asked again.

"Nobody likes me, Anne."

"Oh, Terry, I like you," she said, a lump filling her throat, her arms reaching out to encircle Terry "Why wouldn't he like you?"

"Cause no man ever has."

"Well, there's always the first time," Anne said in a near whisper. "So he kissed you and now you're not a virgin..." she giggled.

"Not a what?" Terry gasped and then laughed, too.

After break time, Terry's mood improved, which had the opposite effect on Gary. He was convinced that her joviality was forced and that she was using it to distance herself from him. He was miserable. All day he continued to mope around the office. By five o'clock he stood a foot shorter.

He saw Anne and Terry walking out the door together, whispering with their heads together. Gary sulked past them.

"Goodnight, Gary," Terry said.

He turned to look at her and stopped walking, letting them catch up.

"Terry, can I talk with you for a minute?" he asked afraid to look her in the eye.

Terry looked at Anne, who nodded her approval.

"Certainly," she said to him. "See you at home," she whispered to Anne, who sped up her steps and passed him.

"Terry, I'm sorry, again, for upsetting you today. Can you

forgive me?" He looked up and met her eye.

"Gary, there is nothing to forgive. I'm having a lot of problems at home and I can't cope with anything else. So if I got upset today, it wasn't your fault."

"Really?" He felt his excitement growing. "Terry, if I can do anything to help you, please let me know. I'll do anything. I meant what I said. I really like you." He reached out for her hand, but stopped, remembering where he was. "Oh, Terry, I'm so glad you like me, too. I know we'd make a great couple," he said with vigor.

"Gary, please. I'm married!" she protested. "I have to go." She turned to walk toward her car again. "I'll see you tomorrow."

"Right," he said, unable to hide the grin on his face. "I'll see you tomorrow!" He gained at least two feet in height while he headed for his car. *Progress. Good progress. Anything is possible now. Especially if she's having problems at home. Hallelujah!*

Chapter 22

The kids waited at the door when Terry arrived home. They seemed happy and peaceful, both speaking at once when she walked in.

"Whoa, one at a time," she laughed, glad to see them happy again.

"Oh, Mom, Sara is wonderful. We played games, and went to the park, and she's teaching us to play chess," Cara said gushing. "And she goes to college, too."

"So I've heard. And what about you, young fellow, did you like her, too?" she asked her son, nuzzling his neck with her face.

"Oh, yeah, and she played catch with us, too," he said, giggling.

"Well, I'd say that was a good day, then, right, guys?" Terry laughed.

"Yeah!" they shouted.

"Okay, then, get washed up and I'll see what Anne has planned for dinner." She shooed them out of the living room and toward the bathroom. "Anne," she called.

"Yes," Anne answered from the kitchen. "I'm out here."

"What can I do for dinner?" Terry asked, rounding the doorway between the two rooms.

"I thought we could have some ravioli and salad. Is

that okay?" Anne asked.

"Fine. Shall I make the salad?" Terry offered.

"Yes, please. The vegetables are in the bottom drawer of the refrigerator. I'll open the ravioli and set the table."

The two women worked in the peaceful kitchen, and Terry couldn't help but think of the difference between this home and her own.

"The kids seem so much calmer today."

"I'm glad," Anne answered. "You all deserve a rest."

"You know, Anne, if it weren't for your husband's...ah...death," Terry continued softly, "this would be an enviable place to live."

Anne shook her head. "Terry, it's a morgue without someone to share it. A morgue may be a great respite after what you've been through, but remember..." she said..."Mack is the one who belongs in a morgue, not you or the kids. You have a chance to make a different life for all of you. And I'm blessed to have your company in the meantime," she said.

"Anne, I don't know how I can ever thank you. Or repay you, for that matter."

"Just bringing life back into this house is payment enough."

"But I can't stay here forever, Anne. What am I going to do?"

"You can stay here as long as you like. Then, if you want to, you can get a place of your own." Anne said.

"A place of my own?" Terry looked horrified.

"But you can stay here if you like," Anne said, amending her statement, hoping she hadn't conveyed the wrong message.

"What about going back to my own home?" Terry said.

"I don't think that's a wise idea right now. I think it'd be dangerous and foolish to go back there, even if he said he'd leave."

"But don't you think things will work out?" Terry asked, her eyes stretched wide open and her mouth pulled way down.

"God no, Terry. How can you think it would? You don't really think things will smooth out, do you?"

"Well, I was hoping…" she didn't finish her sentence. Tears choked off her words. "What will I do then?" Terry mumbled.

"Start over," Anne said.

They finished dinner by 6:30 pm and Terry thought about putting Tommy into the tub. Then she remembered their scarcity of clothes.

"Anne, I want to go home and—"

"No!" Anne cut her off so quickly that the kids looked up from their TV program..

"Just to get some clothes," Terry said, finishing her sentence.

"That could be dangerous, Terry," Anne whispered after the kids went back to their program.

"Well, we can't live on a single set of underwear each, and the kids have only one change of clothes. I've got to get them back in school tomorrow. What else can I do?" she said.

"I'll call Mr. Hansen and ask him." Anne rose from her chair and walked toward the telephone.

"What if he says I shouldn't?" Terry asked.

"Like they say, we'll cross that bridge when we come to it," she said.

The office phone rang twice before the switchboard operator picked up, announcing that the office was closed for the day. Anne hung up before speaking to the operator.

"Damn, I forgot the time," she said aloud. "What was that home phone number he gave me?" She was annoyed with herself for misplacing it. She didn't like speaking with this man. There was something about him that irritated her.

"Here it is," she said, pulling the card from her wallet and dialing the number. Three rings later, he answered.

"Hello."

"Mr. Hansen, this is Mrs. Craig." She waited for recognition.

"Hello, Anne."

"Mrs. Craig, Mr. Hansen," she reminded him. "Mrs. Woods," she said for emphasis, "wants to go back to her house for clothes for herself and the kids. What shall we do?" she asked.

"Well, I would suggest she call the police and ask them to escort her into the house, just in case her husband is home," he said.

"Terry, go pick up the extension in my bedroom and listen to Mr. Hansen's advice," she ordered.

"Steve," he reminded her, laughing.

"Mr. Hansen," she said annoyed that he kept insisting on a friendlier relationship, "please repeat what you just told me."

"Hi, Terry, are you there?" he asked.

"Yes, Steve."

"I don't think you should go back into your house without a police escort. It's just not safe."

"I don't want to involve the police. I appreciate your advice and all your help, but really, I think I've made too much of all of this. Even if Mack is home, he won't do anything stupid. He made a mistake the other night, and I escalated it. But thank you for all your help."

"Terry, look, I realize it's hard to take this thing seriously, but it is."

"Thank you for your help. I'll be perfectly fine, even if he is home," she said.

"Then I'm obliged to go with you," Steve said, surprising Anne with his commitment.

"Me, too," Anne said, chiming in.

"Fine," Terry said. "We'll meet you there at 10:00 p.m.," she said.

"Okay," Anne said.

"Okay, fine." Steve said. "I'll be driving a blue Ford and I'll see you there."

Anne ran into her bedroom once the two women had hung up. "What do you think you're doing? It's dangerous there, and you know it."

"I don't know anything of the kind," Terry said.

"Well, let's hope you're right. Now what do you want to do about the kids?"

Terry stood silent for minutes. "All right, we'll take them with us," she said.

"Heaven help us." Anne shook her head. *What's wrong with this girl?*

Chapter 23

Turning onto Terry's street the women saw the house, looming before them, beckoning their foolhardy adventure. Anne shuttered, thinking of a haunted house at a carnival where spooks and scary things lurked in every corner. The kid's whimpering in the back seat, frightened Anne and her hands trembled — her whole body going numb.

Anne pointed out Steve Hansen's car parked on the opposite side of the street. It sat a few houses down beneath a grand old oak tree, whose wide girth held back most of the light around it. She blinked her high beams at the car, and he signaled back.

"I may not like the man, but I have to admit, I feel better with him here," Anne said, watching him walk to the car.

When he joined them he said, "I've been sitting here for a while and I didn't see any movement in the house."

Anne breathed a sigh of relief. "Good."

"His car isn't here, so he's probably not at home," Terry said. "I'm going in. Do either of you want to watch the kids or should I bring them in, too?"

"Mom, I want to get some of my things," Cara said.

"Me, too." Tommy bounced on the seat.

"Then why don't we all go in," Steve said.

"Okay…" Anne looked wary. "But this seems dangerous.

Are you sure I can't change your mind."

Terry climbed out of the car and headed across the street.

They were about ten feet from the house when Cara whispered. "Mom, I hear voices." They all strained to listen. Sure enough, a conversation was going on inside the house.

"Here, let me go to the door." Steve pushed past them. "You stay here."

He stood at the door listening, ringing the bell at least a half dozen times to no avail. Then the conversation inside the house changed and loud music replaced it.

"It's okay, it's the television," he whispered.

Sighing with relief, Terry led the way up the steps. She fumbled with the key in the lock. When she finally opened the door, they burst into the front hall, and gasped. Smashed furniture lay strewn about the room. Dishes, food, clothes, toys, all lay piled in the center of the living room floor, with the television blaring. Terry stood speechless, and the kids stared wide-eyed and shaken.

"Look at this place," Steve said. "It looks like a cyclone went through the room."

"I wonder if there's anything left worth taking," Anne said.

Terry moved into the fracas first, stepping over large piles of clothing and debris. She pulled a favorite sweater from the wreckage, and tears sprang from her eyes.

"I waited a month to buy this sweater." She clutched it to her chest.

"Terry, let's hurry and see if there's anything left in the kids' rooms," Anne said, taking charge of the situation.

"Okay," Terry headed off. "This way."

"Steve, would you mind staying here with the kids?" Terry asked.

"Sure."

"No, Mom, don't leave us down here." Cara's face was wet with tears. "We'll all go upstairs." She ran after her mother, her brother close behind.

"I don't blame them," Steve said, following the troop climbing the stairs.

The upstairs also lay devastated. But, Terry and the kids were able to salvage some of their clothes. It wasn't until Terry stood on the stairs looking down into the living room that the carnage really hit her.

"Oh, God, look at this place," she whispered. "My home is destroyed! Goddamn him!" She looked at her children and saw they too cried when they joined her. "I don't want to start over again, goddamn it." She pulled one thing after another from a pile, seeing years of accomplishments destroyed and discarded in a single rage. *What had it all meant? All the days of working and struggling to make ends meet. All the days of exhaustion, trying to combine work and home and family. What had it all meant? Nothing.*

The sacrifices, the pain, the exhaustion, the hope... especially the hope...hope that one day she'd have gotten it all...she'd have done her part and finished providing for others and could then do something else. The effort she'd put into her marriage became like feeding a hollow, insatiable monster with holes in his feet. She poured everything into him and then he let it drain out of him. Nothing had stuck or nourished. Nothing had lasted. And now here lay the evidence...the pile of waste where he'd left behind the feedings.

"I don't want to start again...I can't." She sobbed, and slipped down onto the floor beside the heaps of her ruined life. "I can't do it all again..."

"Terry, please! We'd better go, honey," Anne said, walking over the piles of trash and reaching down to cup Terry's elbow in her hand.

Terry let Anne pull her from the floor. She saw the pity in Anne's eyes, and Steve shaking his head. At that moment, she hated Mack. *How could he do this to me? To us? To the kids? How could he destroy everything we've worked so hard for? How could he destroy everything we've accumulated in our struggle to have what others have — to be what other families are. How could he destroy it all and still say he loves us?*

The kids hadn't spoken or moved much since they came downstairs, and now they sat just as subdued in the car.

"Terry, were you able to get enough clothes?"

"Some stuff," Terry answered from far away.

"And you kids...did you get any favorite toys?" Anne asked.

"No," they answered in quiet, flat voices.

Anne fell into quiet reflection, making the ride back to her house endless. Steve had restated his fear about going back to Terry's house again. Anne agreed on both counts. She checked her rear view mirror and there he was, following them back to Anne's home.

I have to admit, he is caring, and he was determined not to let Terry or the kids go in there alone. Perhaps there is one other good man in this world. Perhaps he's handled this just as well as Sam Gregory would have, if he'd been at the office the Saturday when I called. God! Could it only be so short a time ago? It feels like years have passed. And surely I've aged years since then, with all this fear we're living under. How could Terry have lived there for ten years and not lost her mind. Why, just being in that house was enough to raise skin from your body and not just in goose bumps! And the destruction! He must be a madman. God help Terry and those poor kids if they had been in there when he started his rampage. Anne shuddered to think of the consequences. She missed Joe more and more. *Stinking life...take the good, leave the grotesque. No justice anywhere!*

Within fifteen minutes they arrived back at Anne's house and still none of them had spoken since her brief attempt at conversation. Just as quietly they got out of the car and walked into the house, Terry bringing the salvageable clothes straight down to the cellar to the washing machine, and the kids heading for the bathroom to wash up for bed. Cara took

Tommy by the hand and led him there. Steve walked in only moments after them and waited in the kitchen. Anne finally realized he stood there.

"Oh, I'm sorry, Mr. Hansen. Please, have a seat," she said remembering her manners.

"Thank you, Anne," he said. "Did she say anything on the way home?"

"No." Anne shook her head and frowned. "I'm worried about her, really."

"We must find a way to keep her away from him and that house until we can get some court action to remove him. Then we'll get her permanent custody of the kids and the property," he said. "In the meantime, it's imperative that we keep her safe."

"What can I say to her?"

"Keep telling her that she did the right thing. And that her kids are safer here. It's very important you get through to her," he said.

Anne felt like crying. All the fear and anxiety mounted in her throat, fighting for recognition and air. "I don't know what to say!" She burst out crying.

He took a step toward her, but stopped. "Obviously you've said the right things up to now. She came to you in the first place and has let you help her. Just keep doing what you're doing."

A little bit relieved, she now understood the awesome, fearful responsibility she'd taken on. "Thank you, Steve," she said, truly grateful for his encouragement. "I'll keep trying."

"Good. That's all anyone can ask of you, Anne."

"Would you like a cup of coffee?"

"No. I want to speak with Terry for a moment before I leave, though."

"Of course," she said, and they sat without speaking until Terry came upstairs.

He didn't leave until almost midnight.

With the kids already in bed, sound asleep, Anne was ready for bed, too. But Terry was too nervous to sleep, and took a cup of tea into the den, closing the door after her. She lay down on the sleep-sofa. She never expected him to destroy their things. Her—maybe, but never their things. What was he thinking? She alternated between tears and anger. Why did he destroy their things? It had taken years to accumulate their property and now, in this short span of time he'd obliterated everything tangible. It was as though, if he couldn't have her, she couldn't have anything they'd worked for. But what if she had gone back? What would they have done then? Start all over again? He hadn't even given her time to change her mind. He'd burnt the bridge behind her and now if she wanted to go back, she'd have to catapult over the abyss. The stupidity and the waste of it all struck her.

She jumped up from the sofa and paced back and forth, her breath coming in short angry snorts. Tears burned their way down her face. She didn't wipe them away. *Let them fall. Who gives a damn anyway? Who gives a damn?* With each step her rage intensified until she wanted to reach out and smash something. But she wasn't in her own home so she grabbed a pillow from the sofa and clenching it between her teeth, bit it and shook it like a dog shakes a bone. She punched her thighs, and dropping the pillow from her teeth, bit her lips and the inside of her mouth.

The more she paced, the more her adrenaline rose and threatened to overflow her body. She ran from the room and out the kitchen door into the night air. She threw herself down onto the cold and damp ground and pounded her fists into the hard earth. She punched and pounded and struck at the black earth until her hands warmed with sweat and blood and her arms ached as though she'd carried the world through the galaxy single-handed. She lay there, spent and sobbing and sore as the last ounce of rage was pulled from her by the cold and unfeeling earth beneath her body, and she thought she would die right there.

Anne had seen Terry bolt outside and went out into the yard and tried to bring Terry back into the house.

"Terry, please get up." She pulled on Terry's arms while Terry lay face down, sunk into the earth. She pulled with all her strength but Terry was dead weight now. "Terry get up!" Anne said, more frightened than angry. "Get up, damn it, or I'm calling the police!"

Terry stirred, finally letting Anne grip her arm. Anne pulled her into a sitting position. Even in the dim light Anne saw the black earth covering Terry's face and clothing. Anne had to get her into the house. "Get up off this ground!" Anne pulled at Terry again. "Terry, get up!"

After several minutes, the two women dragged themselves up the backstairs, into the kitchen. Once inside, Terry dropped down onto a chair, her face covered with dirt and blood. The front of her dress, Anne's dress really, was covered with grass and earth. Terry's arms and fists were caked with filth.

Anne went to the sink where she ran lukewarm water over a cloth and brought it to the table.

"Hold still now," she said. "This may hurt." She washed away some of the dirt and blood from Terry's face and neck, using short gentle strokes.

Twice Terry winced. "Ouch! For crying out loud, Anne, that hurts."

"I'm glad!" Anne said. "Because if it felt good, you'd go out and beat up my backyard again tomorrow night!"

They both laughed.

"You are a weird broad, Anne."

"I hope so." Anne turned her head side-ways and raising her nose into the air. "How else could I manage these midnight forays into fantasy?"

"Fantasy?"

"Yes, my dear, fantasy. Two weeks ago I couldn't have believed such pain existed in the world, so this must be fantasy."

"Yes, pain and fantasy. It's like a horror movie starring me." Terry sobbed. "Except this is a rotten script, lady."

"But you can rewrite it!" Anne said.

"How?"

"By changing the ending. Constantly rehearsing this play won't change the ending. You've got to get out of this one and make a whole new one."

Terry moaned again. "But how?"

"Don't go back to Mack! Do something for yourself. You can make it. Honest. And I'll be there to help…and others too, if you want them. Just give yourself a break by getting away from that maniac husband of yours!"

"You're right." She reached out and embraced Anne. "Please help me…help me be strong."

Anne squeezed Terry, "I'm on your side and I'm not going anywhere, honey…" Anne said.

Chapter 24

Anne saw him coming before he reached the door. He weaved and pitched and she watched him reach for the door handle twice before catching it.

She pressed the alarm button to summon security when he lurched into the reception area.

"Hey, you!" he bellowed.

"Can I help you, sir?" Anne asked, seeing the man's arms flying from his sides while he sought to gain balance. *I hope the guard hurries.*

"Where's my wife?" the man said, lunging toward her desk, his breath arriving first.

Anne recoiled. "Who's your wife, sir?"

"Terry! Now getta for me."

She pulled back and rolled her chair out of his reach.

"I'll try to find her for you," she said, rising from her console and rushing to Clark's office. "You just wait right there, all right?"

"Hey, where ya going?" he said, following her. She sped up and ran through the foyer.

Mack was so unsteady on his feet that he couldn't keep up with her and used his voice instead.

"Terrrrrrrry!" he screamed. "Hey, Terrrrrrrrry. Get out here!"

The secretaries came running from their desks in the inner office.

"What's all this yelling about out here?" Mr. Clark shouted, pulling his office door open and entering the reception area.

Shaking, Anne ran behind him.

"Who the hell a you?" Mack said.

"I'm Mr. Clark! The Manager here. Now, what's all this about."

Anne watched Mr. Clark stand taller and straighten his shoulders. "Who are you?"

"I'm Terry's husband." Mack teetered and tried to lean forward.

"Ahem, I see. Well, Terry is working right now. She can't see anyone. Now, you better come back later, Mr. Woods," Mr. Clark said, crossing his arms.

Mack bolted at Clark who leaned backward into Anne.

She ran to the other side of the room watching in horror.

"What...what are you doing..." Clark whimpered when Mack caught the old man by the collar, pulling them both to the floor.

"What the hell." Clark squirmed under Mack's weight.

Mack struck out, catching Clark's chin with the edge of his fist.

"Help...help," Clark yelled, blood spilling over his lower lip.

Anne stood transfixed, not knowing what to do.

"Watch out, Anne," Gary shouted from behind her and pushed his way to the men wrestling on the floor.

He freed Clark from Mack's grip and pushed him out of the way. Yanking Mack to his feet in a single sweep, Gary punched him in the face twice, blood splattering across Gary's face and shirt.

The drunken man slumped beneath Gary's hold, unconscious, and Gary let him fall to the floor.

"Where's that security guard, Anne?" Clark yelled, crabbing his way across the floor.

Anne ran to her console and pressed the button over

and over again. "Come on, come on," she yelled.

From the corner of her eye, Anne saw Terry standing in her office doorway, watching, her mouth agape and tears running down her face.

The security guard finally arrived, and Anne saw Terry slip behind the door and heard her engage the lock.

Anne heard the siren whipping through the parking lot and the front door burst open.

"What's going on in here?" A commanding male voice said.

"Over here, officer." Mr. Clark pointed to the unconscious man.

"He came in here looking for his wife, and, he's...well...a little under the weather." Clark nodded.

"What's all this blood? Was there a fight?" The cop asked, looking around.

"No, no, just a misunderstanding. Isn't that right, Gary?"

Anne saw Gary's mouth drop open and his eyes darken.

"Gary?" Clark said.

"Yes...yes, that's right. We just kept him from hurting himself."

"Is the wife here, now? We'd like to talk to her—find out what's going on."

"No, she's not here right now. I sent her to the post office an hour ago. I think that's why the husband was upset."

"Do you want to press charges, then? We can hold him for the night."

"No. No charges, but I think he should sleep it off somewhere safe." Clark winked at the officer. "I'm sure everything will be fine tomorrow."

The cop called to his partner, who'd been standing nearby. "Looks like we have a guest tonight, Bill,"

Anne watched them cuff the still unconscious Mack. They half-lifted him by the armpits and dragged him out of the building.

"What the hell was that, Clark?" Gary whispered. "He beat on you, and me, and he would have beaten on Terry, too, if he'd gotten to her."

"Gary, you don't understand. You're not married. Husbands and wives have little tiffs from time to time and sometimes things explode, but they die down. Do you want to condemn a man before he can make things right at home? Do you?" Clark inclined his head. "You'll understand, one day, son, when you're married. Now, go get cleaned up and take the rest of the day off. You look like hell."

Anne realized her mouth still hung open and closed it. She watched Gary run to his office and then charge through the reception area, eyes blazing. He bolted to the front door, yanked it open, and ran out.

Clark walked to his office and closed the door.

"Oh, God..." Anne whispered and moved back to her chair, still shaking.

Heart pounding, Terry huddled in her chair with her back against the locked door.

Oh God, what have I done? He's going to kill me. Stupid, stupid woman. I brought this on myself. Oh my God, what's going to happen to me...to the kids? I wish I were dead.

She tried to muffle her sobs, but hic-cupped between them, making it hard to catch her breath.

Please God, just let me die. I can't face Mack or Anne or Ga...

She pushed his name from of her mind—that's what put her and her children in jeopardy! *Stupid, stupid woman.*

The sound of a knock, gentle as it was, caused her to jumped from the chair.

"Terry?" Anne whispered. "Terry, honey, are you all right?"

"Is it over?" she whispered. "Is Mack gone? Is everyone all right?"

"Yes, everything is fine now, please come out and let

me talk with you. Please?"

"I can't right now, Anne. I'm sorry, I just can't."

Clark had cleaned up his bloody face, but his lip was swollen and turning an ugly color when he found Anne at her desk. "Is Terry still in there?" He motioned his head toward Terry's office.

"Yes, I'm afraid so, sir." Anne's voice caught on her words.

"Well, get her out of there and bring her to my office, now."

"I tried, sir, she won't come out."

He hissed and charged over to the office door. "Terry? Come out here, now."

"I can't." Terry's voice trembled.

"It's alright, now. You can open the door," he said softening his voice.

The door opened just a crack. Terry looked out into the reception area before opening it all the way.

Anne thought Terry looked smaller, somehow crumpled and weak.

"Oh, Mr. Clark, I'm so sorry...really." Terry burst into tears.

"Now, now, that's all right."

Anne watched Clark reach out to Terry, but he pulled his hand back.

Eyes widening, Terry said, "Mr. Clark, you're hurt." She wiped at the fresh tears.

"Yes, he did hit me, but I'm all right, now. Your husband was just drunk," he said, waving the offense away. "But what's going on? Are you two having problems?"

Her shoulders dropped. "Yes."

"Why didn't you tell me? I could have helped."

"There's nothing you can do, sir," she said. "I have to work this out myself."

"Nonsense. I could have given you some time off to be at home," he said. "You know, Terry, a man likes to have his wife's attention and maybe if you spent more time at home, it would all work out. I mean, I appreciate how hard you work here and the late hours you sometimes put in, but I can't be selfish. Your husband has to come first."

"But, sir, I try to take care of everything."

"Now, now, that's in the past. Tonight, your husband will be sleeping in the pokey, but I won't press charges. He might be out by tomorrow morning. So, why don't you go home and make it up to him?" He smiled.

A rage swelled within Anne. *Don't you get it, you moron? Her husband was drunk. He came in here to hurt someone and that someone would have been Terry if you and Gary hadn't intervened.*

Clark had gone into autopilot again, just like when she'd interviewed for the job.

You're a moron. But worse than that, you're going to send Terry back into a death trap? Don't you get it?

Terry said, "I don't think that'll help right now—"

"Nonsense. Nothing like a little home-cooked meal and a little…ah…attention. Now you scoot out of here and get the home fires burning again, all right?"

Terry obeyed and retrieved her coat and purse from the office, while trying to hide her sniffles.

When she returned, Clark smiled at her and winked. "That's the ticket, my dear. It'll all be fine. Take whatever time off you need. All right?"

"Yes, Mr. Clark, thank you." She nodded and turned to the reception area. "Anne, I'm going home." She rolled her eyes toward Mr. Clark, who followed close behind. "If I get any calls or if anyone looks for me, call me there. Okay?"

Gary ran back into the building. "Terry! Wait!"

Terry stopped. Mr. Clark stood behind her, motioning her to go on home, while Gary blocked the exit.

"Terry, are you all right? Where are you going?" Gary said.

"She's going home, Gary. It's where she needs to be, so let's let her go, shall we?" Clark winked at him. "She's pretty upset and embarrassed."

"But, are you all right?" Gary stared at Terry.

"She's fine. She just needs some time to calm down and to make things right at home." Clark waved away Gary's concern.

"I'm fine, Gary, really," Terry said, moving past him and reaching for the door handle.

"Wait!" Gary moved to follow her through the door. "But I have to talk to you, Terry," he called.

Terry kept on walking.

Clark had gone back into his office, but not before showing displeasure with Gary's upstaging. Anne watched them both with wonder.

And poor Terry is worried that no one will help. She doesn't know how entitled she could act, never mind be. If she'd just open her eyes to who's interested in her. But that's good. The more ammunition I can get to use against that drunken husband of hers, the better!

Terry reached Anne's house long before the kids came home from school, so she made a cup of tea and headed for the bathroom to take a scalding hot bath. She needed something for herself right now. Maybe a good strong drink would have done more than a bath but she tried not to use alcohol when she needed it. Otherwise, she might end up like her mother.

Her mother. Oh, God! She'd forgotten to call her mother. It'd been at least a week since she talked with her. Damn. One more crisis.

She started the water and went to the kitchen. She dialed the number anxious to get it over with, but deep down she knew better. The phone rang five times and Terry was about to hang up when a groggy voice answered.

"Hello?"

"Hi, Ma, it's Terry."

"Well, if it isn't a voice from the past! And who might this be, calling me and waking me up in the middle of the freaking night."

"Ma, it's me, Terry. It's the middle of the afternoon."

"Well, well...now that name sounds familiar? Didn't I used to have a daughter by that name?" she said.

"I'm sorry I didn't call, Ma...but...I've been sick and—"

"Well, isn't that too freaking bad—you been sick! What about me? I'm a sick old woman, left all alone, no one to help me. And my goddamn daughter can't even call me. Nice. Real nice! What if you'd called and I was dead? Then what?"

"Ma, you could have called me, too, you know." Terry defended herself.

"Oh, I could have called you? You no good, lousy bitch. And I suppose I could have talked with that stinking son-of-a-bitching husband of yours, too, huh?"

"You know he doesn't answer the phone, for heaven's sakes!" Terry's voice rose.

"That's it! Make excuses for him...and for not calling your sick mother! But who gives a damn! I can just rot away here, no company and no money. And I can watch the goddamn TV all day and read my goddamn papers, if someone will brings them to me, and I can go hungry, too, because my goddamn daughter is too busy to bother with me! Just wait'll your kids grow up and see what it's like. See how you'll like it then, Miss High-and-Mighty. Just see how often they bother with you, Your Highness," she said.

"I'm sorry to have bothered you, Ma. I just wanted to see how you were doing," Terry said.

"Sure, you wanted to take care of your freaking conscience. That's all you wanted to do. You don't give a goddamn about me or my welfare or what I need or whether anyone in the world bothers with me? Do you, you bitch?" She ranted on.

"Ma, you know I care about you, but—"

"Yeah, but you're too busy to help your poor, sick mother. Well, stay the freak away from me! No help is better than waiting and hoping you'll come around and then never hearing from you or seeing you. So just do me a favor. Stay the hell away from me!" Silence filled the receiver when she hung up on Terry.

When Terry smashed the handset down onto its cradle, she hoped she hadn't broken it. *Why did I have to call her? And especially now! I knew better, but no…I had to call her today. Why am I so stupid?* Terry stormed into the bathroom, hoping the tub hadn't overflowed.

The bathroom had filled with steam, and the visibility was poor, but the warmth and coziness of being blind comforted her. Terry undressed and twice her rings caught in her sweater. She had the urge to rip the sweater to shreds, but then remembered the piles of ruined clothing at the house the night before. It was bad enough one of them had a temper. She wasn't going to add to the destruction. But now her mother was angry at her, too. So it must be her fault.

Why do I always antagonize everyone? She cried, playing the old record in her head, getting more and more angry with herself. Her stomach burned and her head throbbed. Everything was so bad, and she had made things worse. She writhed and moaned until the pain threatened to consume her.

When she thought about lying down under the water and letting it take her away, a strange thing happened. Her mind stopped letting the thought in, and with the pain of self-denigration blocked, a new thought got through.

My mother didn't asked how the kids are or how I am or give me a chance to tell her about my problems. She only demanded attention and help for herself. If she couldn't bother asking, does she even care?

Terry realized that she had tried to keep peace with her mother and Mack and their needs, hoping that once they were taken care of, they'd take care of her. It was now clear. She didn't count. She never would. She was only as good as what she could give them.

Anger took hold of her. The reality of Mack's visit, and her mother's disregard for her welfare hit her. They didn't care about her or the children. *Bastards. Selfish bastards.*

Her rage grew and so did her awareness of what Mack had done today.

He actually came to work drunk and tried to find me. What if he had? Would he have killed me?

Her new anger and the old fear collided and she became incensed—at Mack, at her mother, about living in someone else's house, and mostly how all she'd worked for had not resulted in a single benefit or blessing from which she could now build.

She welcomed the anger, took it in and used it as a solid foundation to rise up and make a stand. Recognizing she was truly alone and had nothing to show for all her struggles, the bathroom filled with her scream of rage.

"I'm tired of them. Tired of her whining and his demands, and I'm tired of feeling bad all the time." Her voice became hoarse. "I'm tired of trying to please them, and I don't give a freak if he kills me or she never speaks to me again. I'm sick and tired of it all!" Her voice broke and she ran out of breath.

She felt like she'd been raped, over and over again, except at her own invitation. She realized how stupid she'd been—how pathetic—and pitiful. She jumped from the steaming bath and drove her fist into the adjacent wall. A loud crack followed the blow. Her hand swelled, but she didn't care. It was her symbolic lashing out at the attackers she had welcomed. This pain was the last pain she'd ever take on their behalf.

She slumped down onto the toilet seat, cradling her throbbing hand, and sobbed. She'd never felt more alone, yet somehow she also felt stronger, finding strength where before there was none.

For a long, long time she sat there. She didn't stir until she heard the kids come in, and their laughter drew her from the bathroom.

Terry threw on a robe and ran toward their voices, arms outstretched, ready to claim them and hold them. Seeing the young babysitter, Sara with them, Terry stopped short, forgetting that she picked the kids up from school.

"Hi," she said.

"Hi, Mrs. Woods, I didn't expect you home this early," the young woman said.

"Mom, are you alright?" Cara asked. Staring at Terry's swollen face, she ran to her.

Tommy stood there, mouth open.

Looking over Cara's head while she hugged her, Terry said, "I'm fine, kids." She held her child tight. She wanted to cry again, but Cara squeezed her tighter.

"Are you sure, Mom?" she whispered.

"I'm fine now," Terry said gently.

"Thank you for taking care of the kids today, Sara, but I have some time off now and I won't need your help after all," Terry said, letting go of Cara and walking over to the countertop. She picked up her purse. "How do you spell your last name? I'd like to write you a check for your trouble. You've been a godsend and I'm very grateful." She smiled at the young woman who smiled back.

"Mrs. Craig already paid me for the week, so I'll have to bring some money back later," she said.

"Absolutely not! You keep the money and I'll reimburse Mrs. Craig. Now how much did she pay you?" Terry asked, and the young woman told her.

"Thank you, Mrs. Woods."

"And thank you, too! I know the kids enjoyed being with you." Terry walked to the door and opened it.

"If you ever need me, just call. Mrs. Craig has my number."

"I sure will, Sara, thanks, again. Goodbye."

"Bye kids." Sara smiled and the kids waved.

"Mom, why are you home so early. Why have you been crying?" Cara asked when Sara had gone.

"Your father came into my work today. I think he was arrested." Terry looked down at her worried daughter. "Mr. Clark sent me home."

"Oh, God." Cara gasped and Tommy's eyes flew open. "Now what?"

"I don't know honey. But I've had it. We're not going back to him anymore."

"All right!" Cara pumped her fist in the air.

For a second, Terry wanted to chastise her, but saw—maybe for the first time—that they had all suffered. She had not been able to protect them—even a little bit—and that made all the difference in the world.

I hate you, Mack.

Chapter 25

Terry stood at the kitchen sink peeling potatoes when Anne walked in from work. The kids were watching television in the living room.

"God, what an afternoon, Terry!" Anne said, dropping her purse on the countertop and smiling at her friend.

Terry shrugged. "Bet you never expected a three ring circus when you came to Hollicorp, did you?"

"It beats the soaps, doesn't it?"

"What happened after I left, Anne?"

"You know Gary hit your husband, right?"

"Yes."

"The police came and took Mack away. That jerk Clark refused to press charges, so the police made Gary give them a statement to that effect."

"I heard all that."

"Well, I think Gary ran after you to say he was sorry for hurting Mack, but also to say he'd protect you if necessary," Anne told her.

"Gary ran after me because he likes me," Terry said annoyed, disputing the embellishments Anne draped over the incident.

"I know he likes you, Terry," Anne said, "but he was also willing to protect you. I don't think you can look a champion in the face and walk away right now."

"I'm not walking away!"

"Well, just remember," Anne said with a note of caution in her voice. "I told you that you were entitled to love, and I think Gary loves you. So do yourself a favor and let him help you."

"Anne, please don't push me. I can't think right now," she said, coming close to tears again.

"I'm sorry, Terry." Anne said. "I didn't mean to push you, honey…I just want you to find a good man who'll take care of you. I don't want you to go back to that bastard!"

"Don't worry. I won't now." Terry said, wiping at the tears spilling from her eyes'.

"Good! And by the way, Gary asked for my phone number this afternoon," she said. "I gave it to him. And I invited him here tonight…" she said, picking up her purse and rushing from the room.

"You what?" Terry called after Anne to no avail. Anne had retreated to her bedroom.

At seven o'clock, Gary stood at the door. Terry's heart fluttered so she could barely speak.

"Can we go for a cup of coffee, somewhere?" he asked.

"I don't know Gary. Why can't we just talk in the kitchen?"

"Because we're going to make cookies," Anne said, nodding to the kids. "And the kitchen is going to be in use."

Terry saw Cara's and Tommy's frown and glanced at Anne.

"Mom, is Gary your boss?" Cara asked pulling her chin into her neck.

"No, honey, but he—"

"Who is he then?"

Anne jumped into the conversation, smiling. "Gary works with us honey, and he's a friend of your Mom's."

Cara frowned. "Can't you stay home with us tonight, Mom?"

"Look, Gary," Terry said, "the kids have been through a lot and I should stay with—"

"Nonsense," Anne said, taking the kids in tow. "We're going to make cookies tonight, so you go ahead and go out for a while, just the two of you."

Cara shrugged off Anne's arm and stared at her mother. With hawk-like eyes she watched Gary wrap an arm around Terry, and led her out the door.

The couple drove in silence for miles until Gary spoke. "Terry, I hope you're not mad at me for hitting your husband today. He was out of control."

"Why would I be angry with you," she answered, realizing how tired she was. "I was scared, that's all."

"I can't believe he actually came into work — drunk as hell, and made such a jerk of himself! Is he always like that?"

"Like what?"

"Crazy? Or drunk?" he said. "What would you call it?"

"Mack's just upset right now. He's just..." she stopped when Gary grunted.

"Upset my foot! For God's sake, Terry, I'm trying to help you. Why can't you give me a little credit here?"

"I'm sorry...I just don't know what to think right now," she said, tears falling again.

He turned the car to the side of the road and shut off the engine. "Terry, I'm sorry. I didn't mean to pressure you."

In the silence, she pressed herself against the passenger door. "Gary, I don't want to talk about it. Can we go back now, please?"

"Let's talk for a while," he said, moving toward her.

"Gary, please, I want to go back to Anne's house." She heard her voice tremble.

"You know I'm leaving in a few days, so why won't you let me help you while I'm still here?"

"Because I need to work things out for myself," she whispered.

"But Terry," he said, turning to face her. "I...think...I... love you, and I want to help you."

Terry pushed back as far from him as she could.

He reached over to embrace her, but she pushed his arms away.

Shaking and sweat pouring into her eyes, Terry, with her heart racing, cowered against the car door. Anxiety racked her body and she tried to retreat farther and farther into the armrest behind her.

"Leave me alone!" she said, but he reached out again. "Don't touch me." She slapped at his hands and pushed them against him.

"Stop it, Terry!" He reached up taking her shoulders and shook her.

Terry gasped and took in a huge breath, hysterical sobs escaping her lips.

He pulled his hands back. "I'm sorry, Terry, please. I'm so sorry. I was just trying to...Talk to me, honey," he said, reaching for her again. This time she didn't resist—her strength gone.

He took her into his arms and rocked her. "Poor, poor baby." He swayed back and forth until the rhythmic motion lulled her into serenity and her gasping cries became shallow puffs.

"Leave him, Terry. You don't have to take his abuse. Come to Bangor with me, instead, and I'll take care of you. And your kids, too. I won't let him bother any of you again."

He continued rocking her back and forth. "And you can work if you want to...I'll give you your big chance...you can work your way up to a managerial position if you want...or you can stay home and just take care of me and your kids. Just come with me, please. I don't want to go without you. Please come with me."

"I can't—"

"You don't have to do anything! I'll take care of everything. I promise." Unwrapping his arms from around her, he pushed her away to look at her. "Don't you worry about anything. I'll do everything. You can just be happy for a change, okay?" He smiled down on her until he pulled her close again, kissing her forehead.

Terry's stomach fluttered and her head spun in confusion.

I don't want to make cookies Cara thought, but she complied. *And I don't like that man Gary, either. What's he doing with my mother? Where did they go? Why did she go with him?*

Cara squeezed the cookie dough through her fingers and let it fall to the floor.

"Oops, sorry," she said.

When the obligatory cookies were done, Cara excused herself and pulled Tommy along, out of the kitchen.

"Go get washed up for bed, Tommy," Cara said once they were out of Anne's ear shot.

"What about you? Aren't you going to bed?"

"I'm waiting for Mom."

"I want to wait, too!"

"No. I told you to go to bed. Now go!" Cara pushed him toward the bathroom.

Tommy grumbled but he moved down the hall.

Cara settled herself, fully dressed, onto the twin bed she'd been assigned in the guest room. She lay awake waiting for her mother.

Anne finished cleaning up the kitchen and looked up at the clock, it read almost nine p.m. She realized she hadn't called the lawyer to let him know about the arrest today.

Pulling out the paper he'd given her, she thought about calling him at home but changed her mind. She put the paper back into her purse, pulled the telephone directory from a drawer and dialed the office number instead.

"Hanson and Gregory," someone answered.

"I don't suppose anyone's in the office right now, are they?" Anne asked.

"No, ma'am, but I can page them if it's an emergency. With whom did you wish to speak?" the operator asked.

"Mr. Hansen." Anne sighed. "It's important that I speak with him tonight, please."

"Fine. Please give me your name and telephone number and I'll page him right away."

Anne provided the information and looked at the time again. She hoped he'd call back soon. She didn't want to be up all night, but he needed to know what happened.

She was happy Mack sat behind bars, but he'd be out by morning and she was afraid of what he'd do when he got out. Mr. Hansen needed to know.

Anne left the kitchen and went into the bathroom to clean up for bed. She had just begun running a bath when she heard the front door open.

"Terry, is that you?"

"Yes."

Anne ran from the bathroom. "So, how did it go?" she asked her voice tinged with excitement.

"Fine," Terry looked tired.

"Tell me what happened!" Anne said, taking Terry's arm and walking her into the living room.

"Anne! For God's sake, you sound like a mother whose daughter just came from the prom," Terry said in protest.

"Oh, stop being peevish and tell me what he said."

"He said he loved me...wanted to take care of me," Terry knew her anger vented through her words. "Are you satisfied?"

"Terry! I have no interest in whether Gary loves you or not—but he can protect you," Anne defended herself.

"To hell you don't. You think love cures everything!"

"What're you saying? Do you think all of this is somehow my fault?" Anne whispered, tears coming to her eyes.

"No, it's not your fault! But stop making it worse!"

"You're entitled to love, Terry, not abuse! Gary is as good as anyone for giving you love."

"Yeah, well, get off my back, will you? I can't think right now! Besides, why don't you concentrate on your own love life and stay out of mine." Terry stormed from the room.

Terry saw Cara waiting in the hall when she came up the stairs.

"Mom, are you all right?"

"Yes, baby."

"Mom, I love you and I'll take care of you." Cara hugged Terry. "We don't need her," she glanced over her shoulder, "or him, or Dad or anyone. We can live by ourselves, Mom. Honest. I'll help you."

"You may be right, honey," Terry said, heading for the bathroom.

All night Terry thrashed in the bed. She felt entombed in a dark box with no windows or door, though, she could hear everyone yelling at her from outside the container.

'Go back where you belong,' her mother said, scolding her.

'You're not a good wife, Terry,' Mr. Clark told her. 'Go home now and do what it takes to make your man happy.'

'Look at Mrs. High and Mighty career-girl,' a neighborhood mother's voice taunted her.

'What the freakin hell have you done to us now, Terry...letting outsiders in to ruin everything.' Mack's voice shouted.

'Terry, run away with me and I'll take care of everything,' Gary pleaded.

'Open up to love.' Anne said.

"Shut up, all of you!" Terry screamed out from inside the dark box. The sound of a blender started up somewhere close.

It was late morning and the sun streamed into the room, when the telephone woke Terry. She reached over to the night table to pick it up. "Hello," she mumbled.

"Well, isn't this nice. The freaking police said you was there, and sure enough."

Terry caught her breath. "Mack, where are you?" she said.

"Don't worry about that, bitch." he said. "You don't need to know where I am, 'cause I ain't staying here long. You really done it this time — you spoiled it, girl. I've had it with you and your freaking kids. I don't want no more trouble, Terry. You hear me? I did my best and you screwed me. You screwed me over good. And I ain't taking it no more." He paused. "You hear me?"

Terry remained silent, too shocked to speak.

"I'm gonna go shoot rats, Terry, and you ain't gonna see me no more. I ain't coming back. No sir, you had your chance and you blew it. I never done nothing to you but try to help you but you turned against me and you turned those kids against me, too. I'm giving up on you, but just remember…if I wanted you back, there's no way you or nobody else could stop me. You understand that, bitch? But that's okay 'cause I don't want you no more. I'm leaving and it's all your fault. You broke my freaken heart."

The phone went dead.

Terry shook. Vomit rushed up into her mouth and gagged her. She ran to the bathroom to flush it away.

Was he gone? Really gone? What did he mean if he wanted me back? I won't go back with him…I won't.

She cleaned the vomit from her nighty and rinsed her mouth. Looking into the mirror, she saw swollen eyes and a haunted look on her face.

I won't go back with him…I don't care what happens, I won't.

She stared at herself in the mirror. *I didn't break your heart, you bastard, I broke your leash. I won't ever go back to you…ever.*

She went to her room, pulled out fresh clothes and returned to the bathroom for a long hot shower before she woke the kids.

"Anne, this is Terry," she said, twisting the phone cord around her fingers, her heart racing.

"What's wrong?"

"Mack just called me — he's out of jail."

"Call the police right now."

"I don't have to do that, Anne. I think he's going to kill himself," Terry whispered.

"Good riddance!"

"Anne! Don't say that. I don't want to live with him anymore, but I don't want him to die, either."

"No such luck!"

"I'm taking the kids and going home, Anne."

"What? You can't. What if he's there? What if this is just a trap to get you and the kids to come back!"

"He's gone, Anne, I'm telling you. He never said he was leaving before. He meant it."

"Please don't go back to that house, Terry, please. I'm begging you."

"I can't stay here, Anne. I'll be just as safe in my own home and the kids can get back to normal. I'm sorry, Anne, but I'm going home."

"Listen to me, Terry, please! I talked to Mr. Hansen last night and he said Mack might pull something like this. Mack can't be trusted. He'll do anything to get you back, or to get back at you…threat of suicide, threats of finding you. Please, Terry, don't trust him. Trust us. Steve said the only place you and the kids would be safe is in a shelter."

"What? Are you crazy, Anne? We're not going into a shelter."

"It's the only safe alternative. If you really want to be free, you have to do it. I swear I won't tell anyone where you are! You'll have time to think and figure out what you want, but you can't go back to your house!" Anne was sobbing.

"You don't understand. He's gone, Anne. I know him."

"He's an animal, Terry and they're most dangerous when cornered. It's not safe to go back there."

"Anne, I've made up my mind. I promise you we'll be safe."

"I can't lose a second person I love, Terry, please. You're like the daughter I never had. I swear I'll help you every step of the way, please." Anne said, pleading.

"I'm just so tired of fighting, Anne."

"I know honey, but we can fight this together. I promise you on Joe's grave, you and the kids will be safe in the shelter until we can make other plans. Please…"

"I'm sorry, Anne." Terry hung up the phone. "Kids, finish breakfast and pack your things, we're going home.

Anne pushed away from the console so quick her chair tipped over and fell with a loud crash.

"Gary!" She raced to his office. "Gary!"

"Anne, what's the matter," he asked meeting her half-way.

Still sobbing, Anne blurted out the news. "She's going home, Gary."

"What? Who's going home? Stop crying and talk to me."

"Mack called Terry and said he was going away so Terry is taking the kids and going home!"

"Call the police and send them to her house," he said racing to his office. In a second, he came rushing out, his car keys jangling.

Terry's heart pounded when she pulled into her driveway. Nothing looked different from the outside, but she remembered the mess they left when they'd retrieved their clothes. *What's one more mess to clean up? Once that's done, it's over. It's all done. Mack's gone, and the kids and I can live a normal life again.*

"Leave your stuff in the car for now, kids. We'll bring it in later," Terry said.

They walked up the path, Terry turning to look left and right for Mack's car. It wasn't around.

She put the key into the door and ushered the kids through it. She turned to shut it but a huge hand grabbed her and threw her to the floor.

"You stupid bitch! Did you really think I was gone?"

Terry stared up and her throat constricted. "Mack!" She turned and saw the kids huddled together, crying. "Kids, run out the back!"

Raising the shotgun, Mack yelled. "Stop right there or I'll kill her."

The kids stopped, their backs to their father.

"You two, sit on the couch—now."

The kids turned and Mack leveled the gun at them while they crossed the room.

"You," he said, pointing the gun at Terry again, "get up off the floor and join your brats."

"Mack, please." Terry whispered.

"Shut up! Did you really think I'd let you take everything I worked for, including my freaken wife and kids? You're even stupider than I thought you was. Now you're going pay."

"Mack...please, no."

Terry looked up when Gary charged through the open doorway. He make eye-contact with her.

"Terry, what the he...."

Mack flipped the rifle and swung the butt against Gary's head, knocking him to the ground.

Terry shot off the couch. "Mack, please..."

"Sit down," Mack said, barking out the command. He flipped the rifle again pointing it at her.

She edged her way to the couch backwards, and felt the kids grab her skirt and pull her onto the couch.

"So, that's why you left me, you pig?" Mack sneered at Gary's limp body on the floor.

"Mack I swear to God, I didn't..."

"Shut up." Mack walked toward them. "This is all your fault, Terry, but now I got no choice."

Cowering together, Terry pulled the kids in tight. She watched Mack coming toward them.

Terry heard a series of clicks and Mack's eyes flew open. He fell forward and landed at Terry's feet, dropping his rifle to the floor.

Three police burst through the open door, guns drawn and eyes darting around the room. One officer rushed to Mack's convulsing body, while another ran to Gary, and the third, a woman, came over to Terry and the kids.

"This one's okay," the first officer said, describing Mack's condition after being tazered.

"This one's okay, too, but he's got an egg on his head. I think he needs an ambulance."

The two police nodded to the third.

"Okay, cuff him, and get an ambulance for that one," the female officer said.

She turned back and knelt in front of Terry. "Are you all right ma'am?"

Terry tried to speak, but her throat was dry and her breath came in rapid, shallow spurts. She felt the blood rush to her head and gasped for air in ragged spasms.

"Get her some water," the woman ordered, turning back toward one of the other officers who scrambled out of the room to find the kitchen.

Within a minute he came back, water sloshing over the top of a glass, which he handed to Terry.

"Drink that," the woman said.

It took a few minutes before Terry could swallow. "He said he was going away…he lied to me."

"Who said that?"

"My husband," She nodded at Mack.

"Wait a minute, back up a bit. Why was he going away?"

"Because I got a restraining order on him and he was very angry with me."

"You have a restraining order on him?" the woman asked, turning and nodding toward another officer.

"Yes, but then I came home and Gary came in and Mack hit him…."

"Whoa. Let's start with your husband's full name."

For the next hour, Terry answered all the officer's questions. An ambulance came and took Gary to the hospital, and the police hefted Mack off the floor and put him in the cruiser to follow the ambulance.

The children still encircled Terry, neither speaking nor moving.

The woman closed her notebook and stood. "Well, ma'am, not only did your husband violate the restraining order, he assaulted the other man, and he held you and the children hostage with intent to murder you. It's safe to say that you won't be seeing him, outside of prison, for quite a long while."

"I hope you're right." Terry said, looking down at her kids.

Judy Shine Logan

After working in the department of psychiatry at Boston Regional Medical Center in Massachusetts, Judy moved to Las Vegas, Nevada. There she donated her time to Safe Nest, an organization and confidential shelter for battered women. When she became a widow, she found herself comparing her life to that of the abused—good love versus bad love. Her contemplations led to the writing of *SHELTER ME* with two hopes: that battered women will realize bad love is not better than no love, and, to educate others about the insidious nature of abuse that steals a person's self-esteem until she has none left.

It's NEVER as easy as "Just get out!"

CPSIA information can be obtained
at www.ICGtesting.com
Printed in the USA
FFOW04n1606170117
31430FF